Galilea, *Galilea*

$$F = \frac{q_1 q_2}{4\pi\varepsilon_0 \varepsilon r^2}$$

$$\Phi = \int B\cos\alpha\,dS$$

$$\frac{1}{\lambda} = Rz^2\left(\frac{}{}\right.$$

$$\vec{E} = \sum_{i=1}^{N} E_i$$

$$\Phi(x)$$

$$P = mg \qquad C =$$

$$= \frac{1}{r} \qquad\qquad\qquad L =$$

$$\zeta = \sigma T^4 \qquad\qquad T = \frac{2\pi}{\omega} \qquad x = \beta T$$

$$x = A\cos(\omega t + \alpha) \qquad \omega = 2\pi\nu \qquad \Phi = BS\cos\alpha \qquad E = m$$

$$\sigma = 5{,}67\cdot 10^{-8}\ \frac{Bt}{m^2\cdot K^4} \qquad W = |\psi|^2$$

$$\zeta = \alpha\sigma T^4 \qquad x = A_0 e^{-\beta t}\cos(\omega t + \alpha)$$

$$\lambda_m = \frac{b}{T} \qquad b = 2{,}9\cdot 10^{-3}\ m\cdot K \qquad T = \frac{2\pi}{\sqrt{\omega^2-\beta^2}}$$

$$\varphi = \operatorname{arctg}\frac{A_1\sin\alpha_1 + A_2\sin\alpha_2}{A_1\cos\alpha_1 + A_2\cos\alpha_2} \qquad \lambda = \nu T$$

$$s = \pm m\lambda_0,\ m = 0,1,2,\ldots \qquad\qquad k = \frac{2\pi}{\lambda}$$

$$A_p = \frac{f_0}{2\beta\sqrt{\omega_0^2-\beta^2}} \qquad W = \frac{1}{2}mA^2\omega^2 \qquad \xi = A\cos(\omega t - kx)$$

$$M = F\delta \qquad \Delta\varphi = \frac{2\pi}{\lambda}\,\Delta r \qquad p = nkT$$

$$\eta = \frac{1}{3}\rho\langle v\rangle\langle\lambda\rangle$$

$$\langle\varepsilon\rangle = \frac{3}{2}kT$$

$$\varepsilon_2 = \tfrac{5}{2}\,\hbar\omega\,(n=2$$

$$i = I\,\Delta\Phi$$

$$\varepsilon_1 = \tfrac{3}{2}\,\hbar\omega\,(n=1)$$

$$q = \frac{\Delta\Phi}{R}$$

$$\varepsilon_0 = \tfrac{1}{2}\,\hbar\omega\,(n=0)$$

$$D = \frac{1}{3}\langle v\rangle\langle\lambda\rangle \qquad \varepsilon = \frac{q}{4\pi\varepsilon_0 r^2} \qquad \chi = \eta\frac{z}{2}\frac{R}{\lambda}$$

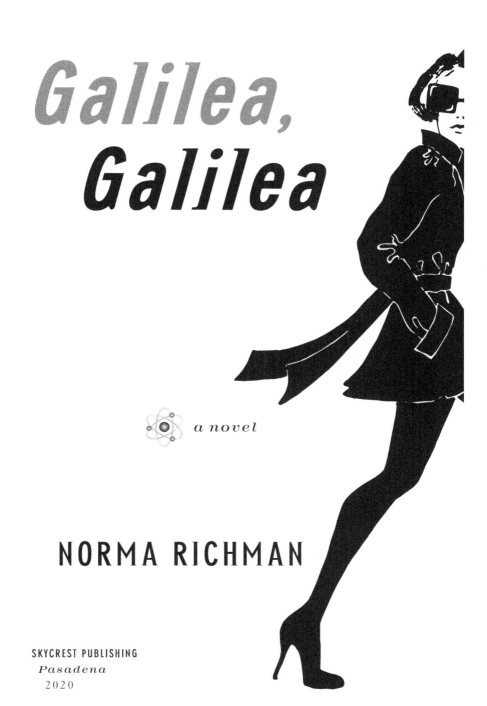

Galilea, Galilea

a novel

NORMA RICHMAN

SKYCREST PUBLISHING
Pasadena
2020

ISBN: 9798676903657

Cover and Interior Book Design by Claudine Mansour Design

Printed in the United States of America.

www.galileabook.com

Dedicated to scientists everywhere.

"The thing that doesn't fit is the thing
  that's the most interesting, the part that doesn't go
  according to what you expected."

— RICHARD FEYNMAN

ETYMOLOGY OF LEE

Name/ Origin	Pros	Cons
Galilea (born that way)	meh	Often confused with the Queen song; also, weird if you are a kid.
Lea	A distraction from the middle school brainiac label and a good reminder *not* to wear her hair in those two goofy buns—or even one.	Middle school peers were not stellar spellers, so they were always confusing her with the *Star Wars* Princess Leia, to whom she bore no resemblance. Lots of teasing. A lot to live up to.
Gal	High school saw the incarnation that stuck for only a brief period. Admirable for the strength; the mental fortitude was there too.	No way to know that fate would have brought her full circle in a few years to the same dilemma: she bore no resemblance to the latest version of *Wonder Woman*, Gal Gadot. And the outfit?
Lee	Denotes male or fe-male—good if you are looking for work in the world of physics. A new beginning with a new name that has few references to the entertainment world. Easy to remember after a night of Happy Houring.	Oh, except Lee Marvin, Lee Ann Womack, LeAnn Rimes, Lee Majors, Lee Meriwether, and other "Lee" people you have probably never heard of. And Lee Harvey Oswald—certainly a negative connotation; don't go there.

CHAPTER ONE
GALILEA, GALILEA

The Sierra Madre Earthquake of 2019 was a definite setback for Lea. She knew the hippie-inspired home her parents willed to her in the Canyon was not built to code—any city's code. The attraction was its stained-glass windows and split railroad timber walls. In the seventies it had been a haven for her parents, Ann and Alexander. Never mind that even a soggy Domenico's meatball would roll across the floor at lightning speed all on its own.

In the sixties the couple had stopped on a whim at Mary's Market, an institution of wonderful made-to-order burgers, and it was love at first whiff—the aroma of the burgers married to the more-than-hint of pot—as they sought out information on available housing. Either the Upper Canyon or the Lower Canyon would do: they wanted a newlywed refuge. Hence, the retreat that became a home when Galilea was born.

Now, Lea surveyed what was left of the family home. The sleepy surroundings belied the moderate quake's devastation.

In this canyon, sandbag barriers would appear in every front yard before the rainy season, and owing to the fire danger, cars were parked downhill for an easy getaway all summer long. This was the quintessential testament to the attraction, the charm, of Southern California.

In an instant the structure had become tinder; the windows became shards of brilliance that sparkled in the SoCal sunlight. And the thrust fault had emptied its contents onto the narrow, winding road. Mount Carter Lane was her closet now. Lea extricated the fashion treasures left to her by her late mother: haute couture dresses and scarves, among them Chanel, Tadashi, Cavalli. She could see that a few items were still usable, though covered in dust. It was a miracle that Lea and her mother were the same size; at least she had a few things to wear. She always thought they were, in fact, nothing alike otherwise. With one exception. They did have those shoes in common—the ones with the red soles that neither could afford to actually buy but loved so much. Now a spiky heel protruded from the flotsam and jetsam strewn across the harsh aggregate roadway, like a beacon. She gingerly pulled it out. Intact but definitely warped.

That night she sat in the bar at The Langham Hotel in nearby Pasadena, which, like most structures in town, had actually survived the quake unscathed. Wearing the cleanest of the rescued (plain) black dresses, Lea presented a study in contrast as she sank into the off-white upholstered sofa that wound around the room. She took comfort in the dark woodwork and the glowing gilt mirrors. Even her injured black shoes, the coveted red stripe running down the back of one heel like a scar, looked presentable in the dim light. A recent reversal of professional fortune meant that she had to get by on the salary of a part-time physics instructor at Pasadena City College, PCC. Lea had grown up believing she was destined to research and teach at the prestigious California Institute of Technology— Caltech, the place that was literally down the street from PCC, much to her annoyance. A good thing her father was no longer alive to see how far she had fallen from her—or was it *his* goal, really? She must have mulled this question over in her mind dozens of times recently, a habitual inner dialogue providing neither answers nor peace. Lea had always been comfortable with intrapersonal communication and enjoyed the sarcastic insight with which she answered herself... until now. *You may never know the truth, Lea. Get over it.*

Lea worked hard to avoid thinking about the last few days as she nursed one of the almost-twenty-dollar cocktails the Tap Room was famous for. It was like slogging through the plasma of a space populated by wood and glass and designer fabric particles. Toss in a rejection letter or two, and here was the cosmic matter of her thirty-two-year-old life. Could this be her "Introduction to Physics" unit? *Not funny, Lea*, she thought.

As she got up to leave, a little unsteady on her feet—part booze, part torqued designer heels—she signed the bill *Lee*, not Lea. Time for the fearless, what-are-they-gonna-do-to-me Lee. Drop the "a" and she could reinvent herself again. This name change opened up a world of possibilities.

=

The blue glass was all that protected her from radioactivity, but it also lent an entrancing otherworldly hue. Lee glowed in the reflection of the radium chloride–filled jar. As she glanced around the stifling storeroom replete with cobwebs and the de-tritus of academic life, she became aware of things she'd only seen in old movies: Steelcase desks, thermal copiers, ditto machines, and shelves and shelves of obsolete scientific artifacts. Dr. Frankenstein would have had a field day here.

Still a little fuzzy-headed from her night of drink and regret—no, not regret—reincarnation, Lee told herself it was time to move on. An overused phrase she disliked, but in this case, she really did have to move on. *Get your act together, Lee. The azure glow notwithstanding, this is no place for a lady.* The radiation alone, with its half-life of forever, could kill, and her only remaining white silk blouse, an eerie blue at the moment, was microns away from certain ruin.

She had come down to this place under the old gymnasium of Pasadena City College looking for those 1930s ceramic tiles, the ones that had just enough uranium in the glaze to set off a radiation monitor. Urban—institutional legend, really—had it that these tiles once lined the walls and floors of all the restrooms on campus until their danger was discovered in the late sixties. Avocado green and black. The trick was to find a few leftovers. Cato, her mentor at PCC, a curmudgeon now but a long-haired hippie back in the day, told of "blowing the minds" of his Physics 101 darlings with the single six-sided bathroom tile and a Geiger counter that goes off like a machine gun.

"Nothing could make them less jaded, less bored than a *wow* demonstration. That lightbulb moment," he had told her one day as they sat in his dusty office, swatting away dive-bombing motes. "I guess we all like flirting with peril, even these kids. Oh . . . and welcome to PCC. I think you'll do well. Let me know how the radiation thing works out . . . unless it doesn't, and we end up with a class of glow-in-the-dark students. That'll be hard to explain to the admin people; I'd have to disavow even knowing you." *He's smirking*, she thought at the time. *He can't be serious.* Then he laughed.

Failing to find the box of tiles would make her lesson plan for tomorrow more difficult, but fearing that she would end up like one of those luminous bedroom ceiling stars she used to stare at in the night could be worse. *Failing or fearing, Lee. Take your pick.*

Radium chloride. That was the magical chemical compound. Strange to think that back in the day, before her time, it was used to create glow-in-the-dark watch and clock hands. An alarm clock could wake you up and give you a jolt of radiation all at the same time. *Good Morning, Starshine.* In reality she knew that the dose was not lethal in such minute quantities, but that jar sitting on the shelf promised something more. It was glowing blue, but it was the blue glass causing the effect, right? What if she opened it, poured a little out into a glass dish? There were a dozen dust-coated petri dishes just begging to be taken off the shelves. She reached for the jar, grasped it tentatively.

In that moment, Lee noticed for the first time how serene the chamber was. Not silent: dripping water way off in the distance and the faint numbing hum of a transformer somewhere were joined by the pounding in her ears. Even her non-glowing watch, a gift from her father, added a slight percussion to the score. For a second a profound sense of peace–not eerie, not scary–filled the room to its three dimensions. That confined place offered a glimpse of its magic. She was alone but not lonely for once, a sensation of lightness she had not felt in a long while and the feeling also that she had company. No horribly dressed floating ghosts like the ones who tortured that agonized soul Scrooge were here, but more like the blissful,

Hollywood-beautiful couple hovering in *La La Land*. She could qualify for the latter. She was dressed for the part anyway. All she needed was a dancing partner.

"Get real, Lee," she said in the darkness. *Leave the jar of radium chloride behind. It'll be here for a while. No rush.*

CHAPTER TWO
WHAT ABOUT THE CAT

The requisite vintage *Campari* poster on the bar's back wall cast a bluish hue on the couple as their second-round drinks were delivered, reminding her of something. She couldn't put her finger on it. But she was here on business, so what was the difference? A week after the quake in Canyon, when Lee was settling in to her new job at PCC, he had called her to discuss her recent failure and she knew it. It should have been a no-brainer to secure a spot at prestigious Caltech. Isaac was not the gloating type, or she wouldn't have come, though the thought of dressing to kill and hanging with Pasadena's glitterati was a reward in itself these days. Curiosity got the better of her, or did it get the cat killed? She was too tired, and approaching tipsy, to care.

Start with a diversion, Lee. Defuse the situation. "So I had this really strange experience with radiation the other night . . ."

Lee could see that Isaac was shifting to get a better look at her in the darkness of the Tap Room. She knew the body language all too well, and tonight she played at being a fitting addition to the ambience. And The Langham played its role too. This place was still called The Huntington Hotel by the well-seasoned locals, a reference to the heydays of Pasadena's founding fathers and the influence of a wealthy railroad magnate who left his mark on the town. Redolent of the moneyed, beautiful people, it offered privacy and luxury, a place to hide or to be seen. Yet here *they* were too. Democracy is great.

"We have something else to talk about. You shouldn't take *no* for an answer. At least not yet. There's a reason it was someone else and not . . ." He recognized a stubborn streak that would always define their relationship. They had been cohorts and friends for a few years now, and he had watched her struggle with the loss of her parents and her family home, and yet she maintained the uncanny ability to bounce back, to be a thorn in his side when he least expected it. He was happy to call her *Lee* now—a phase or a turning point? He didn't know. Isaac trusted that she had her reasons, but her judgment in the case of this Caltech thing could be her undoing.

"I don't think so." *Head him off at the pass, Lee.* She couldn't bear it, not a do-over of her humiliation. She noticed at that moment that this impeccably dressed man, a friend, a particle physicist, had a single white cat hair on his leather jacket. A single one: somehow his black jeans and shaggy black hair had escaped the fur shower. *Is this the curious dead cat thing, or just a coincidence, or just too much to drink?* "It was someone else because I wasn't qualified, or experienced enough, or any number of reasons."

"That's just it. Don't you see? He's *less* qualified. He was originally only a research assistant. The most the guy did was . . ."

"No, *that's* just it; he's a guy." She hated to play the gender card, but it just came out that way. Slow down. Take a sip. The

Rose Bloom, a cocktail famous in Pasadena circles, though no one knows why, tasted of sweet sugar cane and bitter disappointment at this moment. "Am I boring you?" No matter how hard a guy tries, he can't hide the fact that he's sneaking a peek at his phone. It's the glow on his face that gives it away. He looked guilty. It was then that she noticed he was not wearing his usual smart watch, a tattoo in its place, peeking out from under his sleeve. That's what people do now. Check the time. An excuse to reach for the phone. "Sorry. You don't owe me anything, not even the time of day." A pun that used to be funny but at the moment sounded just plain bitchy—something she regretted immediately.

"I think he's actually a threat to the university. It's not just about you, you know. This business of looking to disprove the theory that no new energy exists or can be produced in the universe could be an embarrassment . . . a danger . . . to the Institute, to all of us."

Lee was getting fuzzier by the moment. "Think about it. *I* could have been the embarrassment. *I* was working on the same theory. Right?"

"No. Not exactly the same. You were on to something. Look, all I'm saying is don't give up. I know you've got work now, and it's honorable work. If you're going to sit around in a bar every night, you clearly aren't happy with how things ended."

"I'm doing okay except for, you know, the earthquake and the rejection letter, and the . . ." She wondered how long she could circle before she runs out of fuel here. *It's like that energy thing*, she reminded herself; only she really *does* think there's a way that energy is destroyed. Period. Not coming back as something else. Kind of like her life for the moment. "You must have better things to do than . . ."

"Look, Lee, I'm telling you. There's more to this." He got up and left, cat hair and all and a quick peck on the cheek. Lee watched him go, not sure if she should ask him to come back. In truth, she didn't have the energy to keep the conversation going—at least not tonight. The thing she liked about Isaac was his forgiving nature, and the thing she hated about Isaac was his forgiving nature. It was impossible to stay mad at him. They could argue big bang theory or the usefulness of nuclear energy till the cows came home. Their two disciplines of study had always been at odds. He was theoretical. The abstract suited him. Lee, on the other hand, stuck with the practical: the laws of motion, electromagnetism, that sort of thing. No ifs, ands, or buts. She liked the concrete physical world. For all the good it did her.

For a few months, Lee (still calling herself Lea at the time) and Isaac had worked side-by-side on a research project at the Institute that combined both streams of physics. He was already an assistant professor, and she was just finishing her grad work. They had both grown up in the Pasadena area, and their paths had crossed, crisscrossed really, many times over the years. And there was her legendary father, Alexander Roberts. Isaac, like most others in the business of physics, assumed she would follow in his footsteps. Isaac encouraged her and counseled her, but something went wrong. When someone else, this outsider, as far as they were concerned, stepped in and took the position both she and Isaac figured would be hers, she walked away without even asking for an explanation.

She was not one to recognize her emotions, let alone admit to others how she felt. Being her father's daughter, Lee immediately began the search for work. Job openings for physicists don't come along every day, but if any city can support multiple employment opportunities in physics, it's Pasadena. Caltech wasn't going to hire her, but Jet Propulsion Lab would have to be a good fit. JPL's response was "Come back in a few years when we have the budget and you have the experience." Lee procured a job at Pasadena City College the next day; they knew and she knew that they were lucky to have her. She figured that she could bide her time teaching there until she figured out what happened at the Institute. Isaac remained in her corner, and that was saying something.

=

Isaac—he always hated that name. Too many connotations attached to it. The fact that it was a good conversation starter, an ice breaker, did not outweigh the need to prove himself and to disavow any curiosity about its origin. You know: Isaac Newton, Isaac Asimov, Isaac of Israelite fame. No good way to come up with a term of endearment or a nickname either. Zacky was a short-lived childhood iteration that lent itself to too many bad jokes. So much so that even the more mature name Zack elicited flashbacks of playground taunts. Best to stick with Isaac and hope for the best. Like Lee, he had lived in Sierra Madre and then later in Pasadena in the San Rafael neighborhood that was situated both figuratively and literally in the shadow of the famed Colorado Street Bridge. Many people, and not with pride, referred to it as Suicide Bridge—another story for another time.

When a quiet, cerebral kind of guy goes into the study of dark matter and antimatter, there's only one way to proceed: MIT. Studying particle physics at the Massachusetts Institute of Technology would have sounded like pie in the sky to any ordinary parents, but obviously, if they named him Isaac, they were not concerned with frivolous things. In fact, in their Caltech milieu, driving around with a bumper sticker that announced "Proud MIT Parents" was just the ticket, and they happily forked over the tuition—enough to finance a small municipality for a year. Paid internships at the University of Chicago Fermilab and then CERN in Switzerland dovetailed perfectly with Isaac's plans. Both labs, in an attempt to prove the invisible, the impossible maybe, hurl subatomic particles at each other like ping pong balls but at way more than the speed of light, with an end to seeing what kinds of matter and energy come from their collisions, and therefore, their origins—presumably the origins of the universe. The Chicago people affectionately named their particle accelerator ATLAS. CERN's people coined the term "The God Particle." No wonder physicists had such egos.

The counterpart to ATLAS was CERN's Hadron Collider, also known as ALICE. Pasadena's researchers did stints there, along with MIT's. They were so dedicated in looking for The God Particle, in fact, that they spent as many as twenty-four hours straight staring into the ether of these chambers and tunnels five hundred feet underground. One goofy crew that included MIT's and Caltech's best had to bust out. They authored a rap designed to explain the collider, complete with lyrics and gangsta moves. The target audience was of unknown description, but the physicists didn't waste any time uploading their rap masterpiece to YouTube:

I'm about to drop some particle physics in da club
Da LHC is supa dupa fly

You know what I'm saying?
Check it

[Verse 1]
Twenty-seven kilometers of tunnel underground
Designed with mind to send protons around
A circle that crosses through Switzerland and France
Sixty nations contribute to scientific advance
Two beams of protons swing 'round, through the ring
   they ride
'Till in the hearts of the detectors they're made to collide
And all that energy packed in such a tiny bit of room
Becomes mass particles created from the vacuum*

It was at about this time that Isaac found himself heading home to Pasadena to look for actual work. There's only so much demand in the universe for a rapping particle physicist, gangsta or otherwise.

It didn't take long before Isaac landed a position as an assistant professor at Caltech with a promised slot car–like track to full professorship. He found the stereotypical bachelor pad just minutes away from work and just close enough to his parents; fortunately, the Bank of Mom and Dad was there to shell out just one more chunk of cash, an arm and a leg, for a down payment. The cost of living in Pasadena was no joke. His tiny studio townhouse was perched above the Paseo Colorado shopping district and looked down on the city's Beaux Arts–styled Civic Auditorium. He liked the minimal look of his place but also had a taste for expensive furniture. It was a good thing there was really only one room, with approximately the same square footage as one of those popular but ridiculous "tiny homes" featured on TV—a trend most people were hoping would die soon. Isaac set up housekeeping with his new roommate Bernoulli, a cat of unknown lineage that could go airborne at Mach speed if a cricket or mouse scent wafted his way.

CHAPTER THREE
CHEERLEADING FOR THE BOMB

Thinking back on her ambivalent relationship with her father, Lee knew that he was proud of her for her academic accomplishments. And she figured he expected her to follow in his footsteps: take the name. It's a name that honors Galileo. You know. The physicist? Not the "Bohemian Rhapsody" guys, though she likes their music. She wondered, *Who does that? Name me something that is sure to make me an outsider at school?* The nerdy girl with a math-physics head forged ahead in her high school classes, outperforming the guys and, in some cases, the instructors. What did she care? Her hand would go up with *Jeopardy*-like precision and fervor in physics lab and always with the spectral image of her father-professor bouncing around in her brain. Among her peers she became persona non grata, so it didn't always end well on the balance beam social scale, but in the ways it mattered to her, it was a zero-sum game. She survived. They eventually left her alone, and she had infinite time to navigate her own life. She got in trouble once in ninth grade because of her name *and* her brains. Her father called it teenage angst. Some understanding from Alexander would have been nice; instead he just laughed when she told him what happened: even at the age of fifteen, she could compute in her head in a matter of seconds how long it would take one of those wretched cheerleaders to reach the apex of a toss in the air and how much she would accelerate in coming back down. And if by chance no one caught her? Newton's Third would kick in. Action—head hitting ground. Reaction. . . . *Don't go there, Lea*, she told herself. She was laughing. Someone said she was taunting them, or maybe they thought she was putting a curse on them. It reminded her of a ridiculous story her father had told her about radioactive jackrabbits. More on that later.

Physics professor extraordinaire. Alexander Roberts, unassuming but an intellectual powerhouse nonetheless, taught at Caltech for two distinguished decades, before surrendering to the ravages of Alzheimer's.

Even before accepting the position, Alexander had paid his dues with years of research in particle physics—that discipline that everyone associated with The Bomb. It was so much more; in fact, it held the answers and the questions (in that order) to all things ordinary as well. Years later, after his death, TV-watching armchair scientists would learn from *The Big Bang Theory* that there were some half dozen fields of physics and that they had a dubious hierarchy of importance. An endless source of humor, even begrudgingly, to Lee. She marveled that something so sacred to her father then was now woven into popular culture. In her own way, Lee resented that: what she shared with her father, what made her a standout, as well as an untouchable in school, was a language all its own. Her gutsy science psyche kept her going through those years, even as she felt entrapped. She would have to discover some new subatomic particle to measure up, she was sure.

In any case, Alexander came up through the ranks, having met, or known someone who had met, the superstar greats of science. Richard Feynman was not the least of them. A resident of Altadena, just north of Pasadena, he held court not only in the classrooms and the lecture halls, but in the tony homes that surrounded the Institute. What a guy: be instrumental in the understanding and designing of The Bomb one day and do a song and dance at a costume party a week later. He, among many of his fellow scientists, grew to understand the consequences of the former; the latter is still up for debate.

Lee thrived during her high school years on stories about "The Gadget," as it was called at the time of its inception. Feynman, J. Robert Oppenheimer, and others convened at the most secret of secret places, Los Alamos, New Mexico. Einstein was there in spirit only, kind of like the Wizard's big head looming above, but the cast of characters was complete as far as she was concerned. She couldn't imagine a place that was officially *not* on any map, a place colonized with brainiacs like herself. What a perfect world for a geeky teenager. No cheerleaders here, unless you count the jackrabbits jumping around for joy out on the test site, collecting a tiny bit more radioactivity on their not-so-lucky little feet with each successive day, their white pom-pom tails distinguishing themselves in the fine gray dust. Oh, if only they had the bodies for short skirts.

Driving over to Twohey's with her father for the treasured "stink-o burger" became a lesson in force, mass, and acceleration. Determine why that car skidded into the intersection and earn an extra greasy but so-worth-it onion ring. An accident on the side of the road made him giddy. Inertia and momentum?

Explain and earn a hot fudge sundae. It's a wonder she didn't weigh five hundred pounds, Lee told herself—often.

The year before Lee graduated from high school, her mother passed away—an untimely death of unrelenting cancer. Ann Roberts was graceful even to the end, and father and daughter took her strength and forged a new team, determined to make their way together. Mourning would come later. But even as dementia began to set in, Alexander was still the control against which Lee measured herself. He could recite the latest theory surrounding dark matter, which in itself sounded like the ramblings of a madman to the layperson. It was their vernacular. "Funny how having a genius brain is no protection. The disease is an equal opportunity plunderer," he would repeat almost daily, laughing as if telling a joke for the first time.

And she would always answer, "I know, Dad, but you're still the smartest guy I know. Who else could recite the periodic table of elements—backward—and still not be able to use a cell phone?" Built into the fun and games, Lee knew, was that smothering imperative that she was expected to carry out: his plan for after he was gone.

While her high school classmates attended surf camp or volunteered at the LA Zoo for the summer, Galilea spent the hot months working on paleontology digs around the country, shoulder to shoulder with students from the Wedd School, a unique boarding school that catered to scholarship recipients or those who could actually afford field trips to parts unknown during the school year. Fortunately for Galilea, the summer programs were open to kids like her. Alexander had insisted that she get "out of her head" for a while, a strange notion but one he told her would pay off. She had yet to see the value, but it was a fascinating time, excavating and reconstructing, and especially hearing from forensic experts. Even her jaded persona was no match for the rush she felt inside when a piece of bone or a ragged tooth made an appearance in the hardened earth and magically fit like a glove into another nearby piece. Alongside would occasionally be a fragment of a spear or an ax. The jigsaw puzzle of life's whodunits. As summer came to an end, Galilea began to envision the physics of movement—forces, acceleration, momentum—as part of the puzzle. How did these pieces of carbon-based material move through water or through air? Better, how did they propel a whole organism through life? She would never admit it, one of the solemn tenets of teenage-hood, but there in the dirt and mud, was born a newfound appreciation for dear Alexander and for the practical application of the laws of physics.

So, in a perfect world, her father would still be here, exerting that subliminal pressure to succeed in a man's field. And she would have had time to fully appreciate what he meant to her. High school gave way to college and grad school, and camps gave way to internships. As one of his final acts, he had secured for her the most fateful opportunity of all. Los Alamos. Lee's life was complete.

CHAPTER FOUR
GIRL MEETS MUON

Hallowed ground to scientists and historians, scene of infamy to pacifists, LANL—Los Alamos National Lab—was the equivalent of Disneyland to someone like Lee. Recalling the stories, she immediately recognized the Ice House where "The Gadget" was constructed. The iconic black-and-white photo in her textbooks depicted a goofy-looking giant metal meatball. Dull, not shiny, it reminded her of that Mel Brooks movie. Was it *Spaceballs?* Wrapped around it, in what appeared to be a haphazard pattern, cables resembling spaghetti strands completed the meal. Beaming proudly were Oppenheimer and other luminaries—the Chefs Boyardee—of destruction. No matter, here she was.

Lee settled into her dormitory for the near future and noted that this construction was relatively new compared to those WWII apartments on legendary Bathtub Row—some story about the only available bathtubs in Atomic City. No need for a tub when you had to take a spa-like decontaminating shower every time you finished work for the day. Bathtub Row was still on the grounds but now off limits to the public. Anchoring the street was the original Oppenheimer home, sort of like Main Street Disneyland, right? From her room she had a view of the dusty hills and the mesas and understood why this place was ideal for isolation. Oppenheimer liked the place because it lent itself to secrecy and because, according to legend, he had seen it as a child when it still housed a school for boys. *Loose Lips Sink Ships,* she remembered from the lore.

The heat created a haze even at this mile-plus altitude, and the infamous Trinity site was nowhere to be seen. Just as well. Loose Lips and all. With a free day before she started work in the labs, Lee decided to take a jog. Less than five minutes into her run she discovered the problem: lack of oxygen. *Really, Lee? Who are you kidding? Jog at this elevation?* But she knew that. The jog was for appearance only. She discovered that the old high school social defense still loomed large in her psyche: *Look like you're a bad-ass so no one will bother you.* Gasping for air destroyed her cover; fortunately, no one was around to witness her folly. Fuller Lodge, dining hall in the secret heydays of this place, loomed ahead. Closer inspection revealed a lackluster community center now, but the walls inside were still lined with memorabilia and gray-tone photos of unassuming family members wining and dining while The Bomb was born. Well, that settled it; she would have to find the local bar and offer thanks. Her chosen discipline for the summer, muon tomography, would have to wait.

=

In a place designed to create and deliver civilization-ending technology in the 1940s, it's ironic that here in the 2000s it was also developing equipment to detect and prevent nuclear proliferation. Lee wondered if this was atonement of some sort. Muons were predicted and then proven in the '50s, but it was decades later when their usefulness was fully defined. As particles—like electrons—they were fundamental, meaning they were complete and basic entities that could not be broken down any further. Lee recalled learning early in her elementary school math classes about prime numbers. She remembered trying to explain this concept to her Highfield Academy classmates, but for most, it was too much information—TMI, as they say. So the idea of fundamental particles made perfect sense to her. It was much the same. No matter (*Yes, a pun*, she thought). Muons possessed a very special property, however: they had about two hundred times more mass than their famous cousins, the electrons. Muons had to be put to practical use, or they would remain the domain of theoretical physics forever. Where there's fame and fortune to be made in the dog-eat-dog academia business, there's a way. Lee didn't care that muon tomography would yield a means to generate three-dimensional images of long-hidden cavities in pyramids, empty stashing places for treasure or bones or nothing at all. Muons distinguished themselves by being able to pass through solid surfaces like concrete or lead—the power of superheroes, for sure, and maybe every teenage boy's wish.

In any case, if muons could pass through all sorts of hiding places, they could also detect nuclear material in underground sites. Lee would, years later, dazzle her own students with the fact that some ten thousand muons would bombard and pass through every square meter of earth every minute, including the human body. But they were also *boffo* at pointing out where weapons-grade stockpiles were hidden for nefarious reasons.

The idea of nonproliferation appealed to her even as her own life had taken a decidedly self-involved turn, but it was an opportunity to revel in research and do the world a favor, Wonder Woman style. And so she settled in for the summer to a place that officially hadn't existed just a few decades before but was bound to become indelible.

=

The glare coming through the blinds was of *Close Encounters* magnitude, a light so bright, Lee expected one of those ovate-headed creatures to slip its long green fingers under her door. Six a.m. and already that first day as an intern at Los Alamos was off to a fantastic start—until she stood up. For a moment, before slight nausea set in, she had forgotten the hours spent the night before at the Quark Bar. Making friends had never been her strong suit, but then there's no greater bond than a girl and her muons. Her seven new cohorts seemed fine, or maybe it was the artisanal tequila talking. They all compared notes: Ivy League schools for some, hard scrabble scholarships for others. Lee fit somewhere in between. One other female. No surprise; that's a typical ratio. She seemed serious enough to earn the admiration of all, including Lee. The others, herself included, were already sporting unflattering olive green LANL T-shirts. A little embarrassing, Lee thought: even the old logo patches worn by the scientists in the '40s—a cross between *Star Trek* and the Boy Scouts—seemed more appropriate, more suited to the honor of being in this place. Except "Other Female" had on a snug black blazer of some sort and the most fabulous (mahvalous, darling) shoes she had ever seen. Clearly those red-soled, black heels that made her a good four inches taller were going to be useless in the lab tomorrow, or almost anywhere, but Lee admired someone who knew how to make a statement.

=

The usually confident Lee felt a little shaken as she walked into the LANL workroom for the first time—kind of like the first day of school, every first day of school rolled into one. Her drinking mates from the night before appeared equally humbled and a little hung over to boot. Other Female had traded her impressive attire for the required mundane lab coat and practical shoes. No scofflaw was she, Lee noted. One thing about Los Alamos: they weren't fooling around. Interns had to go big or go home when it came to applying themselves; this was an opportunity that led to long lists of applicants just waiting to skip to the head of the line and push out a lax performer. *No pressure here, Lee*, she told herself.

Syllabus:
Muon Tomography LANL Research Project

Task 1:
Learn everything you can about muon tomography—portable muon tomography, to be exact—by tomorrow.

Task 2:
Build a working portable power source (from scratch) that increases the voltage to power this mobile device. Due one week from this date.

"We've got this," Lee remembers someone saying, and she hoped it was true. The muon tomography contingent would be attached at the hips for the foreseeable future, forcing Lee to become a team player, something that did not come naturally to her. Foreign as it was, the sense of mutual respect for each member's intellect was the glue, the attraction, in physics terminology. They all felt that they had a pretty good handle on the basics. These tiny fundamental particles were unmatched in their ability to leap tall buildings in a single bound and penetrate concrete and lead, if need be. They produced three-dimensional images and ably beat out ordinary X-rays as they sought to ferret out hidden nuclear materials. The need for mobility was obvious: take this handy dandy cosmic ogler anywhere.

The next part of the assignment was the MacGyver/Inspector Gadget challenge, the one that intrigued the team the most. Lee, and probably the others, had those childhood roots: take apart anything with more than one component and put it back together perfectly—or better yet, as any self-respecting toddler can do, improve upon it by adding Play-Doh or a spoon or an errant Lego block, all the while careful not to shove anything up your nose. So the Muon Tomography Drinkers Club brainstormed a list of supplies and, by day's end, knew exactly what was available from the bins at the back of the lab and the machine shop next door. Their jokester egos took hold as they congregated again at the Quark Bar for an evening of debriefing and imbibing, and they generated an even longer list of items to be had on Amazon. Unnecessary components but good for a laugh. One click and they could have an absurd miscellany of parts delivered in a couple of days: uber-sized scotch tape, Milk Duds, a shower squeegee thing, a bobble head of Einstein (a serious consideration for the group), a bamboo back scratcher . . . you get the idea.

Other Female offered her own take on the list: "Don't forget chewing gum. Nothing's better for sticking things together than gum. Almost as good as a soldering iron for completing a circuit. Right?" *She has a sense of humor*, Lee thought. *Or was she serious?* This suggestion took off as the group ordered a second—third, for some—round of drinks and posited on the best brands of gum for the property of adhesion.

Much to Lee's relief, the giddiness of the night before faded, and they set about compiling their actual grocery list, most of which was available on site:

Diodes
Capacitors
Resistors
Copper wire
Wire leads/alligator clips/banana plugs
Circuit boards
Soldering irons and solder
Circuit breakers
Transformers
Solar cell/battery/generator

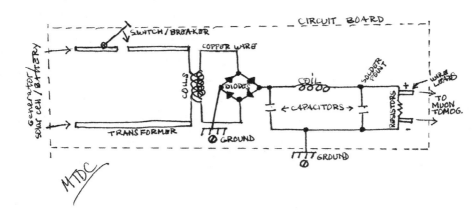

Work went quickly. Over the next week all parts were soldered together as planned; Lee was gratified that the group members all pulled their weight and seemed up to the task. No condescension on the part of the male contingent, no animus or grandstanding on anyone's part—all intellect.

Much to their chagrin, the MTDC (Muon Tomography Drinkers Club) had failed the test the next morning. Lee knew why. Where do you put all of these assembled components so, as they generate electricity, they won't spew lightning bolt–like arcs in every direction? The device had a particular purpose, other than being portable: increase the original voltage. This power needed to be contained, harnessed. And more importantly, not lethal to its users. A box—metal and big enough to house the whole thing. Considering the power requirement of a mobile tomography apparatus, a metal case the size of a shoebox would do.

In the final days of the LANL internship, an experience that would stay with her for the rest of her life, even if she didn't realize it at the time, Lee relished the satisfaction of having solved the big how-not-to-shock-the-daylights-out-of-yourself conundrum. The metal housing for the mobile power source was the solution, one that her cohorts also quickly recognized as the "Duh!" moment—not the "Aha!" moment. There's something to accepting the value of the straight line, the simple path. The Occam's razor theory in action. Lee had forged an alliance with seven other people, and in doing so, set a neuron path in her stubborn brain that would serve her later.

=

For months after Alexander's death, she had had to steel herself even further; the gutsy go-it-alone girl hated to admit that she did need other people—not to problem solve *for* her (she had that nailed), but to acknowledge her ability to problem solve for herself. An affirmation, of sorts. Food for the science-geek's ego. With Alexander and Ann gone, Lee found herself having to forge some new relationships as she returned home to Sierra Madre and that quirky canyon home. The girl was human, after all. A series of revolving college roommates, with varying views on the meaning of tidiness and the usefulness of deodorant, served as surrogate family and gave her spending money, to boot. It was here, in this wood-and-glass retreat and then, at this stage in her life, that she grew to appreciate further the legacies of her parents. She spent days at the Institute in classes that by turns fascinated and frightened her. Such power, such egos, and such responsibility; thank goodness she was her father's daughter. And nights? Most nights after class she roamed around the house, tracing the footsteps of her late mother as she went room to room, raiding Ann's closets of sartorial splendors. Unaware of her resemblance to her mother, she was, in fact, a paler, blonder version—a beautiful, reluctant ghost. The black Valentino with the draped front and back and the tiny silver belt, the Longchamp scarf with its rose and black flowers, the fitted Chanel jackets with their woven threads of gold and silver. Gradually, she culled the collection of items that didn't fit or that were clearly "not her," visiting the full-length mirror for confirmation and comfort. *Not bad. Thank you, Mom*, she said to herself, thinking she hadn't said it often enough.

CHAPTER FIVE
M IS FOR MOTHER OF NECESSITY

Like one of those female leads in a Netflix comedy, Ann Roberts was a beguiling mix of wisdom and bumbling charm. For the older generations, Mary Tyler Moore and Diane Keaton blended into one stunning package. For the rest of us, maybe the beautiful Anne Hathaway. She was a born nurturer, kindhearted, indulgent, and a fierce defender of her child. And Galilea needed defending—often. The daughter was nothing like the mother and everything like the father, and Ann recognized early on that the terrible twos would be a decades-long issue for this little girl.

Ann was not the University Wives type, particularly at the Institute, where pressure to be a high-performing adjunct to her mate was expected. She was up to the task but not interested in fitting the mold, preferring instead to do volunteer work or pursue her passion, photography. On some days she spent hours in her own private darkroom and emerged smelling like the chemicals that created the magical images, holding a dripping black-and-white photo by one corner. Even as digital photography started to take hold, she preferred the tactile experience of processing her own shots, the tell-tale developer's stain always on her fingertips.

Ann had grown up in the village of Sierra Madre, the seemingly sleepy town that cloaked lots of intrigue, real or imagined. Once its claim to fame was serving as the backdrop for the original '50s flick *Invasion of the Body Snatchers*; two decades later a less-famous remake woke the beast, and the town became the scene of renewed, frequent homemade alien "pod" appearances, particularly in Kersting Court—a tease and a testament to the quirkiness of its inhabitants. Residents at the time took their enthusiasm to the Nth degree, volunteering for open casting calls, wearing gruesome make-up and parading up and down Baldwin Avenue, hoping for a role as a zombie. To the outsider this bit of excitement appeared to be just a lark, but to the hopeful extras, it was dead serious (yes, but not a pun). The more fateful production was, in fact, a film named *Testament*, an artifact of the '80s that saw an American mother watching her children as they try to live normal lives in the aftermath of a nuclear detonation that would eventually kill them. Everybody in the town at the time saw this production as a serious reflection of national concerns about The Bomb, and there was, thankfully, less chicanery—no glow-in-the-dark bodies appearing in the town square.

Ann got started with photography in her teen years as a school newspaper photographer at Delverno Girls' School. The use of black-and-white print at the time served to train an amateur eye in the ways of composition, and soon she was winning local awards for arts photography. The school itself was a work of art: housed in an Italianate villa, its architectural style presented a classic backdrop for movies, music videos, and fashion shoots. This is where Ann was first exposed to that world—not a natural affinity but a compositional one—contrasting solid and gossamer, juxtaposing minimalist and flamboyant. All the stuff of haute couture. Beautiful in her own right, she stood on the sidelines in her spare moments taking in the stunningness: a career in the making.

A decade later, a career later, Ann met and married Alexander. Until Galilea was born, the two lived as blissful complements to the canyon culture in Sierra Madre. Alexander dove into his work, and Ann traveled with a contingent of fashion models, snapping shots for every couture publication. She studied Cavalli and Chanel, and she could spot a Louboutin heel at fifty paces. She was in the right place at the right time: the day's sartorial choices would be tomorrow's cast-offs, and the models who loved her so much made sure she was in line to catch what they tossed her way, laughing as she grabbed her camera with one hand and airborne treasures with her other. The scene, a ballet complete with pirouettes and feline leaps this way or that.

This fashion house fortune would become Lee's legacy—a conduit to a designer wardrobe that was worlds apart from her grown-up, daytime life of science and research. And she liked it that way.

CHAPTER SIX
KIT KAT

She arrived just before sunset. The light streaming into the Blue Room was not doing it any favors. Isaac had not made it through the Colorado Boulevard rush-hour traffic yet, so Lee had a few minutes to look around and postulate about his reasons for texting her. The whole Caltech job topic was dead as far as she was concerned, but any excuse to haunt the bar at the Constance Hotel. It had a shabby charm about it that attracted a crowd on the weekends, and its proximity to the Rose Parade route on New Year's Day made it the go-to place for visitors and locals alike. The original vision must have been that of a chic, minimal vibe—the blue mirrors, fading to a greenish-blue. *Someone should have known that blue is not colorfast*, Lee thought. The gray booth seats were interspersed between the large windows. No frills here and a different crowd from the Tap Room, to be sure. In the withering daylight, Lee spotted several patches of peeling fabric on the seats, and the mirrors had that old cataract-like film on them. People poured in and out of the lobby which, in the open plan, provided a bustling backdrop that bounced off the hard mirror and glass surfaces. Lee's phone vibrated on the small tabletop:

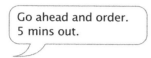

Go ahead and order.
5 mins out.

You don't have to ask twice. The Happy Hour Arroyo Mojito looks good. Still impeccably dressed after a day's work, Isaac looked more like a Lake Avenue financial advisor than Bill Nye the Science Guy. Lee sensed uncharacteristic agitation on his part and knew instantly that this meeting would not be about her. He didn't even look up when the server came.

"Gin and tonic on the rocks . . . please." Isaac pulled out his smartphone, not to check the time, just to keep it handy on the table. Now that the sun had gone down, the recessed lighting and mirrors prevailed, casting a strange hue over the few patrons seated around the bar's perimeter. Lee's slim white Cavalli jeans—inherited from her mother's treasured wardrobe—glowed blue-ish as if born that way. Not a good fashion statement, she decided.

She could wait him out, not sure that she wanted to know where the conversation would lead. They drank their first round in silence—a relief, really. Finally, "How's the cat?" Lee knew that was a lame way to start, but it seemed to set him at ease. He loved that cat.

"Bernoulli's fine, thanks.

How's work?" Lee also knew he didn't really care, not any more than she cared about the cat, but the conversation was the modern-day version of polite discourse. So many other topics were taboo these days.

"Well, the best part of the job is the lab work, just as you'd expect. I'm updating Cato's old lesson plans. You know, peppering them with twenty-first century lingo and working on objectives to fit the new standards. Some things never change . . ." At this point, Isaac had already tuned out—not rudeness. Something else, she decided.

"Uh-huh," he said, checking his phone. A sudden ramp-up in activity and chatter at the reception desk broke the spell, and he looked up. "So, you remember my sister, Kat?"

She did know Kat. She didn't care for Kat. Lee had little patience for her type. Here was a young woman who couldn't get out of her own way, couldn't lift a finger to help herself and left those who cared for her in the wake. Isaac included. In another life and time, they could have been improbable friends, or lab mates maybe: Lee the nerdy, friendless one and Kat, the ditzy cute one who attracted other people with her magnetic personality—just like a Disney TV series. Call it *Kat and Friend* or *Kat and the Other One*. That *was* another life and time, Lee decided, and in her newfound reincarnation as *Invincible Woman*, she was struggling here to be more generous for Isaac's sake. She owed him that much.

Kat did have a presence about her: slender, with dark curls that framed delicate olive-toned features. A feminine version of Isaac, to be sure. She garnered magnetic attention as she moved, an almost rhythmic sway in long skirts and ballet flats. Her appearance belied her approach to life. While she commanded considerable notice, she would truly do anything to disappear into the woodwork, preferring to be an onlooker. Her all-encompassing commitment to the spiritual communities she adored was her strong suit. Beyond that, she bumbled through life, depending on the kindness of bohemians.

"She called the other night. Called, not texted. No happy

emojis. So I knew something was wrong. There seems to be something about a death up in Santa Ynez. Someone in her . . . uh spiritual group up there. The local paper said the police found evidence of an electrical explosion but no clear source. What they *did* find sounds like it's right up your alley. Unexplained death or an accident, I'm assuming, that has her really rattled." Isaac looked rattled himself, partly because Kat was his baby sister and partly because he was about to ask for her help, Lee supposed. She reminded herself to keep that poker face she had cultivated. *Look like you care but not like you are worried*, she thought. In truth, she didn't care all that much, and she wasn't worried all that much either. Projecting compassion was still a skill in progress, one Lee hoped could be learned rather than faked. Eventually.

Lee did care about Isaac, though, and so she put a hand on his sleeve, a decidedly awkward move for her. "What do you need?"

=

Kat, too, was a native of Sierra Madre, getting her fateful start at Mama Pearl's Nursery School and the local elementary school. She grew up in a neighborhood of old craftsman homes below the Canyon. The quintessential small-town aura of settled high expectations mixed with free-wheeling renters. It wasn't long before she began to feel different, restless. The family move to Pasadena only served to unsettle her further. Her brother Isaac went off to MIT, which felt like an abandonment, despite the fact that they were years and worlds apart in every way as far as she was concerned. She made it through high school and her first year at the University of California, Santa Barbara—UCSB. Kat was smart but struggled to conform, even by UCSB standards. As much as her parents recognized that she was a "seeker," they hoped she would grow into something more stable with time. It was up in Santa Barbara's wine country a half hour north of the university—the Santa Ynez and Los Olivos junction—that she started on the path that would eventually spell trouble.

At first it was all a lark. Taking cover in horse ranches-turned-vineyards, cults of every size and stripe called to her; Kat referred to them as spiritual communities. It was innocent enough, as long as she had no money or worldly possessions to hand over. It started with recruitment in Love Is Everything Sisters. LIES. The acronym alone was enough to send most everyone else running. They advocated for every kind of Ponzi scheme they could get away with: Gifting Circles, the equivalent of chain letters, only with some other poor dope's money, were their fuel. Meditation classes were offered in never-ending tiers of increasing tuition and commitment, all the while selling the sense of family that its adherents sought. Next came the food factions: uncooked food—even meat—was promoted by Raw Unprocessed Foods Forever. You figure that one out. The adherents of RUFF ran around the hills of wine country, the same wine country made famous in that movie *Sideways*, practically baying at the moon. Worshippers strove for who-knows-what, but RUFF offered the perfect retreat from reality as far as Kat was concerned. Out of that spiritual experience grew the next logical offshoot: algae. Blue algae. The secret to eternal life. Finally, here were *her* people, a ragtag bunch promising to fill every void, imagined or otherwise. Blue Algae Reactant Factor, complete with its own acronym, sold all things algae in the shops on Edison Street and Alamo Pintado Road and out of the backs of pickup trucks on the small ranches in between. It was already known that green algae had practical applications as food and fuel, but *this* form of algae was magical, a means to attain power, beauty, and almost eternal life.

Kat subsisted on every kind of low-paying employment she could find; anything under her ability and pay grade offered the downward mobility and stress-free existence she desired. Her first job was as a dog walker—until she discovered that she was allergic to dogs. Something about the mysterious hives that erupted on workdays. She had an affinity for cats, but who walks a cat? Besides, it was known that cats made good snacks for the coyotes that roamed the hills north of the highway. Not urban legend. Serious business if you are a cat, or a Kat. The next job search led her to a shop on Edison Street. It was a busy place, selling lacey dresses and Native American jewelry to the tourists and locals alike, and she thought she had found her forever job as a "sales associate." Kat promptly quit when leather moccasins were added to the inventory. Her vegan lifestyle had begun when she left the RUFF community. Or maybe she left the RUFF people because she was really a closet vegan. In any case, it was a matter of principle. Kat eventually found her calling: she would market Blue Algae for Pets. She figured she could sell it without having to get near her blotch-inducing clients. Her business plan needed some tweaking, a lot of tweaking, since she didn't actually have a business plan yet.

Companions, some romantic, some whose relationship to Kat couldn't be defined, came and went for the next two years, and she was reasonably satisfied that this was all she should need or desire. There was the dude, whose name was actually Dude. He hailed from Goleta, complete with a surfboard and a quest for spiritual peace. They were soul mates until they weren't. Then there was the bearded mystic from Avila Beach whose name was Stuart. It turns out he was hiding from two of his three wives. And the rolling hills of the Santa Ynez–Los Olivos junction were the perfect place to do just that. Rounding out the collection of suitors was the most normal of the bunch. Antonio had inherited a small olive grove and an olive oil tasting shop to go with it. He had a kind demeanor, which sometimes put him at a disadvantage in the ruthless business of olive oil. A half dozen olive oil emporiums lined the town's main drag, each distinguishing itself with a different infusion—garlic, basil, lavender, blue algae—and with a different proprietary cheese or cracker. Antonio dealt with the pressure by seeking meditation in all its forms. That led him to Kat. Although a few years older than he was, she never appreciated the wisdom of spending time with such a kind soul, and she soon wore him out.

Kat settled into a secluded commune of sorts housed off of "the Pass," as the old Highway 154 was called. Originally a stagecoach route through Indian territory, the Pass now wound its way through wineries, olive groves, and kids' camps. The almost-daily Central Coast fog would rarely make it up into the hills, but this bohemian dwelling was nestled so deep into the trees, that it had a gloomy forest-like ambience all day long. Moss grew on all the north-facing edges and walls and dribbled down the eaves like green icicles. This is probably where the algae craze was born, Kat figured. She never asked.

CHAPTER SEVEN
MENTOR

Aside from Isaac, Lee's other friend in the *phys biz* was her mentor at PCC. Some thirty-eight years her senior, it was Cato Klein, the tetchy head of the physics department, who first interviewed her for her current position. He held the enviable status of imminent retirement after decades of teaching and had seen the groups of students morph just slightly each successive year—into what, he wasn't quite sure. At least, he thought it was the students and not he that had changed. It's hard to know when you are exposed to all sorts of invisible forces, benign and not so benign over the years. His inauspicious start in the early '70s came with an unexpected perk: every other kid who sauntered into the classroom offered up some form of weed, pot, what-have-you. Kind of like an apple for the teacher. Cato Klein took pride in announcing that, as their instructor, he could not accept bribes in class.

In his early days, Cato sported long hair—partially to fit in with his students, but he was also truly a product of the sixties with all that entailed. Not content just to take the classroom lecture approach, he encouraged all sorts of sanctioned and maybe non-sanctioned experimentation, tossing things through the air, sending students diving for cover. Lee pictured him, hair flying in all directions until it became plastered to his forehead with sweat, holding back a laugh. He created the school's first holography lab. Holograms are the stuff of *Star Wars*—that image of Princess Leia popping out of R2-D2's head—but also basic to understanding how 3D laser images work. It was down in the basement, away from light and the vibration of passing trucks on Colorado Boulevard that he built a rudimentary contraption on a steel lab table and coined the term *holographic platform*. The trial-and-error approach captivated his students and made for one of his best and most satisfying memories as a teacher.

Even as he aged, with shorter snow-white hair now, still tall and lanky and with pale blue eyes, he fit everyone's image of Greek Mentor who counseled Odysseus—minus the toga. It was Lee's good fortune to walk into his office. She needed a mentor, or Mentor, right now. As weeks went on and she settled into her teaching routine at PCC, she frequently sought him out. Lee knew Cato had another life, a job that he could slip into at the end of the day, and she envied his ability to escape into something just a little on the edge. At the end of her days, if she could muster the stamina, she slipped into one of her mother's sleek sheaths, usually the Ted Baker with its placed-just-right cutouts over the shoulders or a clingy vintage Tahari, and headed for the Tap Room at The Langham or the Blue Room at the Constance. In the dim atmosphere she looked like a million bucks. All she had waiting at home most other nights were drawstring sweats—a depressing sign that on this day she had given up.

As she got to know Cato, she developed an admiration for his endless imagination and enterprise. What fascinated her most was his second self, one into which he had fallen quite unexpectedly a couple of decades before. A former student came to him with a story and a plea for help: he'd been in a truck accident on the 101 just south of Santa Barbara—easy to do in California traffic. The kid had been injured. The other driver died, and insurance would not pay up. The kid had taken a job as a big rig driver, had the training, the license, and all. What he never counted on were the numerous ways in which the driver of such an eighteen-wheel megalith could *not* see what was going on around him. Nowadays neither Tesla nor plebeian Ford could get away with selling a vehicle that had so many blind spots. He remembered a discussion in physics class about all the forces that come into play during a car accident and also about reflection and how side mirrors work. Lab experiments had further cemented his knowledge of how the mind's eye sees, as well.

Who better than Cato Klein to the rescue? Together, the kid and Cato used principles of motion, forces, and energy—along with a bit of common sense—to figure out that the side mirrors were skewed at a barely noticeable wrong angle, a slight manufacturing defect, and on a very windy day, the on-ramp was partially obscured by swaying foliage. Cato and the kid took meticulous measurements and detailed photos at the crash site, relishing every moment, and a new vocation was born. Federal highway standards were clear but rarely followed. The internet, while in its relative infancy compared to today, offered just enough stats and weather reports, and the truck drivers' manuals, enough diagrams, that the insurance company had to relent. It was a win for the kid.

Cato poured himself into the training he needed to become a forensics investigator with a specialty in accident reconstruction. He took specialized courses on the weekends and in the summer and applied for his license from the ABFE— the American Board of Forensic Engineering. His ace in the hole was his computational physics background and his uncommon common sense. He felt empowered and soon learned how valuable his expertise could be to lawyers—and how lucrative for himself. The kid's situation had been pro bono, but the insight he himself gained was priceless, and soon Cato was pulling down more in one case than a year's worth of salary as a professor.

CHAPTER EIGHT
CLOSE ENCOUNTER OF THE OBNOXIOUS KIND

Following on the heels of a magical mystery tour in radioactivity—the experiment with the bathroom tiles and the Geiger counter weeks before—Lee was feeling pretty smug. She had blown their minds with archaic equipment and old glazed tiles, a coup really. Cato had been right about the wow factor and its attraction. The morning's lesson promised to be equally stunning, but there was nothing in the dusty basement at PCC that she could use, as far as she knew.

The parts needed for a superconductor investigation were pretty easy to come by, if you knew where to look, and some were surprisingly mundane. Good old Carolina Biological was the science teacher's go-to company for classroom kits. Lee recalled working with dozens of those kits as a student in middle school and high school. Her lab partners invariably let her do all the work; rather than feeling put-upon, she was conceited enough to think they couldn't do the assignments to her standards anyway. She could easily gin up one of those hands-on kits to fit community college standards. Small magnets were easy to come by too. But liquid nitrogen was another story.

"A frozen rose bud is no laughing matter, people. Yes, it's matter, as in an organic substance, but picture your fingers holding it while I blast it with liquid nitrogen. It's so-o-o not funny." With that Lee grabbed the flower with a long pair of wooden tongs and blasted away. The class watched as the beauty of the petals faded and then disintegrated, falling on the floor with small clinking sounds. The rapt look on the students' faces (*try not to laugh*, Lee told herself) reminded her of the perilous scenes in *Snow White* or *Beauty and the Beast*—the evil witch condemns the fairytale heroine further toward death with each slow-motion spiral of a petal. "So, who has fingers they don't need?"

Just as Lee figured. After she circulated around the room to chill ceramic saucers with the liquid nitrogen, students got right to work following the lab book instructions and explanations on attracting and repelling magnetic forces. Both classes frolicked around the room with abandon as they got magnets to levitate above the ceramic saucers. The more academic groups managed dignified high-fives, while the typically jaded bunch whooped and hollered. *Give 'em a few minutes*, Lee told herself. The best is usually yet to come: experiential learning. She knew they wouldn't be able to resist poking at the magnet to see if it would do more, and sure enough . . . poke one edge or corner and make it spin in place.

"So, class. What is happening here? What's in the ceramic saucer that repels the magnet and makes it hover?" Blank stares from too many students. *Come on, people.* "Think about

Galilea, Galilea | 45

it. Electrons that are embedded in the ceramic material—in all materials, really. They need to get *excited!*" As she expected, that got their attention. *You lustful little creatures.* "Cooling to such low temperatures with the liquid nitrogen allows electrons—electricity—to flow effortlessly around the saucer. No resistance, right? You need the motion of the electrons, the moving electric current, to repel the magnet, and up it goes." *Another prurient reference ought to get their attention again.*

In a matter of minutes, though, the magnets would begin to sink, and the levitation, falter. Another lesson. The cold liquid nitrogen—the material Lee made sure to keep out of the hands of these students—was warming and dissipating. A lesson in itself on the value of keeping the ceramic conductor cold enough for the electrical charges to do their thing. All in all, a successful day in the life of a physics instructor. As Lee locked away the liquid nitrogen canister in her classroom, she noted how much safer it would be downstairs in that basement. "It can wait," she said to nobody in particular as she headed out. *Will this be a drawstring sweats evening or a dressed-to-kill night out?*

As the end of the semester approached, Isaac's Kat story still weighed heavily both in her dreams and in the waking minutes before coffee. Lee pulled on a mood-lifting pair of jeans and a pseudo designer off-one-shoulder black sweater; it was Casual Day for PCC faculty, but she also threw on an old Lauren knit blazer for effect. One thing she had to learn to do—and soon—was compartmentalize her life. She knew there was no surviving the job if she was consumed with the Kat saga.

The day's two classes were polar opposites: one group represented the serious students bent on transitioning to a four-year school, preferably UCLA or similar, and the other, fortunately smaller, class consisted of kids who just needed science units to graduate and had no idea what Basic Physical Science was when they registered. Lee felt sorry for the latter group, even though they were a tough, largely unmotivated audience; she imagined they were expecting something akin to physical education. She recalled the obvious disappointment on their faces, the dejected body language when they sank into their seats the first day of the semester, and she knew with certainty that some would drop the class during the withdrawal period. Those who stuck it out learned more about the Me Too Movement than physics in the early weeks of the semester.

Lee was older than most of the students in her Basic Physics section, but not by much. Her slight stature was deceptive, and both the male and female contingents tested her at every turn, even going so far as to invite her out for drinks and more at the local Lucky Baldwin's pub. Even if she wanted to, decorum dictated no socializing with members of the class; Lee was grateful. Some were the great unwashed masses, the hoping-to-get-lucky population at the city college. While many young people were on the serious two-year transfer track, a consequence of the costs of higher education, there was still this group, determined to play to their audience of like-minded peers. That extended to wisecracks and exaggerated yawns. The I'm-going-to-invade-your-personal-space move was the worst. Lee's investment in proving her chops to this group was tempered with a desire for self-preservation. Usually she could ignore and rebuff innuendos until the cows came home.

That evening after class—the daylight savings period when it is shockingly dark by 5:30—she had a close encounter of the obnoxious kind with one of her charges. As Lee headed to the faculty parking garage, she spotted him waiting at the entrance. She always had a head for details, and she had noted weeks before how the garage was laid out and where the best lighting was. Her math/physics brain had also mapped out the best parking spots for a quick exit. Tonight she added a description of this kid to her mental compendium of facts—just in case. She knew his last name, pictured the roster entry in her mind, and to her surprise she could even recall part of his student ID number.

As Lee got closer to the structure, she confirmed in her mind that he was waiting for her. *Black hoodie. Dark hair visible underneath. Some remnants of acne. White Adidas track shoes—how do these kids afford those? What more, what more? What's in his pockets? What time is it—exactly? Who else is around? Don't take your eyes off him, Lee.* Peripheral vision told her that they were alone. If this were a bad movie, there'd be screeching tires somewhere and a pounding heart. Halogen lights struggled to come on, in that blinking stage. She made an exaggerated point of looking up at the security camera nearby, hoping he would get the hint. If he followed her inside, they could be out of range, but his image would still have been captured beforehand. Always a false sense of security really, cameras don't prevent an assault if the perp doesn't think that far ahead, doesn't care about consequences. If only she'd had one of those key fobs with the panic button, she could also make a show of that. No such luck, but then again, who pays attention to those blaring alarms anymore? If she pulled her phone out, it might end up the shattered victim here; protect your phone at all costs if you can't afford a new one, she figured. And then there was the handbag—her late mother's unassuming but oh-so-expensive Moynat. What would she give up to keep it safe?

Finally, the sink or swim moment arrived. How is it possible that no one else was around? Lee knew she could run circles around this guy when it came to wits, but she was at a disadvantage physically. *Go with the wits, Lee.*

"So, Mr. Jacobs, ready for your final exam on Monday? Last chance to pass the class, right?" Lee desperately hoped this would be enough to throw him off. Never passing up an opportunity to mess with the heads of her lab mates in high school, she loved seeing the look of panic on their faces when she tossed out an imaginary exam date or project deadline. For a moment she thought she had gone the wrong way with him: *Did he even care about a final exam, passing the class? Did he possibly, improbably, know that the exam date was actually a couple of weeks away?* If so, she needed another dog bone to toss out. As she spoke, she became aware that he was leaning in closer, definitely an "in your face" stance, complete with that twisted upper-lip sneer. Lee hated that. One form of intimidation she had experienced herself over the years as a woman in the male science arena.

In the meantime, she dug down deep into that handbag; if price tag were any indication, she should find the Hope Diamond in there, or at least Yoda's original lightsaber. Suddenly: "Uh, is there like extra credit I can do?" Mr. Jacobs had blinked in a moment of confusion, and Lee felt relief and an adrenaline rush all in the same split second. For confirmation she wanted *him* to back off first. *Patience. Stand your ground, Lee.* She made a show of grabbing on to something hidden in the recesses of her bag, careful *not* to pull it out. She wasn't even sure what it was, but he didn't know that. That did it. As the distance between them normalized, "Uh, maybe not a paper, but like an extra project or something?" She had him now.

"We'll talk next week, Mr. Jacobs." Lee headed off to her car—quickly—so she could get some momentum going before her legs turned to rubber, not glancing back but sure he was heading in another direction when she saw his reflection in the windshield of a parked car. *Thank God someone actually shelled out money for a wash at the Rose City Car Wash Express.*

Lee practically hurled herself into her own front seat as the delayed fight-or-flight reaction kicked in. The first thing she vowed to do tomorrow, after identifying that unrecognizable life-saving gadget in her bag, was to get her car washed and then sign up for a self-defense class—in that order. This was a night for drawstring sweats, to be sure, and she headed over to the drive-through at Tops Burgers for guilt-inducing sustenance before heading home.

There in the dark of the passenger seat, as she reached into the bag for her wallet, she felt it. Heading off to class one day, she had dropped a Causemetics 12-Hour Extreme Super Mega-Lash Midnight Black Cruelty-Free and Vegan mascara into her purse, the kind guaranteed to make one's lashes struggle to defy gravity under their weight but look fabulous for any occasion. You never know when you'll need a little mystique. Fortunately, she supposed, she had forgotten about it. Who knows where it would have ended up if she had taken it out in the car or the classroom on any given day? At any rate, this turquoise, probably dried-out and expired, makeup tool would now go everywhere she went, a lucky rabbit's foot, only not quite so furry.

CHAPTER NINE
WELCOME TO MOUNTAINVIEW GARDENS CONDOMINIUMS

Lee's recently purchased '60s-era condo had neither a mountain view nor a garden. "I'll take it. It's perfect," she declared to the realtor, whose fingers had been crossed behind her back. "What's the least I can offer? What are the HOA fees? There can't be much; there's no pool, no gym . . ." She was looking for a sensory-free environment. This was her only real requirement—aside from price. It's silly that more people don't include that quality on their checklists when buying a home.

The one-bedroom-one-bath place had been mercifully updated to at least a '90s look somewhere along the way. It was clear that it had originally been a far cry from the coveted mid-century expression, so no loss there. The industrial look was a miss too. The walk-in closet, shown in the ad as a "walking closet"—probably the earnest effort of someone not familiar with English or relying too much on auto-correct—was everything she had hoped for, though. Plenty of room for her own pedestrian wardrobe and the fabulous Ann Roberts collection as well. The Chanels and Cavallis had never looked more at home. Even Mr. and Mrs. Louboutin (left and right, size eights) settled in nicely on an upper shelf.

Pasadena's real estate market remained out of sight for many people, but Lee was determined to stay in her comfort zone on this issue. Fortunately, Alexander had taken out an earthquake policy, something that should be a given but is often considered a luxury, even in Southern California. The demise of the Canyon home in Sierra Madre had assured her of a future. Of course, her new "digs," this brick-and-stucco building on Del Mar Boulevard, was the worst kind of construction in a quake zone. The Mountainview Gardens Homeowners Association had done the required retrofitting; steel diamond-shaped bolts running along the exterior of the structure, parallel to the roof line, were supposed to anchor the walls to the roof and the different floors in the interior. At least that was the theory.

This four-story edifice had survived some small quakes, obviously, but age contributed a distinctly westerly slant to the whole place, more noticeable the higher up one went. On the third floor, Lee's slight sense of vertigo soon wore off as she walked around her new (old) place. Before long it was nonexistent, her brain doing the adjusting for her. Adding some throw rugs over the wood floors blunted the effect too. At this point the only problem was in her bedroom: her bedframe, which was on casters, tended to drift to the western-facing window over a matter of days. She would move it back, but she knew one morning she would wake and find herself in bed, hanging over a ledge just like one of those accident scenes in a disaster movie. Maybe *Armageddon: Last Days of Pasadena*.

Tones of gray added to Lee's feeling of contentment. Gray

tile, gray countertops, gray cabinets. Stainless steel in the galley kitchen. Some well-placed "pops" of white worked well with the interior and reflected off an old arched window that looked like it would leak if Pasadena ever got rain again. The furniture left behind by the previous owner had an IKEA sensibility to it—set to self-destruct soon, she assumed. That was fine; she'd have time to redecorate as each piece disintegrated, and a few well-placed throw pillows in the meantime were a good distraction.

Even though the traffic had a steady pulse on the street below, the building itself was reasonably quiet. Many units were subleased by bookish Caltech students, who only had to walk or bike a half mile to reach campus. Others were inhabited by decades-long owners, their furniture and walls still reflecting the year they had moved in. A few—the ones being renovated in the minimal style of the day—belonged to young hopefuls expecting to attend the new medical school nearby. While the neighbors were quiet, the plumbing gave off a symphony every time a toilet was flushed, and the shower water chimed all the way down to the basement. Lee prided herself on being able to pinpoint which unit initiated the flow, applying a bit of physics as she listened and counted.

The downside to her new refuge was its walking proximity—or lack thereof—to her favorite haunts. Not near the Tap Room, nor the Blue Room, and a little too far from trendy Old Pasadena. Even the shops and restaurants on Lake Avenue were out of reach without a car, she decided. So she would drive or ride-share for now; sometime in the future the Metro line would surely connect Lee and her neighbors with other parts of the city.

=

Heading out one evening for a "confab" at the Raymond, Lee made her way on surface streets to the very edge of town, skirting the rush-hour traffic and wending through what were once the quiet streets but now served as alternate routes when the freeways backed up. To her surprise, she was the first one to arrive. This was going to be a deep huddle to determine the next step. After Isaac had related Kat's cult saga to Lee, she had taken a brief version to Cato. Not a betrayal of confidence: a necessity. They had all agreed that they could each bring something to the table here, but it would go no further until they determined the seriousness of the incident. The bar at the venerable Raymond Restaurant was more of a dress-down kind of place, despite the prices. Locals knew about the happy hour discounts and packed into the small, dark room as often as they could. Brown coppered ceilings and frosted glass doors were not the originals, nor were the gas lamp–style fixtures; but the bar's name *was* "1886," an homage to the historic Raymond Hotel that was erected there in the late 1800s and to its rumored hidden "speakeasy." Pasadenans love their history, but a trendy bar menu takes precedence when it comes to a successful business, and so the interior was vintage while the drinks were hip. Lee noted that the attached dining room had a different vibe altogether: quietly staid and expensive. The two rooms had a symbiotic relationship of some sort.

Pricier cocktails, such as the Whiskey Rose Parade, and inexpensive wine and well drinks sat side-by-side on the bar menu. They featured gin and bourbon as the bartender's choices tonight. The noise, even this early in the evening, was bordering on deafening, and Lee figured they would have to move as soon as the guys got there. Not because they could be overheard but because they would have to read lips to understand each other. Isaac and Cato filed in through the narrow doorway and slid in next to Lee, a vision in contrast (old timers would say like *Mutt and Jeff*, though no one knows where that came from). Visually they were a mismatch: Cato, tall, pale, seventy-ish and thirty-something Isaac, shorter with dark hair and olive-toned features. But they both had a sensibility that appealed to Lee, and she hoped they could pull this off.

It became clear as drinks arrived that they would indeed have to move to the dining room. Both Isaac and Cato offered to foot the bill for dinner, and Lee felt fortunate to be with them tonight. In fact, she felt right at home seated between these two salt-and-pepper bookends. There were few tables since most of the seating consisted of leather-clad banquettes running around the perimeter. The history of this room was clear: nothing much had been done to renovate other than adding electric lighting, but that was its charm. It was the food that drew people in.

"So, Isaac, from what you told me, Kat is pretty convinced that this friend of hers died from some kind of foul play—not a heart attack, not a freak accident, as the police are claiming. And you said he had told her on several occasions that this cult, this blue algae group, was into something shady?" Cato took out his trusty notebook to record their thoughts as Lee continued. "He was a young guy, right? That doesn't mean it wasn't from natural causes, but if he truly felt like something nefarious was going on, that sounds like we need to take Kat's concerns seriously. I'm telling you right now I'm not a big fan of cults, spiritual communities, what have you," she added. Her body language, sitting back, arms crossed, confirmed her point of view. "I'm not impartial in that regard, but I can definitely look at the technical stuff."

Cato looked up from his notebook to see how Isaac would respond, and he was rewarded: Isaac nodded intently, and mirrored Lee's same posture. "I know, I know. I feel the same way, but I can't say it hasn't been helpful for Kat. These groups are providing something. My parents actually rest a little easier knowing she's not living alone up there. For better or for worse." Dinner came: crusted salmon, dry-aged steak au poivre, mussels in an earthy brown sauce. A white wine, a red wine, a rosé. A veritable feast that they had agreed to share around, only they were regretting the sharing part at this point. The food was five-star quality, they all agreed, and gluttony was setting in. Good thing Lee had worn her old jeans, the ones that sagged after two or three wearings. Her suede jacket, with four-inch fringe all the way around, was also great for hiding a multitude of sins—no designer duds tonight. *Eat away, Lee.* Halfway through the meal the group was beginning to slow down, and their thoughts on a possible murder began to filter in again.

This time it was Cato who spoke: "I think we need to get up there and take a look at the scene. My investigator's license should get us in. But I think Lee should take the lead. She has a lot of practical experience in electrical engineering. Okay with you, Isaac?"

"Isaac, I was thinking that you should avoid going up altogether at this point. They may make the connection between you and Kat," Lee added. "I think Cato and I can handle it. There's this unusual electrical component that we both recognize, and Cato's experience in the field is worth everything.

We'll keep you in the loop by text. Really. Right, Cato?" It sounded to Isaac as if the two had decided in advance that this is how it should go. Normally he'd be insulted or annoyed at least, but he had to admit that it made sense. The second glass of wine was kicking in too.

"I see your point. I'm fine with it. I'll get some contact names from Kat for you. Just be careful. When?" Lee recognized Isaac's speaking style—short, concise—no time for messing around. It had always been that way, and she figured that's why she found it easy to be around him. She really didn't enjoy small talk either, though her mother's gift of "mindful" communication was in her DNA somewhere. It would creep out at the worst times, so Lee was on guard for anything that smacked of too much sensitivity or unwarranted concern on her part. She called it her BS monitor (she envisioned a dial and a clicking sound, not unlike her favorite Geiger counter, only red—Chanel red).

Cato leaned in. "Lee and I will do a little research online first. We do have to be careful, though. Texting, emailing, phone calls. We don't know how deep this goes. From this point on, the best communication is face-to-face. Barring that, we'll have to come up with some fake news names if we're texting. I'm stuck with my real name; it's on my license. You two can pick your own, and I think the cult should just be referred to as *Blue Öyster*." He was watching for a reaction, and seeing none, he sighed. "Too young to know *Blue Öyster Cult*? I was kind of just kidding about fake news names, but you never know when they might come in handy. By the way, it's a hard rock band from the sixties." At this point Cato was grinning ear to ear.

Not to be outdone, Lee said, "Can I be Individual 1? Or wait

. . . how about . . . Jane Jetson. I always wanted to be Jane Jetson. Anyway, Cato and I should head up to Santa Ynez in a few days for some fact-finding. Isaac, can we get those names and numbers from your sister before then?" Isaac did look a little dejected or maybe overwhelmed at how fast things were moving. "You need a new identity too." She knew how sensitive he was about his given name. "Hmm. Bernoulli, after your cat. A good scientific name. Fitting for an aeronautically gifted fur ball, don't you think?"

CHAPTER TEN
A HALF LIFE IS BETTER THAN NONE, OR THE PIG IN THE BASEMENT

A pig in a poke, a pig in a blanket, when pigs fly . . . counting pigs. Sure, it's really "counting sheep," but Lee had spent hours trying to sleep (enumerating pigs, sheep, what have you) to no avail. She was at that point where the pigs had taken over her dreams: a frustrating loop of pig images surfacing and retreating. Not that there's anything wrong with pigs. In reality, she figured, they were a metaphor for something. But she was now going into her third night of sleep deprivation, and it was driving her nuts. The only conversation she had had recently about *pigs* was a discussion involving radioactivity.

She was planning a lab activity for the final physics class of the semester—another one of those "blow their minds" lessons. Cato had given her an idea that involved the old Geiger counter of which she had become so fond. Could they measure serious radioactivity and its half-life in an ordinary setting, an ordinary classroom, at Pasadena City College? There were no lead-lined walls anywhere on campus, even in that glowing-blue basement of marvels. While Lee knew that this could be done safely, she was also well aware of what could go wrong—the old "What can go wrong will go wrong" thing.

Cato left her a page of handwritten instructions; most notable were the admonitions:

1. Don't forget to get the Geiger counter from the basement. And . . .

2. Get the pig out of the basement while you are down there, but be careful with it.

It was that last item that had provoked the midnight angst, she decided. One more day before she would be on campus to assemble her supplies. This lab activity would serve as the kind of performance-based exam science teachers seem to like: follow the directions, observe, graph, and come to a conclusion. Doable by every class member, she was sure. Even Mr. Jacobs. In Lee's mind the issue was resolved, and she would conk out as soon as she got into bed.

Sure enough, by about 2:00 a.m. pigs were on the move again, drifting in and out of her sleeping-dreaming-waking state, with mouths open, silent (at least). But Alexander was there too, her father's face younger than she had remembered him. *What did he want?* She hoped it was to relive a carefree moment: maybe a trip to Twohey's for a "stink-o burger," maybe a tour of Los Alamos. She regretted never having the chance to thank him for that, or never *taking* the opportunity anyway. Is this some cosmic karma? He was gone, and then so were the swine. Obviously he had tracked her down from heaven, or wherever old physicists end up, and she figured he knew at this point that she was now a part-time instructor at a community college. Not the Institute. But then, Lee slept.

=

Even a Starbucks Double Espresso Caramel Macchiato, light on the caramel dribble, heavy on the foam—her drink of choice in the morning—was not enough to get her brain cells firing. She probably needed an IV drip directly into a vein to make up for the mostly sleepless nights. As she elbowed her way through the crowd of coffee zombies that had congregated near the door of the small Starbucks on Lake Avenue, Lee worked hard to push the images of the night before out of her head as well. Most dreams are long-forgotten within a few minutes of waking, but she knew the pig thing, and, most especially, the appearance of Alexander would stay with her for a while. The scientist in her had a reassuring slant on the situation: the pig would be of great interest to her students because they lived for any moment of peril in the classroom, particularly when the teacher was the one at risk. It was natural, really. Kind of like the time her high school physics instructor walked around the classroom lab with a piece of trinitite in her hand. The kids gasped as she dropped it on the floor and then picked it up: the reaction she planned for as she feigned clumsiness. Even Galilea (still Lea at the time) couldn't help herself—what a way to go. Little did the kids know that the amount of radiation absorbed from this little piece of green-brown rock was comparable to standing out in the bright sun for a few minutes—nothing more. Nowadays, Lee thought, the gauntlet of cell phones she had just plowed through on her way out of Starbucks gave off more radiation. The trinitite story had always fascinated her though.

After the detonation of the atomic bomb at the Trinity test site outside of Los Alamos, the desert floor erupted into a slow-motion wave of melted sand that rose above the site. As it collapsed, it became what looked like an ocean of green glass as far as the eye could see. In truth this "sea" was more grit and minerals than actual glass, but what a poetic image. Some inhabitants of Los Alamos, children included, ventured out weeks later when the ground had cooled and collected pieces without regard and, most likely, understanding of radioactivity's potency. Fifty or sixty years later, the trinitite, named after that infamous place, had lost most of its already-minute amounts of radioactivity and existed almost exclusively for the purpose of being displayed—and dropped—in classrooms everywhere.

=

Old Tupperware bowls, blocks of paraffin from Michaels craft store, and a few silver dollars rescued from her father's collectibles—*check*. The prep work was finished too: paraffin slabs jammed into the bottoms of the bowls, with two slots the thickness and the diameter of the coins carved into the surface of the wax, approximately an inch apart—*check*. Now, the hard part, or at least the part Lee was thrilled about and dreading all at the same time. The source of her pig dreams, she assumed.

Down in the basement below the gym floor, the untouched tableau of old furniture mixed with scientific implements of another time and place seemed more familiar to Lee now. *Get the pig out of the basement, but be careful*, she repeated to herself.

It was clear that no one, with the exception of an errant rat or two, had been there recently. She knew this immediately. She did have an uncommon eye for details: no footprints, no palm prints other than the ones she had left months earlier, nothing out of place. In a weaker, less confident mood, she might have imagined an extra set of prints somewhere. All equipment was present and accounted for, even that azure jar of radium chloride, but she forced herself to look closer—just an exercise in observation skills. And guts, maybe. And maybe she noticed something too: the contents of the jar seemed lower than she remembered, a kind of bathtub ring of blue around the sides. *Get real, Lee.* Her favorite self-admonishment.

The original yellow Geiger counter—devised to measure radiation—had been actively used in Cold War drills up until the sixties. They're still stashed away by the dozens in defunct Civil Defense sites all around the San Gabriel Valley, and newer versions, available through Amazon, are available to measure a variety of more friendly radiation sources today. Lee remembers, as a kid, looking at a map with Alexander and remarking how the many below-ground cavities around Pasadena resembled catacombs. The closest center for her own family had been, in fact, near Eaton Canyon. They would pass by the now-repurposed entrance every day on the way to her middle school. Civil defense officers and radiation safety advisors had been charged with keeping the monitors and the shelters in working order. Never mind that one blast from the Russians would have wiped out every living thing, realistically speaking.

Somehow PCC had one of the old shelter Geiger counters too. She made a mental note to ask Cato where it came from. In any case, it was hers for the time being and she grabbed it off the shelf, grateful that it still worked. *Now the pig.*

=

Radium beryllium was way more potent than those glazed tiles. It truly represented radiation that was the stuff of atom bombs. In fact, a Brit named James Chadwick worked with Ra-Be at Los Alamos while consulting on "the Gadget." Funny about that six degrees of separation thing, Lee thought. A small quantity is great for a demonstration on the half-life of radioactive substances, only it seems to be hard to come by at your typical community college. Enter Cato. Somehow he had procured a tiny cache of Ra-Be decades ago for a lesson on transferring radiation from one element to another and on measuring the radioactivity as it weakens, the so-called half-life. His students immediately had an appreciation for the dangers, and that living-on-the-edge feeling made a lifelong impression on them. Lee was hoping for the same great light bulb moment with her classes—if she could only find the pig he had stashed in the basement years ago.

So here's the pig issue: Lee knew she was not actually looking for swine—dead or alive. Radioactive materials have to be stored in a lead container to prevent leakage. For some reason these containers, resembling thermos bottles rather than porkers, got the name *lead pigs*. Cato had only mentioned to her that inside this pig would be several capsules the size of Tylenol casings, each containing some Ra-Be. What he couldn't tell her was exactly where he had stashed the stuff. He remembers moving it around in the basement several times over the years for security reasons, but like looking for a car in a parking lot, it could be anywhere now. She was on her own here. *If I were a pig, where would I be?* A moment of uncharacteristic silliness set in; it must be something about this place: *Here, piggy!*

Being alone in a subterranean vault, where no one would ever find you, is liberating but dangerous. Lee shuddered with that realization and set to work looking in the most logical spots first: cabinets, desk drawers, lockers. She was feeling a sense of urgency now, and she quickly pried open every desk drawer, locked or otherwise. Her handy mascara would be of no use here; good thing she spotted a screwdriver on her way in. A tremor in her hands. Dust raining down on her skirt and boots as she moved from desk to desk. Sounds in the dark recesses of the basement. Something like the *Mummy* movies. *Not amusing*. Lee spotted an old gym locker plastered with school decals. Freestanding, not attached to a wall, and leaning to one side for some reason. She would have to be careful that it wouldn't fall on her as she attempted to open it. Lee imagined some archaeologist centuries from now—maybe a graduate of the Wedd School—finding her cobwebbed skeleton pinned beneath this strange metal sarcophagus. What a field day trying to decipher the message on it:

G–O–P–C–C–L–A–N–C–E–R–S

A stroke of luck: Lee was able to pry the locker door open enough to see inside. There it was—the pig. She took a closer look, wanting to assure herself that the lid was on, the whole thing intact. *Thank you, Cato!* It was about the size of a small thermos, as expected, and surprisingly dust-free. All she needed to do at this point was pull it through the opening without causing a disaster. She thought she heard the resident rats scatter for the hills as she reached in. *They must know more than they let on.* It would be heavier than it looks, owing to the lead outer shell. It's cylindrical, and so it could be easy to grab hold of. Bracing the locker with one hand, Lee reached in with the other. As she grabbed the lead container, she dropped the screwdriver and then let go of the locker; she would need two hands to pull out the pig. And out it came. A little lighter than she thought, but there was no time to reflect on its condition. It would fit in one hand, so she knew all she had to do was grab the Geiger counter and go. Coated in dust and feeling a little like a victorious tomb raider, Lee left the basement behind and headed home, the pig in her trunk. Foolish maybe, but dinner tonight with Isaac.

=

Wood panels, interrupted by shelves of leather-bound volumes—science books of the 1900s—seemed to dampen the conversations in the dining room. Or maybe it was that people spoke with reverence for the legacy of the Athenaeum. Lee glanced around at the portraits on the walls; all, as if religious iconography, had some historic connection to Caltech. This room could have been very dark, somber really, but it was rescued by the outsized arched windows that looked out on the campus.

"Someday you'll be hung here, Isaac," she whispered. A jest and a triple entendre, to be sure. She wasn't at all confident that he caught the tease. "Kidding, really. You look miserable." *Where was that waiter?* This conversation was definitely going south, and it was all her fault. Even her vintage (slightly frayed at the cuffs) Chanel jacket, threads of silver yarn, rhinestone buttons and all, couldn't illuminate the mood: his and now, hers. Lee scanned the wine list, this being a venue more suited to uncommon wines than trendy mojitos, she figured.

Isaac issued a faint smile, just to let her know he was alive and astute enough to catch the snark. The early diners looked toward the patio every few seconds, as if they were counting down the seconds before the legendary prime rib buffet opened; the aroma of rare meat was enough to clog the veins and lighten the mood all at the same time. A good white Albariño from Spain could surely cut the cholesterol, she suggested. Lee knew Isaac would go with red, as any self-respecting meat eater would, so she was expecting a rise out of him. A small concession to make him feel better, she hoped.

"Not taking the bait, Lee. I know what you're doing. Honestly, I'll be fine. Just tell me that you have some good news, a plan of some sort." Saved by the waiter, and sure enough, Isaac ordered one of the recommended "cabs."

"So, it's a good-news-bad-news kind of thing." She was already losing her nerve; this gutsy girl had a heart after all. She darted out of her chair. Perfect time to surf the buffet table piled high with all things seafood and the rarest slices of prime rib. She grabbed a couple of desserts first, anticipating a bad ending to the meal, while Isaac kept his eyes on her. It was clear he was waiting. Lee worked her way around the buffet and back to their table in silence. The slight quiver in her own voice unnerved her. "We went over the police reports and their photos and some online sites. So there is clearly something going on in Santa Ynez. It looks deliberate, or maybe some quirk of the laws of electromagnetism. I'm leaning toward deliberate. So is Cato. Nothing that your sister could have been involved in. So that's good. We're going up Saturday to get a firsthand look. Cato's taking all his equipment. I'll get those contacts from you tomorrow if that's okay. Can we meet at the Blue Room after work? It's close to campus. Besides, I'll have to walk off this dinner." A pause as the wine came. She wondered how many

Athenaeum food servers had been greeted with an interruption in conversation, suggesting they were less than worthy. This observation was unnerving as well. *When did she begin to care?*

CHAPTER ELEVEN

SMOOT! SMOOT!

"We can even measure in Smoots, as a backup." *There it is, his reluctant smile.* Smoots are a real thing. Lee had heard about them in one of her high school math classes years before and had discounted the term of measurement as a joke—and it had been an ongoing gag among her muon compadres at Los Alamos (true geek humor, she figured), but here it was again. An opportunity to make someone laugh about the deeply serious business of measurement doesn't come around every day, so she decided to run with it. *Besides*, she thought, *if anyone would appreciate it, it would be Isaac, and he needs a laugh right about now.* "Smoot me now, Isaac! You can actually convert standard measurement to Smoots; there are a lot of apps that do that, and even Google Measure has gotten into the act. Take a look when you get a chance. Seriously."

Of course, he would know what a Smoot was. Isaac had spent most of his time actually studying at MIT, but it's pretty hard to miss the significance of Smoots when you cross the Harvard Bridge near Boston. It was called the Massachusetts Avenue

Bridge back in the day. The contribution of Ollie Smoot was legendary. As a fraternity pledge prank, he and a gaggle of classmates had decided one night to figure the official length of the bridge—in Smoots. The story varies as to whether they had flipped the 5'7" Smoots head-over-heels-over-head all the way across, or whether he had gotten up between each carefully measured length. Either way, the group meticulously marked every Smoot with a stroke of paint. To this day all 364 marks remain, refreshed every year by each new class of freshmen. Isaac included.

"I get it, Lee. Thanks for the effort. Sometimes you are a funny gal." *If you only knew, Isaac, how close I had come to actually being a Gal. The etymology is a story for another time,* she decided. "What's the plan for Santa Ynez?"

"Isaac, let's order first. Okay?" There they were again. The Blue Room. At this time of night, it looked even more glaringly like a scene from *Avatar*. Still charming in a sci-fi sort of way. The blue worked well with Isaac's dark hair and eyes but not so much with her own pale coloring. Her gray silk Prada blouse with the red collar, especially suited to her mother, couldn't compensate for Lee's pallor in this setting; even the really low neckline would not be enough distraction. She would have to remember that next time. Maybe back to the Tap Room if he was paying. The two-piece band was setting up, so it was only a matter of minutes before conversation would have to come to an end. *Maybe that's a good thing.* "So drinks and an app?"

The ordering process was a brief respite from the necessary discussion. Over gimlets and the signature exotic cheese platter, the two talked in general terms about the upcoming foray into Blue Algae country. The Blue Room seemed an apt location for planning. "We'll go up tomorrow. Just for the day.

Cato's bringing some equipment, namely the camera with a macro lens and a couple of meters. Should be simple."

"I have the latest contact info for the Blue Algae people, as far as I know. Texted it to Cato too. Be careful tomorrow. Okay? Stick with Cato. Don't roam around there. I get the feeling these cul . . . er . . . spiritual communities mean business." Lee nodded. Not a guarantee that she would follow his suggestions but that she would try. She knew better than to promise; no telling what they would find, or what Cato would decide to do. "Wish I could go with you guys, but I understand your thinking on this matter," Isaac added.

Lee didn't get a chance to respond, but she figured there was nothing she could say anyway to quell his concerns. The duo began to play, and considering the marble-and-glass environment, they sounded pretty good. Acoustic guitars paired well with any setting, even a sci-fi bar peopled with Avatars, she thought.

CHAPTER TWELVE
DO YOU KNOW THE WAY TO SANTA YNEZ?

The drive to Santa Ynez was eye-opening for Lee—not the picturesque roadside scenery, but the interior of the Land Cruiser. She marveled at how much Cato's old SUV resembled his office. Dusty and cluttered. *Strange for a man of the (physics) cloth. Or is the bachelor thing the dominant trait?* "I see you've got a library in the back seat. What are the manuals for?" She figured the answer would be simple: she could see what looked like binders of accident reports, car and truck specs, a photo album, old Thomas maps. That last one was a surprise—but not really. It's easier to deal with a paper map than a googled cell phone map, especially outdoors in the light. She also imagined they would be good for marking up with red ink. Lee really only asked to keep the conversation going, but she had to admit there were some other interesting, unidentifiable gadgets back there too. "What are those other gizmos? I get the camera and the lenses, but what's in your yellow toolbox?" He did have a fantastic camera and an assortment of lenses lining the floor in the back. That was a no-brainer for an investigator. It was clear that Cato was organizing his thoughts—so very like him, and when the traffic slowed on the 101, he launched into an animated two-handed pantomime to explain his back seat filing system.

It was great to see Cato so excited about something; Lee only hoped that when the traffic sped up again, he would put his hands back on the steering wheel. *Let's not end up a deadly traffic statistic, Cato. Someone else would have to investigate us. Hands back where they belong. Thank you, Cato!* Just as she figured, the manuals and maps were what they appeared to be. It was Cato's explanation of the photo album that caught her attention: "The photos are details of the accidents or, in some cases . . . uh, probable crimes that I've worked on over the years. I have to warn you, the crispy critter pics are hard to get used to, but once you do, you'll be hooked." He laughed. *Really, Cato? Fried chicken? Fried shrimp? French toast?* Then it dawned on her, and she paled. "Yeah, it's what you think. There's not much left to work with in a car fire or . . . uh . . . an explosion." Lee could feel Cato steal a sideway glance at her, so she put on her poker face and was glad that she had chosen her oversize sunglasses for the drive.

Guess I'll have to remember that technical term—crispy critter. "We won't see any . . . uh . . . crispy critters today, right?" *Go ahead, sound like a wuss, Lee.* "At least not before lunch anyway?" she added out loud, managing a half smile, but just for show. Funny, she was hungry and appalled all at the same time. Kind of like those frog dissections she did in high school right before lunch. Nothing like rubbery chicken tenders drenched in barbeque sauce to chase the formaldehyde scent away.

As their speed picked up and the turnoff to Highway 154 came into view, conversation segued into a restaurant rundown. "Sustenance before sleuthing," Cato offered. Lee knew that smile. "What do you feel like eating today? It'll be a good half hour before we get to Santa Ynez and another ten or fifteen minutes to Los Olivos, where the best restaurants are. No crispy critters. Promise."

Lee couldn't hold back a laugh. This was turning out to be one of the best days she'd had in months. "You pick. I trust you." *Say that, Lee, and he'll have to live up to your expectations . . . or you'll have to grin and bear it.* "So tell me about the other gadgets back there. Not for autopsies, I presume."

Sides Restaurant, in the heart of town, was crowded with both locals and foodie tourists. It was genuinely old but with a contemporary menu. Lee noted the grainy black-and-white photos of farm life on the restaurant's walls and thought of the Dining Hall in Los Alamos—there, physicists of the forties were also preserved under glass. Farmers of the land vs. framers of the atom bomb. Over glasses of a light viognier, described by the waiter as subtle but welcoming—this is wine country, after all—Cato and Lee waited for lunch and avoided talking about their approach to the Blue Algae Reactant Factor cult property. No reason to ruin a good meal and a buzz.

Cato posed a question: "Lee, uh, I'm curious about your recent name change. I never asked, but I feel like if we bonded over crispy critters, we could talk about this." Lee knew she owed him this much. He was here with her as a favor, and so she quickly recounted the whole earthquake and starting over thing, including the epiphany at The Langham Bar. Not that she needed his approval, but she was gratified that he seemed to accept her second coming as Lee, no longer what-are-they-gonna-do-to-me Lea. "I get it." That's all he needed to say. This opened the door for her to ask Cato Klein just about anything that came to mind. *Save it till you need it, Lee.*

Back in the car, they used cell phone navigation to find the BARF cult property. They could tell from the police aerial photos that the entrance was unmarked—already an ominous sign. As they started off, Cato began to explain the other equipment stashed in the back of his car, both hands on the wheel this time as they took to the winding road off the highway. An attempt to distract Lee . . . or himself?

"That toolbox back there is full of old measuring equipment. Some of that has been replaced now by handy apps on my phone. But a phone can't replace the meters. I keep a gas detector. Always. I have a thing about odorless gas creeping up on you. Methane is a main component of natural gas, but it is everywhere." Lee recalled some of the cases Cato had told her involving explosions that came out of nowhere. Not a bomb or explosive device in sight. There was the exploding elevator door when an unsuspecting delivery man hit the Up button. She could see why odorless gas was no joke. A leaking line below the office building had filled the elevator shaft with gas, and the button on the panel had caused a spark. That's all it took. *A crispy critter story.*

"The other one is a tiny multitasker. Detects radiation, water contamination, and oh . . . nitrates in food. You never know." He looked amused, and Lee knew for a fact that he never met a hot dog he didn't like. "There's a voltmeter for testing live wires. There's also a telescoping measuring rod. Kind of what it sounds like."

"Is that for measuring distance? Or do you use your phone app for that?"

"Yeah. The phone's at least as accurate as the old measuring devices. The Total Stations, we called them in the day. But the telescoping rod is handy because you can set it down in a scene and take a picture. Like put it next to skid marks and take a shot of it. Show the diameter of a blood splatter. That kind of thing." Lee could see that Cato was in his element here. *Let's hope we won't need this stuff, Cato.*

As they approached the road leading to the BARF compound, silence settled in. Lee had no idea what was on Cato's mind, but she began to reflect on Isaac's sense of family—that he cared so much for his sister was causing a lot of grief and trouble to boot. He was that way about his parents too. He had told her time and again, especially after a drink or two, that they were beyond generous to him, the salt of the earth, as they say. They had high expectations, and he didn't disappoint. The first born and all that. Her thoughts turned to Alexander and Ann. Lee wasn't the jealous type, but it was hard not to compare the two families. There was an abundance of love in hers, she was sure, but less obvious affection. Ann did her best to raise a headstrong child who seemed to speak a language all her own, and Lee knew this. Gradually, she was beginning to recognize her mother a little more every time she looked in the mirror, especially on those nights when she zipped up a couture dress or slipped on those shoes. And she missed her. And, of course, Alexander.

In the scheme of things, the inexplicable bond between Lee and Alexander made up for a lot. He expected so much from her, and his pragmatic approach to everything, from teaching her to ride a bike (Newton's laws of motion included) to patching up the resultant scraped knees (more Newton's laws of motion), offered up his own kind of affection. *We were so much alike*, she thought.

"I guess this is it." Cato made a U-turn and headed about twenty yards back the way they had come before pulling over. He grabbed the camera and took a few shots toward the entrance and the road in both directions. Then he picked up his cell phone and did the same. "We might need a handy reference for a quick getaway." He wasn't kidding, and Lee suddenly felt the air go out of her. Cato handed her the toolbox and pulled an old backpack from under the seat. It was an original kid-sized *Star Wars* bag with Han Solo and Chewbacca grinning through the folds of canvas. *Why am I not surprised, Cato?* She hoped Chewie would still have reason to smile at the end of the day.

"Grab the portable gas sensor from the toolbox and put it in the backpack. You'll recognize it when you see it. Then grab that macro lens and throw it in. And the radiation meter—just in case. See if the measuring rod will fit too. Oh, and the voltmeter. And one last thing: see if there's a cigarette lighter in the glove compartment and zip it into the side pocket." Lee did as Cato instructed, happy for the rapid-fire instructions and some physical activity to chase away the shakes. She was also trying not to think about the Niçoise salad that hadn't quite settled in yet. "It's easier to carry the backpack. Frees up the hands," he said. Lee slid her own phone into a back pocket and shoved her purse under the seat. As she crossed the road and headed toward the property, she thought, *It's times like this that a girl could use that life-saving mascara or maybe just some dumb luck.*

=

The possibility of an electrified fence and gate loomed large. Fortunately, a padlock on the gate appeared to be unlocked—*appeared* being the operative word. Not one to take anything for granted, Cato grabbed a fallen branch and maneuvered the lock so that it fell onto the ground. The next step: determine if any portion of the metal gate would shock him into oblivion. Enter the voltmeter; if there was a current running through the chain link, the meter would light up like a Christmas tree. The problem is that it would also beep. "Do you have a Kleenex on you?" Cato whispered. "Something to muffle the sound?"

"If there are hidden surveillance cameras, it won't matter anyway. Right?" she whispered back. But she took off a shoe and, hopping around on one foot, offered up a white sock. "How's this?"

"I like a girl who thinks on her feet—no pun intended," he whispered as he grabbed the sock. "Doesn't hurt to be extra cautious. You never know if someone is actually watching the monitors . . . or listening." With that, he wrapped the sock over the top of the voltmeter, leaving only the metal prongs exposed. "If it lights up, we'll still be able to see the glow." *And if this were some movie, the script would call for me handing you my T-shirt instead of a sock*, she thought. *In fact, Cato, if this were a movie, we'd probably already be crispy critters at this point, so no clothes needed.*

No glow. No beep. A good sign. Nonetheless, he shoved the gate open gingerly with the tip of one shoe. Lee jammed her sock into a back pocket to keep it handy, and then figured out which movie: *Indiana Klein and the Mystery of the Blue Öyster.*

A pockmarked roadway led them through a series of turns

until another gate came in to view. "Great," they mumbled simultaneously. Lee pointed to a wooden sign overhead. What looked like newer cut-out letters had fallen off, leaving faded script in another color and font exposed. The smaller letters Z.U.M.B.A. & H.O. had been painted directly on the wood, and lying on the ground, in a different font and color, were the letters R, A, and F. Further complicating the scene was a round metal placard nailed to a nearby post. A seal of some sort, like a mandala or a shield, with the letters S.O.S.O.S.O. circling the perimeter. The scene reminded Lee of the summer she spent unearthing artifacts with her Wedd School campmates. Or maybe an episode of *Sesame Street*. (*Today's show has been brought to you by the letters Z, U, M, B, A, H, O, S, R, and F.*)

When she heard Cato's digital camera clicking away, Lee quickly pulled out her cell phone and began to do the same. A backup might be needed. A crackling sound drew their attention to a drought-tattered thicket of trees on the right. It was at this point that they noticed a golf cart rolling through the branches toward them. She was thinking there would be more carts appearing on the hill above, lined up like a legion of warriors. The Golf Cart Brigade.

Lee thought about snapping a picture of what looked like Yoda on the Ninth Hole but remembered Isaac's warning: *These cults mean business.* They both looked in astonishment at this new character in Lee's imagined movie. For once, Cato was at a loss for words. And Lee's inner dialogue failed her . . . well, almost: *You've got to be kidding me. What's with the cape and hood? The Imperial Army went thataway, guy.* The guy was bigger standing up. A lot bigger. As he approached they could see that he was actually sporting an oversize olive green plastic poncho (of the trash bag school of fashion) and a matching rain hood. On one side of his chest were the letters SOS. On the other, the logo for REI, the sporting goods store. *Man, I'm sick of this alphabet thing.* Cato must have been reading her mind: "Hey, Pat, can I have another vowel?" *Who knew he was a Wheel of Fortune fan?* "Or can I spin the wheel?" he said in feigned seriousness.

That's it, Cato, confuse the guy! Using her wits had worked for Lee, but she clearly didn't invent the tactic. Garbage Bag Guy looked like he was about to smile, but then a grimace was all he could muster. As Cato pulled out a plastic ID card, Garbage Bag Guy got ready to dive for cover. The investigator's license, Lee supposed. Though, it looked more like the PCC Faculty card. She'd have to remember that one. She had the same card. Garbage Bag Guy grabbed it and tossed it toward the golf cart, where it disappeared into the weeds. *That makes sense now. Don't be too quick to give up something valuable.*

=

It was clear that they were approaching a "Take me to your leader" moment. At least they didn't have to deal with another guessing game regarding the gate. As Garbage Bag Man opened it, Cato and Lee glanced at each other. Nothing resembling wiring appeared to be attached at the hinges or elsewhere. Not a guarantee, but something nevertheless. For the time being, it was not electrified. *I've got to remember that on the way out, if I make it out*, she thought. Cato stumbled backward over a broken patch of concrete walkway, and Lee grabbed on to him, glad that she had chosen her oldest Converse shoes for today's little outing. "This place could use a little maintenance work," Cato mumbled under his breath. Lee was hoping Garbage Bag Man was not the maintenance guy. *No need to insult this fine gentleman, Cato.*

The glass entrance was etched with the words "Tourist Information"; it clearly was not original to the building—a portable trailer of some sort. The transplanted door was sporting a new handle and deadbolt that appeared state of the art, and Lee noticed what looked like the kind of door alarm that relies on breaking the circuit, the connection, between the door and the frame.

"Cato, I think the tourist thing is weird. Maybe they stole the door from somewhere else." He nodded in agreement, looking more grim than amused.

"The Hotel California, 'where you can check out any time you like, but you can never leave,' " he replied. *I have to look that one up, Cato.* In the meantime, they both made a point of looking around. Lee spotted surveillance cameras and motioned to Cato. He had already seen them. Garbage Bag Man ushered them inside with a kind of comical flourish, and Cato said, "Thanks, guy. Where's your master . . . er . . . boss?" *Let's hope that went right over his head.* It hadn't. A hand went up, and Cato and Lee flinched. G B Man reached for his hood and snatched it off, tossing in on a nearby desk, this time with better aim. Then the SOS/REI poncho came off with the same fanfare. Lee was in shock, and apparently so was Cato.

"Welcome. My name is Zin. Zin Ishara. But you can call me Gabe. That's my given name. Gabriel. Visitors are more comfortable with that, usually." His features were stunning, Lee thought. A kind of where-have-you-been-all-my-life stunning. Well-coiffed sandy hair, gray eyes, white-white teeth. The whole package. And grinning from ear to ear, to boot.

What was even more shocking was his suit, a slim-fit gray wool, and fit it did. This time, Lee had no inner dialogue at her disposal, and she wished she had dressed better. She looked at Cato, who seemed equally impressed, his head in a character-istic double take, only backward, not side to side; in fact, Cato had to take a step back to balance himself.

Lee stepped forward to shake Zin/Gabriel's hand, not really caring what he called himself. She did want to get closer for her own reasons, but she also wanted a closer look at the lapel pin he was wearing. Gold and the same design as the placard outside. She hoped it was something innocent: a gym member-ship, a frat pin, even a sober living medal would do. Still not a clue and kind of creepy in a spy cam or evil eye kind of way. She could feel Cato's hand on her arm pulling her back. *I've got this, Cato. Or maybe not.* A cool head prevailed, and Lee moved aside for Cato.

"Mr. Ishara . . . Zin, can we find someplace to sit? It's kinda been a long day for me." Cato playing the age card. No seat-ing in this reception room of sorts meant an office somewhere else, and more to see. Lee avoided glancing at Cato. Looking at Zin/Gabriel was fine for now anyway. Sure enough, they found themselves following Zin through a side door (key card required), where seating consisted of two of those great Bar-celona chairs in black leather and chrome—originals, as far as Lee could tell. Facing the chairs was a slab of the thickest of thick green glass mounted on an equally thick glass base. A minimalist chrome desk lamp offered no useful lighting, but the effect was an artful addition to the room. A room out of *Architectural Digest* embedded in a trailer. Aside from some contemporary artworks—probably also originals, the walls hosted a collection of certificates and a photo that needed closer

inspection. Cato began to cough in heaving fits. "Zin . . . uh
. . . Gabe, can I impose further and ask for a drink of water?" A
raspy voice—not at all like Cato. *A ruse or a medical emergency,
Cato? Should I be worried?* Zin was up and out in a flash, and
Cato snapped a few cell phone pictures of the walls, returning
to the hacking cough to cover the click of the phone. He had
forgotten to silence it, and as soon as Lee realized what was going on, she reached into her pocket and felt around for the little slider on the side of her own phone. They were both taking
a chance that there were security cameras aimed at them, but
there was also the possibility that a secretive cult leader might
not want surveillance of his private lair. Either way, the photos
would sync with their computers back home. *Well played . . .
so far, my friend.*

When Zin returned with a decanter of water and two glasses,
he had that look: the cat is out of the bag look. They should
have known he would be keeping his eye on them somehow.
Play dumb, Lee. She hoped Cato had the same thought. She
glanced around the room, looking for one of those Renaissance
portraits with the eyes that were really spy holes. No such thing
here, and the modern art offered nowhere to hide—not an eye
in sight, though with abstract art, an eye could look like an ear
or a foot. You never know. Cato was doing the same, though
she was sure he was actually looking for a lens, not a wander-
ing eye.

Bottled H$_2$O wasn't a guarantee of un-poisoned water, but
it offered a slight sense of comfort compared to an open carafe.
Zin poured, and Cato and Lee gulped air out of nervousness.
Lee figured they had to play along, so she took a sip and set
the glass down. Cato actually managed to spill a little on his
pants first. He watched as the wet spot spread on his pant leg.

No obvious signs of disintegrating fabric, no smoke or sizzle, no burning. *What a clever guy*, she thought. Still, he motioned to her with a slight shake of the head, as in *don't drink. Really, Cato? I'm dying of thirst!* To her surprise, *he* did take a sip . . . and another, but it was like wine tasting. That rolling around on the tongue thing to determine the subtleties of the ingredients. Here in wine country, one is not expecting a hint of arsenic or a dash of ricin. He was stalling, looking for dried residue on his pants. Finally, the all-clear. They both drank.

May the Royal Order of Water Buffaloes come to order. Lee was trying to figure out where she'd heard that, other than in her head just now. Satisfied that Zin Ishara was not going to kill them right then and there, Lee sat back. She could see that Cato was still on the lookout for something but feigning a look of trust with his big grin.

Zin began: "What can I do for you? It must be something important to compel two strangers to trespass on ZUMBA property." Emphasis on *trespass. Wait. I thought we were trespassing . . . uh, visiting . . . Blue Algae Reactant Factor property. What happened to BARF? The GPS must have screwed up or something.* Lee's look of confusion mirrored that of Cato's. *He must be thinking the same thing.* But Cato recovered immediately. He put on his introspective stone face, stroking his chin so hard she could hear the five o'clock bristles from six feet away. "Yes, I see I've caught you off guard. Better you than I, my friends," Zin said as he rose from his chair. Lee's arm hairs rose to attention simultaneously, as if in a salute. *The Flintstones. That's it! The Grand Pooh-bah.* The old cartoon channel lived in her psyche. *If only Fred and Barney had a way out of this office.*

"So, we were asked by the family to look at the scene of

your accident. They're having a hard time with closure. They miss their son, and they know what a devoted member of your spiritual community he was." Cato smiled as he continued. "They have permission from the county for one last look, but they asked me . . . us . . . to take a quick gander for them. I'm sure when the county offices open Monday morning, someone'll be happy to explain, though you might want to check all the regulations and make sure you're in compliance here before you call. You guys don't want to open up a legal hornet's nest. You'd have inspectors all over the place." Cato looked at Lee for agreement. She nodded but mostly in awe of his quick thinking. *He's done this before.* "Do you need to see my credentials, Mr. Ishara?" Cato motioned as if to fish his investigator's license out of his pants pocket, but Zin waved it away. *He bought it,* Lee thought. *Not so smart after all, Mr. Pooh-bah.*

Think, Lee. What can I add to keep this thing going? "I'm sure the family will thank you for your kindness; if Mr. Klein and I spend just a few minutes here, we can bring that closure to them, and they won't feel the need to bother you again. I know you have a lot of important business to take care of here." *Can you suck up any more?* "Can I ask, though, about the name change? ZUMBA and Blue Algae Reactant Factor? I don't get it."

"We do have to get going, Ms. Roberts." Lee had never heard Cato call her that before. She recognized that he was getting antsy or maybe sensed something she didn't. He got up, and she followed suit.

"Wait here." *Authoritative. Used to bossing people around,* Lee noted. With that, Zin opened another side door and slipped inside, but not before Cato and Lee caught a glimpse inside: a bank of monitors. They looked at each other. *That question answered.* Lee supposed they'd never know what the two names

were about; at this point her mind was on overload. *If I never see another acronym again, I'll die happy . . . er . . . poor choice of words. Never mind.* She imagined Zin leading a Zumba class. And then again, the blue algae thing was bonkers too. His Grand Pooh-bah-ness seemed more business-like than hippy-dippy, and the décor in his office suggested an urban—no—*urbane* sensibility. A creepy what's-wrong-with-this-picture feeling was percolating. Cato was looking around, noting the vents in the ceiling and a small window to the outside world. *Cut that out, Cato. You're making me nervous.*

Zin appeared with a key and a post-it note. Handing them off to Lee, he said, "This key will get you into the garage where the most unfortunate death happened. Keep the note handy in case anyone stops you; it has my signature. That should be all you need. I trust you can get "a gander" within the next hour and be on your way. Say by four o'clock?" Cato looked at his watch while Lee and Zin both noted the time on their cell phones. The generational thing. "I'll have someone show you the way and return exactly at four to pick up the key from you." Lee knew at that moment that she had to handle the post-it with kid gloves; actually latex gloves would be better. If all those years of watching *CSI* taught her anything, it was that DNA was everywhere—even on a post-it note.

"Well, we better get going. Thank you, Mr. Ishara . . . uh . . . Zin . . . Gabe." Lee put on her most endearing smile. *You never know.* Time was of the essence here. A four o'clock deadline meant that they had less than an hour to get in and out, and Cato was already halfway out the door.

"May Ishara shine on you," Zin responded, and a chill ran through Lee. *Sheesh! What was that? The Grand Pooh-bah has spoken.* Cato was several yards ahead, taking long strides to catch up to a garbage bag–clad guard of some sort, and she figured he hadn't heard Zin's blessing, or was it a curse? G B Man #2 was smaller in stature than the Pooh-bah, but something foreboding was clanking around under his poncho. It could have been anything; nevertheless, Lee's imagination was getting the better of her.

G B Man #2 was not a talker. Nor was he much of a walker, apparently. Once out of view of the trailer, he stopped, and Lee and Cato piled into him. A rear-end collision with Cato in the middle and Lee bringing up the rear, post-it note gingerly held by one corner, flapping in the breeze. He motioned toward an old corrugated metal shed and retreated back down the road toward the trailer. *In a hurry to get out of there*, Lee thought. Like the rats in the basement at PCC, a little too eager to get away. They were alone but still silent as they headed toward the shed.

Lee broke radio silence. "Cato, two things: Why was this guy in such a hurry to get out of here, and did you hear Zin's send-off? 'May Ishara shine on you'? Really creepy. Seriously creepy." The look on his face was not particularly reassuring. *Don't fail me now, Cato.*

"He let us keep our phones and the backpack. That's not a good thing."

=

She was afraid to ask but figured she already knew why it was "not a good thing," as Cato put it. Zin never even wanted to see what was in the backpack. Any self-respecting cult leader would be suspicious . . . unless he knew that the contents and its owner would never see the light of day again. Lee knew exactly what Cato was getting at. It was like those mobster movies: the intended victim gets to keep the payola until he is dead, joyful and relieved up till the very moment someone pulls the trigger. She heard Isaac's admonition, "Those cults don't fool around." And for a second, she wished she had listened to him. But really, she figured, she and Cato were doing just exactly what Isaac would be doing if he were here: figuring out what Kat had gotten herself—and them—into.

Lee watched as Cato dropped the bag on the ground and started rooting through it. The voltmeter came out first, no sock needed this time. Before they stuck a key in the padlock, they'd better know if it was wired up. No light. No beep. No current. The key had worked on the first try. No rust. That meant that the lock had been accessed several times recently— or that it was a brand new replacement. Before Lee could push open the door, Cato grabbed her.

"We still don't know if the door is rigged to set something off when it opens," he explained. Next he pulled the telescoping ruler out of his bag of tricks and opened it all the way out—all twenty feet of it. *What the . . . ? Cato, what could you be measuring?* Then it dawned on her. They both stationed themselves behind the nearest bunker, a pile of rocks—not the best protection because the mass and inertia of one big boulder would have worked better. Lee was shaking in her tennis shoes, trying not to lose her lunch. Cato grabbed one end of the telescoping rod and rammed the garage door open with it. The laws of physics would have told him that, to compensate for the thin rod with relatively small mass, he would have to exert a bit more energy into poking the door. Surprisingly, it swung open pretty easily. A sign that it, too, had been accessed several times recently. "So far, so good," he told her, though he didn't look particularly convinced, Lee thought.

A few slats of wood and metal fell to the ground inside, broadcasting a cloud of dust and bits of paper in every direction. "No slivers of sunlight inside," Cato announced. "That means that the structure is pretty airtight. A good thing when it comes to preserving evidence." He used the rod again. This time to flip the light switch with the two of them standing just outside the structure. One of those swaying light fixtures went on, and all was quiet. Except for the pounding in Lee's ears and maybe some stomach churning. And next to her, Cato's whiskers sounded like a power sander as he stroked his chin furiously. They closed the door behind them to keep the breeze from disturbing the scene further and set to work. It was obvious that the setting was ground zero for something. Not a big explosion. Something subtler had left scorching in the center of the garage. While Lee examined the ground, Cato set out a few instruments that he thought would come in handy, most notably his gas meter and his camera.

"This looks like part of a label with that seal on it. It's got those letters, SOS," Lee said, looking around for something with which to skewer it so as to leave any evidence intact. How did the cops miss it? Then she realized it had fluttered to the ground when they shoved the door open. It must have been under a coat of dust. She collected some dirt in her palm. Then pieces of a jigsaw began to emerge, like the images on photo paper her mother used to share with her in the darkroom: some copper wire, part of a circuit board, a coil. Things that in themselves would mean nothing. *Nothing, Lee? Don't go crazy here. Stay calm.* Cato handed her a ziplock baggie from the bottom of his backpack. It had a Fritos remnant in it. Not sterile but the best they had. He snapped pictures of everything he could see, seemingly not aiming. Just snapping. She sat on the ground, collecting pieces of solder—like little gems in the dust—and then, the remains of a crystal diode and a small transformer. *Be still my heart!* "Cato, look!"

But Cato was not looking, at least not at her. He had set the gas meter on the ground a few minutes before when fishing around in his backpack, and nothing had registered then. But now he was staring at it, growing paler by the second. "Uh. Lee, grab your evidence bag and get up slowly. Careful when you pick up your phone. Avoid creating any friction; don't even let your pant legs rub together." Her legs had turned to rubber at this point, so no guarantees. Peripheral vision told her that Cato was doing the same, except he had that blasted Star Wars bag to carry. *Chewie, sorry, and Han Solo, you too.*

Lee's fingers had turned numb, and she struggled to hold on to the baggie. "Cato, whatever it is, leave the backpack. Come on. I'll buy you a new camera and a new meter thingy." She knew what he was going to do: grab the bag and make a run for it anyway.

The only thing Cato had to say was, "Don't. Don't turn off the lights!" He pulled the door open carefully, then grabbed Lee by the sleeve. Running while not allowing your pant legs to touch each other: that's a ridiculous vision. They looked like bow-legged cartoon cowboys as they dove behind the familiar pile of rocks. That wasn't good enough, apparently, because Cato kept looking around. He wanted something more substantial. Meanwhile nothing had happened in the garage, and Lee was wondering if he had imagined the whole thing. Then he said, "We left the door open; air got in. That was a mistake. With no explosion they will know we are still alive." Before she could respond, Cato ran back to pull the door closed, but not before snapping a picture of an exterior side wall of the garage. Something had caught his interest, but no time to discuss it now. "We've got a few minutes till gas fills up the garage again. Can you hand me the cigarette lighter . . . and . . . can I have your sock again? I have to let you know you won't get it back. Sorry." Lee fished the grimy sock out of her back pocket and handed it to Cato. "Let's get some distance between us and the building." He didn't have to say it twice. She was right there with him as he grabbed the backpack again and headed into the trees. She realized why the bag was so vital: they might not be able to get out of the compound without the voltmeter and maybe some of the other handy-dandy equipment.

Cato was rooting around in the undergrowth looking for something. As far as Lee knew, they could account for everything they had come with plus the evidence bag. *Cato. . . . What the . . .*

"Found it!" Cato held up a grapefruit-sized rock, but before Lee could ask, he jammed it into the sock. *This can't be good.* "Stay here, get low to the ground. I'll be back." *This really can't be good.* "We need a spark," Cato said as he held up the lighter. *Oy.* Cato took a quick look at his watch and ran back to the shed, sock-clad rock in one hand and lighter in the other. Lee could see him through the branches but only if she stood up. *Just for a second, then do as you're told for once, Lee.* She watched as he carefully opened the door to the shed—six inches or so—and then he ran back behind their rock bunker. Not far enough from the garage, possibly, but a reliable distance for launching a flaming sock missile.

Not a really loud blast but concussive enough to bounce off the eardrums. No flames but enough heat to destroy any further evidence and, of course, two "trespassers."

"It's not four o'clock yet, but then they probably had no

intention of collecting the key and escorting us out. At least not without body bags," Lee whispered. She was picking leaves out of her hair and emptying the dirt from her shoes. They sat in the bushes near a perimeter fence. Cato looked like a swamp thing. Thin branches with equally thin leaves hung from his jacket and pants and over one ear. She looked at him. *What next, fearless leader?* Then she saw the resemblance. *Cato, I'm buying you one of those Indiana Jones hats if we ever make it home to Pasadena. There's that hat store in Old Town. . . .* "Can I text Isaac? He should know where we are—just in case." Lee didn't wait for Cato's nod.

> Hope to leave Blue soon. Will text when we are out.

"Whew! It went!" As they scrambled to the fence, she was thinking how it was that she couldn't rely on a text getting delivered to Isaac from her place in Pasadena, but here it was, out in the middle of nowhere, on its way.

She knew the drill. No light. No beep. No time to think. She was sure she could get over the chain link with her little baggie, but not so sure about Cato. He whispered, "Go for it, Jane Jetson. I'll toss the backpack to you when you're on the other side. Don't give it a second thought—I'm a fence climber from way back. No worries, as they say." It was about eight feet to the top, and Lee scaled it quickly, evidence baggie hanging from her back pocket, along with her phone. If Lee were a praying person, she would have let loose, even praying to the Grand Pooh-bah himself.

Fate—and physics—intervened. Distribution of mass. Cato pulled out the camera and hung it around his neck, facing backward. He threaded the telescoping rod through the fence and stuck the voltmeter in his jacket pocket. The gas sensor and the small radiation/contamination/nitrate sensor remained in the bag. Cato tossed his macro camera lens over the fence to Lee. *He has no idea how bad I was at softball*, she thought. *Just think of it as a pair of Jimmy Choo heels.* That's all it took. "Good catch, Jetson! Another!" He heaved the backpack over the fence. Just enough mass and momentum to make Han Solo and a still smiling Chewie go airborne. With that, Cato began to climb, shoving his clumsy shoes into the largest of the gaps in the links. Not there yet, and they could hear voices. And what sounded like a golf cart.

CHAPTER THIRTEEN

Made It Out!
On Our Way Home

Lee could see how tired he was. In fact, she worried about the drive home. They were in the thick of rush-hour traffic on the 101 South, and Cato had made a few questionable lane changes already. At this rate it could take two hours or more to get back to Pasadena. *Think.*

"Hey, Cato, I don't know about you, but I'm about ready to pass out. I need food and water . . . and a bathroom." She watched for a reaction. Nothing. Then, the first words since he had landed on the other side of the chain link fence:

"Yeah, I know. Me too." He looked a little dejected. That jump had taken a lot out of him. They cut it a little too close for comfort as they dove for the foliage that skirted the roadway and slithered their way back to the car. Cato was pretty scraped up, and he had to be thinking how much easier this kind of thing used to be "back in the day." He said, "Let's stop for a bite at least in Santa Barbara. Maybe at the marina or that place on State Street. The Mexican place." Lee was secretly hoping that he would opt for a good night's sleep too. Two rooms at the Franciscan Inn wouldn't cost much, and breakfast is free.

Like many of the places on State Street, the Mexican cafe was gone, replaced by a Thai restaurant. Parking on the marina at dinner time was always a challenge, but they lucked out and headed for the best shrimp, fries, and slaw in the city. Brophy's was a local favorite, and the bathrooms were clean. They both needed to wash up as best they could. Lee resisted the temptation to stick her whole head under the faucet in the hopes that a hot shower was in her near future.

The food, served with a craft beer, had a healing power. Cato and Lee both felt like human beings again. They made a point of *not* discussing their recent near-death experience, choosing instead to make small talk. The view from the restaurant was spectacular: masts as far as the eye could see. Every size and class of sailboat bobbed in the coastal waters, and there was still a remnant of sunset tinting the sky orange. Finally, the conversation turned to plans for the rest of the evening. "Drive home or stay over?" Lee asked.

"I'm feeling pretty good right now," Cato grinned. "But you can drive if you want. I think traffic'll be a little lighter . . . at least until we get closer to LA. Up to you."

Lee was still feeling a little out of it. *The beer, no doubt.* "Let's walk around the marina for a few minutes, and then I'll be happy to drive." *There's always something to be said for waking up in your own bed*, she thought. A few minutes in the sea air and Lee felt recharged. She had to admit that tackling the drive home was probably worth it. "I guess we'll have to get an early start on the lab analysis in the morning. Do you think two different labs for quality control? Maybe Isaac can arrange one with his Caltech buddies." Cato nodded but looked like he wasn't up for a one-and-a-half-hour crime debriefing on the 101 South. She felt the same way. "Let's go over everything tomorrow," she said. "I need to sort of think things through myself."

Cato looked relieved. She didn't blame him really. It was a rough escape, but she recognized in herself a familiar rush of adrenaline as she replayed it all in her head. It was like that summer dig site that offered so much mystery, only with a good dose of added peril this time. And a flaming sock. She understood Cato's attraction to forensic investigation and hoped he would feel better about the experience after a good night's sleep. *You did pretty well for an old . . . uh . . . mature guy, Cato.*

=

The hot shower only served to remind her of how bruised she was. Lee watched a stream of dirt and sand circle the drain, and she told herself *not* to time the water flow as it made its way to the basement. She knew exactly where it was coming from and why. Her ears were still ringing from the concussive explosion, and the climb up the chain link fence had done a number on her arms, but all things considered, it had been a pretty gratifying day. And it was still early enough to pour a glass of wine and catch up on the news. Lee hoped, also, that she would eventually be able to sleep tonight.

An hour later she climbed into bed and slept. But 2:00 a.m. came, and figures began to swim around. Not pigs—green garbage bags with identical little bobbing heads that looked familiar. *Zin!* A dozen of them. In her half-awake state, she wondered if he was really reaching out to her, controlling her mind with that Ishara stuff. *That's ridiculous, Lee. You are just exhausted.*

When morning rolled around, Lee was relieved. She took inventory of her aches and pains as she lay there in bed, but the replay of the previous day's caper wouldn't run in her head. In the light of day, it was too soon to think about how perilous it had been, she guessed. Lee had a lot to do: text Isaac, sort out the ingredients of her evidence baggie, get in touch with Cato for a debriefing session. She grabbed her phone from the nightstand, happy that it had survived its adventure, but before she could text Isaac, two messages came in from Cato. He was clearly raring to go too.

> Morning! Can I bring coffee and bagels over?

> And evidence.

That's all she needed to hear.

=

"I think I can get one of my contacts at Western State Analytical to handle the dirt samples and a section of that SOS label you found. And maybe the post-it. Give me some of those solder pieces too. You never know. You can give the rest to Isaac. Having two sets of results is a good practice. The best scenario is that they will match each other. I emailed you some photos this morning. Take a look and see what you think." Back to the old Cato, though the Snoopy bandage above one overgrown eyebrow was a little distracting. And no backpack today. She hoped Han Solo and Chewie had survived. It could have been a lot worse for both of them, she realized. This gig wasn't even

Cato's responsibility, and yet she wouldn't have known where to start without him.

Lee grabbed her laptop and pulled up the pictures. Cato knew just what to photograph; there *was* a method to his madness. He had cropped and enlarged a few shots, and some details showed up that she hadn't noticed before. She figured he must have slipped the macro lens on while she was crawling around on the ground. Then she spotted the photo that Cato took outside the garage on the north-facing wall: a gas meter and two valves. She hoped he'd get around to explaining it later. "Can we get a close-up of the SOS label? And the diode and transformer too?"

They made a pretty good team. Lee cleared the bagel crumbs and coffee cups, while Cato zeroed in on more photos. His macro shots of the label and the diode popped up in Lee's photo folder in seconds. They were so sharp that enlarging them even further was still possible with the Edit tool. *One of those tricks of the trade, Cato. You are the true Yoda.* He played around with the Contrast and Sharpen tools, and soon they could make out a few words on the label. A brand name on the diode was discernible even with all the burn marks. "You are in your element, Master Klein," she said with a flourish. Lee thought she detected a little blush under those whiskers, but it could have been an abrasion from yesterday's mad scramble.

"How much do we share with Isaac? We don't know much yet ourselves, and if he blabs to Kat, she could be the next one in danger." Lee knew she had a valid point, even as she was saying it, but it didn't give her any satisfaction to think about Kat as the next victim.

"If you give him those samples for testing, you're going to have to say something. Just talk in general terms. And tell him *not* to say anything to his sister yet. Lee, the time will come when he's going to have to get her out of there, but in the meantime, keeping her out of the loop is the safest way to go. Do you want to print out a couple of pics so you can work with them?"

A text from Isaac vibrated on the kitchen counter.

> Cato over there? Can I join you guys? Really need to know what's going on

Lee looked at Cato for the go-ahead. It was a tough call, but she texted:

> Sure and we have bagels.

She was not an emoji kind of person, but the temptation to cheer Isaac up this morning with a goofy happy face was compelling. He would probably need some cheer very soon. Lee's sensible brain prevailed and rescued her from certain embarrassment—no emoji, and she hit Send. Cato shrugged. It was clear he didn't like the idea of including Isaac today. So much raw material, without analysis, could lead even the most seasoned investigator down the wrong path. A worried big brother had no chance.

"We've got to get our stories straight about Zin," Lee said. Even the mention of his name a day after their escape sent a chill through her body. And the thrill of his good looks had worn off too. Maybe it was the Ishara blessing or maybe it was the odorless gas. Then again, there was the dream of bobble-headed garbage bags she'd had the night before. Cato nodded. "Yeah, let's not get into that yet. Maybe just mention all of those acronyms, those new names. He might have heard Kat talk about them. It's worth a try. We could start some research on that. Don't say anything about the garage or the gas."

Isaac arrived with more coffee in hand and a laptop bag over one shoulder. Starbucks was making a killing today on the Blue Öyster Crew. Lee was glad she had kept her parents' wobbly but charming dining table and chairs. Not fashionable, but they offered plenty of room for the three of them to work. Cato took the lead in sharing info with Isaac, and it was evident to Lee that he was choosing his words carefully. She was sure Isaac realized that too, but for whatever reason, he didn't press them for more details. He hadn't heard Kat mention the additional acronyms or the name Zin Ishara, but then again, he told them, she was pretty protective of the group. Perhaps some brainwashing mixed in with defensiveness about her life choices. He would tactfully ask her about all that tomorrow, and in the meantime, he took on the task of researching the names.

"You guys look pretty beat up. Was it really that rough?" He looked uncomfortable at the thought that he had drawn Lee and Cato into the whole thing.

"Well, it was actually kind of cool," Lee replied with a smile and a shrug. Mixed body language, but she wasn't kidding. Isaac was not convinced, though he figured he would hear more later. The three of them—one seasoned investigator and two amateur sleuths—sat huddled over laptops and photos until late in the afternoon. Leftover cold pizza made an appearance and so did the rain, plopping onto the old arched window. The room alternated between light and dark when large clouds skimmed by, and Lee was hoping the guys would take a hint from the weather and head home. It wasn't that she was tired or bored even; she was sore, running on overload, and beginning to crave her own quiet space. By the time the guys came up for air, she was curled up on her gray IKEA sofa under a gray IKEA wool blanket.

"I'm just resting my eyes," she said.

CHAPTER FOURTEEN
RA-BE IN THE CLASSROOM

Lee pulled into the faculty garage but drove around before settling on a spot. Ever since the encounter with her errant student, she had a habit of looking around to see who was coming in behind her. She also scoped out the lined-up cars to see which ones had been washed recently. You never know. She hated the idea that Mr. Jacobs was still taking up a little bit of real estate in her head.

The pig had spent the weekend in her trunk, but it was no worse for wear. As far as she knew. When she reached in to grab it, Lee realized just how sore she was. Long sleeves and a high collar covered the scratches and bruises, but her fence-climbing muscles needed more time to recover. And she wondered how Cato was doing today.

An hour to go before class, which allowed for time to set up and test run the Ra-Be half-life experiment. Fortunately, Lee had set most of the supplies out the Friday before, along with hand-out instructions. There was one new thing that hadn't been there when she left that day, though. On her desk was the screwdriver she had grabbed on her way down to the basement. It was an old flat-head tool with a wooden handle. Three dots in red paint were marked on it, like the way some people mark their more expensive golf balls. She remembered dropping it on the concrete floor near the locker when she pulled the pig out. *Think, Lee. Did you actually pick it up again? Did you bring it upstairs with you?* Her answer caused an involuntary shudder. When she closed her eyes, she could still see it lying there in the dust.

Students weren't due for a while, but there was no way Lee could get ready for the day if she didn't get to it immediately. This was the last performance exam of the semester. It was important for her own academic review and for her pupils, including Mr. Jacobs. She set duplicate supplies on each lab table: a Tupperware container lined on the bottom with paraffin wax, a snack-size baggie, pencils, tweezers, lab write-ups sheets. On her demonstration table were the same supplies, with a notable difference: her paraffin block was larger—and she had the pig. The Geiger counter and a long pair of tongs were at the ready. She turned on the document camera, an Elmo, and made sure that it projected onto the Smart Screen above her head. Fifteen minutes until Lee had to open the doors. She figured it would be a good idea to check the contents of the pig. Just as Cato had described it, the pill-sized capsules were in there. She took one out with her tweezers and shook it. No way to know how much material was in each capsule. There was so little mass. She would have to use the Geiger counter to get a reading. She must have earned some good luck today: the meter was clicking away. In fact, it responded loud and clear.

She wrote "Radium-Beryllium: Half-Life Measurements of Radioactivity" on the screen and opened the doors. For once

the group looked eager to get started. Maybe they were actually interested in their physics labs at this point in the year, or maybe it was that the semester was coming to an end. Or maybe they were hoping something would go very wrong. Lee had already impressed upon them how privileged they were to be working with Ra-Be in a community college lab, and she had explained more than once the importance of following directions. *Okay, people, we'll see.*

"This will be your last lab for the semester, people. You'll be turning in the lab packet for a grade, and I'll be watching as you work to further assess your understanding of the concepts. Don't be surprised if I ask you questions as I move around the room. You may confer with your lab partners, but the written work must be your own. Any questions?"

"Uh, Ms. Roberts, will we lose our hair or something from the radiation exposure?" The girl with the big hair.

"Yeah, do we all have to take a shower together after class—to get the radiation off, I mean?" The class clown.

"Is this a big part of our grade?" Mr. Jacobs. *What do you know!*

"No, No, and Yes. Now let's get started," Lee replied. "Grab a pencil and take notes on the first page of your lab packets. Copy the title of this activity onto your papers and write your full names and group letter at the top right. Answer the Guiding Question first: What does the term half-life mean and how does it apply to this activity?" Still a challenge for some students. She allowed a couple of minutes for the groups to agree on a response and record their answers. Lee placed her Tupperware container under the camera and grabbed the putty knife, checking also that it was all projecting clearly on the screen. "Next, I'm making several slits into

the paraffin, around the edges of the wax. Yours are done for
you. The slits are about 5 millimeters, enough to accommodate the silver coins. I'm placing the opened baggie into each
slot and pushing the dollar down into it. Next, I'm going to
measure the radioactivity of the silver dollars by themselves
before adding the Ra-Be to the mix. Listen carefully. No reading on the Geiger counter. Correct?" Lee demonstrated each
step as she talked. *So far, so good.*

Lee shoved silver dollars into her own setup and waited for
everyone in the class to catch up. She dug a hole into the center
of the paraffin, just big enough for the capsule. Carefully, she
opened the pig and fished out a capsule using the tongs. There
was no doubt that she felt a little intimidated herself by the
power of this little casing, and she hoped the students were
not seeing the slight tremor with which she worked. "I'll come
around with the silver dollars after I have exposed them to
the Ra-Be and place them in the slots for you. Pass the Geiger
counter around quickly once. Each table will have a few seconds to record the time and measure the radioactivity of just
the silver dollars. Record measurements in your books. This is
the important part. Listen carefully. Really. No joke." She had
their attention. "This next step goes quickly. Pass the Geiger
counter around again, recording the new time and a new reading. You need to be careful not to touch the silver directly. No
fooling around with this." She was sort of joking about that,
but she paused to see who was listening. All eyes were on her.
"So then, illustrate your setup on the blank page of your lab
book first, labeling all parts. While you are drawing, I'll come
around and check on you. Work fast. I'll be looking at your lab
book illustrations while you are working. We have to keep the
Geiger counter moving around the room, noting the time as

exactly as possible. You can use the wall clock—it has a second hand—or use your cell phones." She paused to see if the class understood. "On the graph, you'll note a place to label everything. Find that page. While you are filling in your books, one person from each table will return the baggie with the silver dollar inside to me. Use the tweezers to grab the top of the baggies and bring them back. I'll call you up one at a time, so listen for your names. Let's demonstrate with Group A first."

With a little prodding at each step, Group A managed to complete the task in a few minutes. Each group managed to follow directions in successively less and less time. They all worked like well-oiled machines. And the capsule went back into the pig. No mishaps. Lee was gratified to see the groups with their heads together, finishing the lab graphs and filling in their observations and conclusions.

"Okay. Well done, everyone. You have twenty minutes to complete the labs with graphs before the end of class. Walk around and check out each group's graphs for a minute; that's all it will take. Compare your results. Your final question is on the last page. One half-page answer, complete sentences required. When you are finished, return all materials to my table and turn in your lab books. Remember to check if you wrote your names on the cover. Good luck."

As students filed out, Lee stood at the doorway with the Geiger counter. It was a joke really, but she was also curious: Would anyone register on the meter? Clean hands for most of the group, but one or two actually made a few weak clicks. She heard nervous laughs as they headed down the hallway, but the whole experience probably left them with a healthy respect for radiation. That was worth everything, Lee thought. Do this one more time today, and the pig goes back into the basement till next semester. In the meantime, she would have to figure out what to do with that traveling screwdriver.

Lab Book—Page 4

Essay Question:

Answer in complete sentences. One-half-page minimum.

Using your graph, explain what your Geiger counter readings represent, and why your readings change over time. Also explain why the silver dollars became radioactive.

(2 parts to answer)

Bonus:

What materials are constants and what materials are variables?

CHAPTER FIFTEEN
DON'T, DON'T TURN OUT THE LIGHTS

The semester came to an end, and Lee was just as relieved as the students. The Kat caper needed attention. Some of the lab results wouldn't be ready for a week or two, but Cato was already working on the photos to see what more he could find. In the meantime, Isaac was anxious to get Kat out of the compound. In addition, everyone had to consider the possibility that Zin—the Grand Pooh-bah—represented a threat to all of them.

The Blue Öyster Crew agreed to meet at Lee's place for drinks and dinner. A celebration of sorts for Cato and Lee, as the semester wrapped up, and an opportunity for Isaac to report back on what, if anything, Kat knew about the various names on display at the BARF property.

Lee threw on her white Cavalli jeans and the Prada blouse and went about setting the table. The pinkish hue of the setting sun, akin to Crayola Blush, colored everything in her living room and dining room. It actually worked quite well with the gray-and-white décor, she decided, and with her own outfit. An improvement over the Blue Room scheme anyway.

Lee opened a bottle of Mourvèdre to let it "breathe." Isaac was in charge of the main course and had promised a hearty beef stew, his own recipe. Cato, who was tasked with dessert, had threatened to drive out to Glendora for the best of the best donuts; The Donut Man on Route 66 had dessert-worthy creations, but in light of rush-hour traffic, his back-up plan was Carmela's for ice cream. Either way, it was a win-win for Lee, who barely ventured into her own kitchen. She took a look at the dining table set with new dishes and wine glasses; the family china and stemware were casualties of the earthquake and probably just as well, she decided. Memories of special occasions in that canyon home still haunted her from time to time. The new, sleek all-white porcelain settings suited her just fine.

Isaac arrived at the door first, though the aroma of his stew creation preceded him by a couple of minutes. Lee put the large pot in the oven to warm it up, and they had a chance to try out the wine. Standing in the galley kitchen, each leaning on an opposite counter, they were quiet, introspective: Isaac still thinking about how bruised Lee looked, and Lee thinking about how to someday break the rest of the cult story to him. The solitude was interrupted by the doorbell, which Lee actually hadn't heard before. She realized it needed some work since it seemed to be buzzing only intermittently. Probably a loose wire somewhere. Is that a homeowners' association thing, or will she need to fix it herself? Funny how the words "Don't, don't turn off the lights" popped into her head. *Where is that from? Was it something Cato said?* She was still sorting out the other day's events, the escape primarily. *I'll have to ask Cato.*

It was a veritable feast. Cato had abandoned the donut idea after all. The handmade lavender-infused vanilla ice cream paired nicely with the stew and the red wine. They decided that only minimal shop talk was in order for the evening. Isaac spoke first: "Kat thinks she heard the name Zin, but she's not sure. It's probably a good thing she never came in contact with him in person. The ZUMBA thing is news to her, and the SOS is only something she heard someone else mention. She never asked about it. Again—just as well. Any news on the lab analysis?"

Cato, still sporting a Band-Aid over one eye, looked well-rested for a change. Lee thought it was the clean clothes and the shave. "Yeah, I've done some research, and it looks like a complicated path through all of those acronyms, but Isaac can keep working on that. We'll sort it out. I'm expecting some prelim reports from Western State in a few days. The DNA takes longer. In the meantime, I tracked down the diode manufacturer. There's probably no way to trace it to a purchaser; they're a dime a dozen."

"They did change designs recently, so we may be able to pin it down that way. I know the ones I use now look more streamlined. Also, there might be fingerprints on it," Lee responded. "It had some residue on it too." Cato nodded but looked like he was done speculating for the night. So did Isaac. The wine was making itself known, and nobody minded.

"Well, friends, I hate to eat and run, but I'm beat." Cato got up as if to punctuate his pronouncement. "Keep the leftover ice cream, Lee. I would just eat it all myself if I took it home." He grinned all the way to the door. "By the way, your doorbell has a short in it. Night."

=

While Isaac poured the remaining Mourvèdre into their glasses, Lee dished out a little more ice cream for the two of them. They were determined to ignore the proverbial elephant in the room: the escape from the cult compound. Instead they debriefed the meal. Where was the wine purchased? What kind of beef was used for the stew? Which shop in town has the best artisanal ice cream? All questions that really didn't need answering.

One question that Isaac did wonder about was how Lee was faring at the community college. They were both sufficiently mellow, and he figured he could ask without risking their friendship or at least the mood of the evening. It turned out to be a good bet: Lee launched into a whole rundown of the curriculum she had put together, including a description of the mystical basement and its dust-shrouded contents. She detailed each lab and its objectives, down to the last procedure and assessment. As she spoke, she was beginning to realize how much she liked what she was doing. Of course, Cato had been instrumental in getting her started. The pig and the old Geiger counter were the source of infinite inspiration. Lee left out the part about the traveling screwdriver and the magical blue jar of radon. Too squishy to relate to Isaac at this point in their relationship, or . . . Relationship. *Not a Relationship with a capital R, Lee! Friendship.* She did bring up the obnoxious encounter with Mr. Jacobs, however. It dawned on her that he was an okay kid, and so the cautionary tale was that you can't judge a college student by his cover—or hoodie. Isaac reacted to the story just as she expected: Is she likely to see him around campus again? Should she file an incident report with the campus police? What good is mascara when things could go so-o-o wrong? At that point Lee was sorry she had brought it up, but it probably wasn't a bad idea to let another person know about it, just as a precaution. The whole death-in-the-shed thing in Santa Ynez was a case in point. It was kind of nice that he cared, but that really was his nature anyway.

The topic of Cato was next, a natural progression. "How did Cato get a hold of radium beryllium?" Isaac asked.

"I'm not actually sure what his source was or is, but he has been in the job for so many years, it's natural that he has a lot of connections. It makes my job more interesting. That's for sure." It dawned on Lee that Isaac had not actually met Cato until this whole Kat thing began, but she was gratified that it was working out so well. Though they seemed like polar opposites, the two men appeared to hit it off. At some point the Blue Öyster caper would come to an end—hopefully, a good one—but Lee was betting that their association would remain solid. *Who knows? Maybe there will be another opportunity for all of us to work together again. But I'm getting ahead of myself here,* she thought.

As the conversation began to wind down, Isaac headed to the kitchen with the glasses and dessert dishes. No fanfare, like most men—just a natural thing to do. This was a hint that the evening was also winding down, and Lee was ready for some privacy and some debriefing of her own. Isaac headed toward the door and, as was his usual habit, gave Lee a peck on the cheek. He pointed to the doorbell and said, "Don't forget to fix that short. It would be pretty embarrassing for an expert in portable energy sources to electrocute herself."

That's it! Don't, don't turn out the lights. She remembered the hasty exit from the BARF, or ZUMBA, or whatever, garage. Cato had been practically yelling at her. Everyone, or almost everyone, knows that when you turn *on* a light switch, it closes a gap in the wiring. It's like connecting one end of a bracelet to the other, making it a continuous circle. The electrons begin to flow in a circuit and voilà. Let there be light. The flow of the electrons also produces a magnetic field. When you turn the light *off*, you break the circuit, and the magnetic field kind of freaks out; it tries to keep a circuit going, sparking as it dies. It's the spark that worried Cato so much. That could have been a deadly oversight on their part had they flipped the switch off. *Thank you, Cato . . . again. Time to sleep; the doorbell can wait.*

=

Quit shaking the bed! she heard herself say in her child voice. Lee had been dreaming about the time her parents reluctantly allowed her to keep the runaway dog that showed up one afternoon on the doorstep of their canyon home. She immediately dubbed her "Chloe," and the dog was only too happy to come when called. It's not that the Roberts were opposed to having a dog; it just never seemed to work out for the busy family. The guiding question was who would be responsible for the care and feeding of a pet. If history proved anything, it was that even a lone Beta fish was doomed to live in a murky bowl, its days inevitably numbered due to an overgrowth of algae and slime and uneaten food. But Chloe was different. The little black-and-white something-mix seemed like a keeper. She had a sweet disposition, and Lee—young Lee—had been dedicated to walking her a few blocks each day, mindful of the coyotes and the bears. The little dog slept in her bed; never mind how filthy the sheets became. Lee was grateful for the company, even if it meant periodic interruptions in sleep: Chloe was a scratcher. Allergy, it seems. Not fleas.

The days turned into weeks and the weeks, into a month,

and soon fliers began to appear around the canyon, tacked onto the phone poles and even on the bulletin board at Mary's Market. LOST: BLACK & WHITE DOG. ANSWERS TO DAPHNE. Lee had to steel herself to take a closer look. Sure enough, it was her Chloe. Scientific proof that even the smartest dog doesn't actually know her own name. Giving up an adopted dog has to be the hardest thing a little girl would or could do, but Lee was already developing that gutsy persona that allowed her to at least look like she was handling it well. She never spoke of becoming a pet parent again.

So who's shaking the bed?

That's the typical "tell" for a SoCal morning earthquake. You think someone is shaking the bed. If it were the Big One, you'd be tossed onto the floor, or hanging over a ledge à la disaster movie. Like Lee's rolling bed scenario. The truth is, dozens of Little Ones happen on a regular basis. If it's bigger than a 3.0 on the Richter scale, or if you are sitting right above the epicenter of the sudden earth shift, you will feel it. Even in your sleep. And funny how you know the minute your brain wakes up that it's an earthquake. Lee didn't even bother to get out of bed. She had anchored the framed painting above her headboard to the wall with extra wiring and a bolt into the stud. It wasn't going anywhere. The scientist in her wanted to see how far the bed, on casters, would actually move to the west. She could even calculate its traveling speed based on how long the tremor lasted. She'd have to reconstruct that last measurement based on her dream sequence. How long had she felt the shaking? That was the inexact part. Then the mass of the bed would be different if she was in the bed vs. not in the bed.

Car alarms went off all around the neighborhood, sending pajama-clad owners scurrying into the streets and down to the parking garages, key fobs in hand. Only a few lucky owners could stay in bed and shut their alarms off with a tap on their cell phones. That could be a handy selling point for the rest of California's drivers, Lee thought. Not just an EQ early warning system, like the new one being tested all over the state, but an app that would automatically turn your car alarm off at the same time. Finally, curious to check out the much-hyped early warning system, Lee hopped up and checked her phone. She'd had it set to Do Not Disturb—a glitch in the system, obviously. Her phone had remained silent, but there was a notification on the screen and a link to Caltech's seismology lab. No matter. It seemed like a nice day to head over to her favorite Starbucks for coffee. No doubt, the place would be abuzz with earthquake chatter.

With her sloppiest sweats hanging on her small frame, Lee looked like a kid. Flip-flops, the universal, all-season footwear in SoCal, completed the ensemble for the day. She decided to take a walkabout up Lake Avenue with coffee in hand. The citizens of Pasadena had recovered nicely from the rude, early-morning wake-up call. And on a Saturday, everyone was dressed alike. Even the financial district workforce was dressed down today. Little cafés were besieged, and cheese shops were empty. Naturally. It was still early.

When Lee reached the Colorado Boulevard intersection, she headed back, assured that everyone and everything was still in one piece. She was resisting texting Isaac or Cato, though she still had a few nagging questions for Cato. As she drove through the neighborhoods between the Lake Avenue shopping district and her Del Mar condominium, her cell began to spasm in a crush of pings, vibrating itself right off the front seat. She couldn't see the screen, but she knew what had happened.

Right after a quake, everyone with a cell phone starts calling and texting everyone else with a cell phone. The cell towers go on overload, and no one can get through until the volume normalizes. Then all the calls and texts arrive, seemingly at the same time. Lee was guessing it was Cato and Isaac. But they'd have to wait until she pulled into the garage under her building. Actually, they'd have to wait until she made it up to her place. No reception in the cinder block structure. The elevator had yellow caution tape across the doors, with a note to please use the stairs until the technician can do an inspection. A precaution, really. Lee bounded up the stairs, caffeine still coursing through her veins. She noticed other residents she'd never seen before plodding in one direction or the other. Some managed greetings, and others still looked a little rattled. The people carrying grocery bags or laundry baskets looked downright put-upon. She was really more interested in the condition of the stairwell walls and the hallways. Things looked okay. Only a few new cracks in the otherwise aging plaster. That was normal. And more would show up in the days to come. Since no one was expected at her place today, Lee figured she'd fix her delinquent doorbell. And return the texts and phone calls.

Lee grabbed her toolbox; it was considerably smaller than Cato's investigator box, and much more conventional too. No gas meter, no telescoping measuring rod. It did have a small voltmeter and the usual plastic-handled screwdrivers. Also a wire cutter and a few twist-on wire connectors—those tiny yellow and red plastic cones that you shove onto the ends of two wires to twist them into submission. The idea is that the exposed wire tips will be wedded to each other and allow for the flow of electrons. Strangely enough, she also found her long-lost favorite nail polish nestled in among some nuts and bolts. There was no explaining that. Not feeling invincible today, even though she had survived an earthquake and an escape from the ominous Grand Pooh-bah, Lee figured she should turn off the power to the doorbell first. Many an electrician had done this kind of job without turning it off, and they survived, mostly. This was one of those don't-try-this-at-home hints: when in doubt, turn off the power. Lodged behind the collection of designer shoes and clothes in her "walking closet" was the electrical panel to her unit. Fortunately, someone had already labeled the switches, so Lee was halfway there.

As she was detaching the doorbell button and pulling it out of the wall, Lee couldn't help but replay the whole gas-in-the-garage caper at the BARF compound. Something wasn't right about it. She tested the loose doorbell wires with her own small voltmeter, just in case. No light, no buzz, no power. The copper was thick and hard to bend, indicating that it was probably original to the building, but she managed to twist the ends together with her wire cutter tool. How could Cato explain that his gas sensor didn't register anything for several minutes, even with the door closed? And then it did . . . suddenly . . . big time. All that was left for Lee to do was to twist a plastic cap on the wire ends and test everything before shoving it back into the wall. Something accomplished today. If there had been a gas leak in the garage the first time, Kat's friend could have been blown to bits along with the shed, or at the very least gassed to death. Instead, the cops claimed accidental electrocution leading to a heart attack. There was a body, and the building was intact. Another thing: What was it about the gas supply and the valves on the side of the garage that caught Cato's attention? *Time to text Cato back.*

Lee hadn't even checked her cell phone yet. She was right: a dozen texts from Isaac and almost as many from Cato. And four missed calls. *Well, Lee, it's nice to know someone cares. Something to look forward to when the Big One hits.* Isaac was first on her call list. He was fine and so was Bernoulli. Their newer construction barely wiggled in the Little One. In fact, the cat slept through it all, probably dreaming of crickets; Lee liked to think that maybe he was dreaming of black-and-white dogs too. Isaac had wanted to try out the new Casa Viño in Old Pasadena, so that was the plan for the evening. Seven o'clock. Calm the nerves before going to sleep. Even seasoned Californians will not sleep well for a couple of nights after a quake. The conversation, as Lee suspected, was short, and she could get to the deadly vapor questions she had for Cato.

Cato answered on the first ring and sounded relieved to hear from her. Like Isaac, he was fine. His Spanish-style casita on Orange Grove Boulevard sprouted a few new wrinkles in its exterior, nothing structural. He lost a vintage microscope that bounced off a shelf, but he seemed okay about it. Lee figured he could handle a couple of questions. "I spoke to Isaac. He's fine too. Glad you guys are both okay. So, something's been nagging at me about the gas readings in the BARF garage and about the photo you took of the valves on the outside." No answer. "Can we talk for a couple of minutes? That's all. Promise."

Cato laughed. "Sure. It's simple. One of the valves on the gas supply was remote-controlled. That means that anyone from anywhere could have turned on the gas."

"Like Zin?"

"Exactly."

"So he waited until we closed the door and were distracted. Then he flipped the valve on? But why didn't we smell it? The gas company has to add a scent. Right? So unsuspecting people would know there was a leak."

"Mercaptan," Cato said, no longer laughing. "Yeah. It took me a while to figure that out. But I remembered a couple of cases that I had. One was natural gas—methane. It bubbled up through a shallow pool of water that acted like a filter. So no odor. The other was gas that was deliberately piped several yards below the surface so that the dirt filtered out the mercaptan. I think that option is the likely scenario here. That's my guess, anyway."

"Son of a . . ." An uncharacteristic comment for Lee, but she was shocked at how close they came to being splayed across the landscape in a Santa Ynez canyon. "I guess you'd have to test the soil beneath the surface to know."

"Lee, I don't think it's worth the risk right now. We've got other things to work on. Don't say anything to Isaac yet, but we've got to get a better handle on the cult itself and on Zin. And soon." Just then, their conversation was punctuated by an aftershock. Every earthquake is followed by dozens, even hundreds, of smaller quakes. The idea is that they get smaller and less frequent as days go on, but it's no less comforting every time it happens. "I guess that's our cue, Lee. We'll talk more later. Keep running shoes by your bed tonight. Just in case."

Lee knew what he meant. Sometimes—rarely—the quakes grow in intensity, and the one you think is the main quake is actually a warning for a much larger one.

=

The Casa Viño patio was jammed with people, probably thinking the same thing Isaac and Lee thought: keep busy until you have to go to bed tonight but stay outside. The lightweight awning and the clear plastic floor-to-ceiling curtains all the way around offered some comfort too. Not much to fall on you if the shaking starts again. The air inside felt sauna-ish with all the bodies crammed in, and the various wines—many of them from Spain and Portugal—broadcast an aroma of grapes and alcohol. Tapas, the tiny plates of Mediterranean fare, were ferried from a hidden kitchen to the patio, which, as the hour went on, began to drip moisture down the inside of the plastic sheeting walls. Isaac and Lee both had to shed their jackets as waiters and patrons jostled by. They'd gotten there early enough to secure actual seating at a tiny table—a perfect fit for the tiny plates of chewy lamb, fried potatoes, and roasted vegetables.

Isaac recognized a couple of colleagues, who promptly took advantage of their much-coveted tiny table and deposited empty plates and glasses with them before moving on. "No use in ordering more food unless someone comes to clear this," Lee offered, not quite as relaxed as she hoped to be at this point in the evening. *Chill, Lee.*

He shrugged, an apologetic shrug actually. Isaac grabbed the dishes. "I can probably get through the crush with these. Just save my place." Lee regretted her whining immediately. She could picture someone spilling food or wine on Isaac's white sweater as he wove through the crowd. Waiter to the rescue before Isaac could even get up.

"I'll take those. Anything else you want, Ms. Roberts?" Lee looked up to see her favorite bad boy, Mr. Jacobs, grinning at her. He was dressed like a food server: black shirt and pants, white apron wound around his waist. "Uh . . . I just started work here. What a day to start. Huh? Earthquake and all. The boss thinks it was like good luck or something cuz we're so busy. So, did I pass? The class, I mean."

"Oh, Mr. Jacobs. You passed. Good job on that last lab. Your grade will be posted online Wednesday." Still a little wary of the kid and wondering if Isaac would make the connection between her retelling of the faculty garage encounter story and their waiter, Lee managed a weak smile. The kid reached over the table and offered a hand to Isaac. *He cleans up pretty well*, she thought. "Uh, Isaac, this is one of my students . . ."

"John, sir. John Jacobs. How's it going? Can I get you another dish or like a glass of wine?" Lee and Isaac decided on another small plate of fried potatoes and the house red. "Be right back with your order." It was Mr. Jacobs's turn for the smile, as he looked back and forth between the two friends. *Uh-oh, Lee. He knows something personal about you.* She had been intent on keeping her personal and professional lives separate. This could blur the line if she saw Mr. Jacobs—John—around campus again. There was no client-attorney, or professor-professor's social life, privilege here.

Isaac had a funny smile on his face too. *Must be going around.* "What?" Lee asked. But she knew that look. He was getting ready to say something embarrassing.

"I'm trying to picture him in a hoodie."

"I'm still not entirely comfortable around him, and now he knows I have a life outside of the college. Not so sure that's a good thing. I'm really trying to see him in a different light, but you know . . . I don't usually overreact. Right? There was something that evening . . ." Lee had said her piece. Closed subject for now. She crossed her arms. No way to cross her legs under that tiny table, or she would have done that too. Besides, the black pencil skirt—a vintage Versace—didn't leave any room for crossed legs or much else.

Isaac knew how to take a hint. The small plate arrived and so did the red wine. Not a great wine, but fine for this evening. It was working its magic. By the time Lee and Isaac got up to go, the steamy enclosure was beginning to get to them. Isaac's hair was even curlier than usual, and Lee's was dangling like a wet wig. She was starting to sweat, and her ears were ringing a little. All she could think of was getting to the fresh air. ASAP. The bigger problem was fighting their way through the onslaught of hopefuls vying for their table. Isaac grabbed her by the arm, and she was glad she had gone without those three-and-a-half inch heels tonight. She heard, "See ya, Ms. Roberts" from the crowd and knew it was John Jacobs.

Lee wobbled to the nearest bench—a low concrete wall curving around a spritzing water feature. Cold air, cold water to the rescue. She could see that Isaac was looking a little green-ish himself. "We got out of there just in time. Either we overdid it with the wine and food, or the steam bath was too much for us," she said, but she had a fleeting thought that she didn't want to even bring up. She couldn't even put words to the idea without sounding like an idiot. It was the wine talking, she was sure, though she also knew how easy it was to pick up a glass in a bar and wonder if someone had spiked it. *You're doing just the thing you swore you didn't do—overreacting. Get real, Lee.*

CHAPTER SIXTEEN
THE AFTERMATH

Cato called. No texting this time. "The early reports are in. Check with Isaac and see what he has. Can we meet at my place today? Noon-ish?" It was clear from the tone of his voice that he was excited, raring to go over all the data with the Blue Öyster Crew. His fervor wouldn't have translated well to text message, Cato not being a native emoji user. Lee tried to imagine what that would have looked like: the happy face with his tongue hanging out, the blue face with his hands on either side of his cheeks (ala *The Scream*), or better yet, the one with red hearts for eyes? In any case, the mood was infectious, and she would have to contain herself for three hours. She texted Isaac with the news—no emojis needed or wanted—and went about the business of the morning. The online newspapers and one cup of coffee took up a whole forty-five minutes. A couple of fig newtons (the cookies—not the scientist) and a second cup of coffee were good for another fifteen minutes. *No use avoiding it, Lee. You need a run.*

Lee fished the running shoes out from under her bed, where

they were standing guard for another quake. Interesting. Did the bed move again during the night? She had measured a good five-centimeter drift immediately after the Little One. Here were another two centimeters. Statistically unimportant, as long as she could keep moving the bed back. The phone went into one pocket, and her key, into the other. She envisioned a dirty white sock in there also. A kind of funny PTSD flashback. The elevator was operational again, but the stairs added more steps to her fitness regimen, so off she went, bounding down the old stairwell and out the lobby door.

The street was relatively quiet. Mostly dog walkers ignoring the admonition to pick up after your pets and mothers with luxury strollers the size of compact cars. A look to the north showcased the view everyone in the country saw on New Year's Day: a crisp mountain scape against an unseasonably blue sky. The envy of the world and the reason so many Pasadenans are conflicted about the televised Rose Parade. Hopefully, the city's good weather in January will *not* encourage a population surge in February. The Crown City, the nickname that predated the City of Roses moniker, referred to the spacious valley and the string of pointed mountains surrounding it. But Pasadena was straining at the seams now, though gracefully, according to the city planners. Expensive can still be high-density, and many of the new townhomes and condos are offered for lease as opposed to sale, owing to the asking prices. Infrastructure is supporting more transportation options: a metro light rail, express buses and shuttles, and bike and scooter rentals (the value of these to be determined, as they are deposited all over the place, including doorways and driveways, when they have outlived their usefulness). In fact, bike lane proponents and car lane proponents are forever at odds. The euphemism "Road

Diet" is an annoying attempt to relieve drivers of a lane, and signs have popped up in every neighborhood advocating one position or the other.

Lee headed east on Del Mar, a straight shot for a couple of miles, and then back again. Some stand-alone homes were sprinkled in among the multifamily dwellings, almost all of them dating from the fifties to the eighties. Homes on the side streets even went as far back as the thirties. One large property once housed a private school and is now the latest development in the neighborhood, with brand new million-dollar-plus townhomes. They are selling like hotcakes, as they say.

A vibration in her rear pocket meant an incoming text from Cato or Isaac. Her guess was Isaac.

> Morning. How are you feeling today? Should we bring food to Cato's?

Lee was reminded of the woozy ending to what would have been a nice evening at the Casa Viño. She was sure they had both just had too much rich wine and probably too much rich food. Add to that the balmy microclimate in the enclosed patio, and it was a recipe for a slight case of vertigo.

> Feeling good. How about salads from somewhere? You pick. No wine. I'll split the bill with you.

Time to head back and take a shower. That's another thing that even survivors of small earthquakes dread doing for a couple of days: getting into the shower. Kind of like that scene in *Psycho*, only no blood if you can help it. You just need to keep those running shoes hand—and some clothes.

=

When Lee pulled up in front of Cato's adobe home, she was reminded of the film noir settings of the thirties. These quintessential Spanish California dwellings, along with the stately Craftsman bungalows, fill the historic neighborhoods in Pasadena. Cato's house was a very faded pink topped off with a red tile roof. The arch of the front porch mimicked the arch of the dark brown entry door, and all the south and west-facing windows had brown canopies to match. Cato had been an early adopter of drought-tolerant landscaping, so the front yard was blanketed in brown mulch punctuated with a whole assortment of brown shrubs. Only a few rosemary and lavender plants offered color. A lone, very tall palm tree provided no shade at all but was striking against the blue sky. Still, the overall look was charming and eco-friendly to boot. Isaac's car was parked across the street, meaning he had approached from the other side of town. Lee, balancing a box of cookies from the Euro Bakery in one hand and a laptop in the other, was about to ring the bell with her elbow when the door swung open. Isaac looked fully recuperated from the Viño incident and was wearing jeans and a T-shirt for once. Even Cato was dressed down. The dining table was filled with laptops, cameras, and piles of papers. But the kitchen table was set for lunch.

Lee headed right in and sat down. "I'm starved. I hope we can eat first."

"Two kinds of salads. Take your pick or mix and match.

And there's zucchini bread." Isaac handed Lee and Cato napkins, but they'd already dug in. "Let's not talk shop until after. I need something in my stomach," he said.

Lee figured Isaac might be better off on an empty stomach, and a look at Cato told her he was thinking the same thing. They ate without much conversation at all. At least two of them were not looking forward to going over the findings. And they all knew they were at the point where they'd have to come up with a definitive plan.

The box of cookies migrated to the dining room with the Crew. Cato started: "Thanks for coming here. I don't often get company anymore, but I thought you'd like to see my lair. It has quite a history actually. This was originally a caretaker's cottage. The main house—mansion—belonged to one of the original orange grove farmers. It's long gone, obviously. The whole thing burned down in the early 1900s, and just the cottage and the small casita out back were rebuilt. It's pretty fireproof now, though earthquakes are another matter." He paused to open up the files on his laptop. "So I'll go over my findings, and then Isaac can tell us about his research. Okay? Then, Lee, if you want to present your results . . ."

Isaac pulled out a yellow legal notepad. "I know it's old school, but we can jot down questions, things we still need to find out, and who should do what. Then I'll type it into a Google spreadsheet for everyone to comment. Okay?" As Isaac said that, he and Lee looked at Cato. She supposed Isaac was wondering if Cato had used the collaborating app. And she was too. Like her father, Cato was brilliant at what he knew—the physical world—and not so much when it came to twenty-first century tech, crime and accident scenes notwithstanding.

"Okay. I get it. You guys are staring at me like I'm from

another planet. Planet Luddite, I guess. Yes, I speak Google, though I'm not too happy with their evil campaign to take over the world." Lee laughed so hard she sprayed mocha chip cookie everywhere, just missing her laptop. Isaac looked relieved. He liked Cato a lot, and the idea of insulting him was almost unthinkable.

"It looks like we have residue of lithium and some unidentified trace compound, possibly another psychotropic drug. It was in the dirt and on that SOS label. And also on the label and in the dirt were remnants of blue algae. I'm guessing that they were lacing the blue algae with the lithium to break down people's defenses. It's a great drug for people who need it but not so much for those who don't, especially at higher than recommended dosages," Cato said.

"They still prescribe that old drug for depression, bipolar disease, right?" Lee asked.

"Yes. So the other trace drug seems to be related to gamma hydroxybutyrate—GHB. It's highly addictive, and the smallest of doses causes a whole host of side effects, including incapacitating its victims." Cato paused to formulate his conclusion. "I'm thinking the combo over a period of time—even in minute amounts—would make it easy for someone like Zin to gain control of large groups of people without resistance . . . and maintain that control."

Isaac had gone pale at this point. "So what is the ultimate goal of this group? Of Zin?"

He stood up, trying to dispel the shakes. "Never mind that. How do we get Kat out of there? This has to be what they were trying to hide . . ."

Lee jumped in: "Isaac, we'll get her out, but first we have to look at what happened to her friend so we can do it safely.

We'll need to be smart about this. And we need to know more about the ZUMBA-BARF-SOS connection. And Zin." She could tell that Isaac was listening to her. He always responded to logic. "Can you tell us what you have? It might be the key to bringing these people down." Isaac sat. He pulled up his research docs, which probably looked very different to him now, considering Cato's revelations.

"This is all kind of convoluted," Isaac said, "and it has origins in other states, like Oregon and Illinois, believe it or not."

=

"Here's what I know. The whole thing began in upstate Oregon with a group known as 'Hope of Peace.' They were anything but peaceful. In the seventies they started out as elitist and secretive. Part of their plan was to subjugate women. And they were into anything that would give them money and power. No surprise there." Isaac paused. "The rest gets even crazier. They linked up with a cult in Illinois called 'Society of Souls.'"

"SOS," Cato and Lee said—in unison.

"Yeah. So here's how we get to Santa Ynez: Society of Souls was . . . is . . . more militant. Maybe that's not the word. Uh . . . aggressive. They've been known to use strong-arm tactics. They still associate with Hope of Peace. They need HOP to launder money." Isaac was noticeably agitated at this point. Lee could see it, and she understood why.

"So, Isaac, where do BARF and ZUMBA come in?" Lee had to ask, even though she didn't like where the story was going. "And Zin?" Isaac pulled up another document, complete with photos. There was Zin. Younger. Strangely, not as handsome. Something was missing.

Cato was the first to respond: "That's Zin all right. What's different? He is the guy we encountered at the compound, but he doesn't look as . . . robust. I guess that's the word. The photo looks like the *before,* and the guy we talked to looks like the *after*." All kinds of things were running through Lee's mind: *What's the connection with these groups? Does blue algae really have some magical power? Don't go there, Lee. You're a scientist.*

"So where does Zin fit in the scheme of things? Maybe that would explain the change. I hesitate to call it a transformation. I guess it's creepy, no matter what you call it," Lee said.

Isaac continued, "According to local Oregon papers, Zin was born into the HOP community. It *was* a community too. They had their own enclave and schools. Uh . . . let me see. Born in 1978 as Gabriel Zinder. Says here he was close to his mother as a child, and when she disappeared or *was* disappeared, Gabriel was only five. He was devastated. Too young to realize that she lived a pretty stoic life. A miserable life as a woman in this group, actually. It wouldn't surprise anyone to think she just left the cult. Within a few years the kid was fully indoctrinated into HOP and made a name for himself as a mathematical prodigy."

Lee piped in, "I can see where this is going. Correct me if I'm wrong. Zin, or Gabriel, was the mastermind behind the money-laundering scheme. So he had—has—a lot of power. Both groups need him. What's the story with his last name? You said Zinder, but he told us Ishara."

"Yeah, so Ishara is some kind of Eastern mystical figure. Zin probably figured if he appropriated the name, it would give him more charisma, more clout. But a lot of members also take that as their last names too. Shows allegiance, faithfulness, I guess."

"That makes sense," she said. "Now just a couple of things, and I think we should take a break. I can go over my findings after that." Lee was beginning to formulate a connection between the garage incident and this evil cult partnership, but she was hesitant to go there—yet. "So, Isaac, can you go over the Blue Algae Reactant Factor thing and ZUMBA?"

"I'm ready for a break too," Cato cut in. He was making some of the same assumptions that the others were, but once it was all out in the open, once they put words to the whole cult thing, it would become very real—and dangerous. They'd have to act soon. "Just go over Lee's questions, and then I'll get us something to drink. We can sit outside on the patio if you want."

"Right. It's simple. Blue algae is easy to come by. It can be turned into almost anything: food, soap, lotions, power drinks, what-have-you. Green algae has been established as useful and healthy, so it's a short leap to blue algae in people's minds. In a place like Santa Ynez—in most places that are thought of as bucolic, peaceful, and wholesome—it's a natural. That's BARF, and that's where ZUMBA comes in also. Zin wanted—needed—to be associated with blue algae. It would be easier for people to accept than shadowy cults from other parts of the country. Cults that are known for less benign beliefs. So, Zin's Ultra Mineralized Blue Algae."

"ZUMBA! You've got to be kidding us, Isaac. That's it? It would be funny if it weren't so devious, so evil," Lee responded. *And so dangerous to Kat.*

=

Lee was trying to recall all the "Before and After" ads she had ever encountered. There were the diet products: *Miraculous loss of 161 lbs. in one week—sure, it's possible!* The hair growth products: *Grow your own hair back!* or *Grow someone else's hair on your head—like a Chia Pet!* The suntan products: *Look like you spent a week on the Riviera in one tanning session (melanoma and white raccoon eyes at no extra charge).* The speed-reading products: *Preparing for the SATs? Read ten pages a minute with the possible bonus that you might actually remember what you read!* The body building products: *Become muscle-bound in no time at all—just like the Hulk, only not green!* And her personal favorite, the wrinkle and under-eye bag removers: *You'll never be able to smile again, but who cares!*

"Iced tea?"

"Yeah, that one is good for burns, right? Or it cures cancer or heart disease or something. That would be a good before and after."

"Uh . . . what? Earth to Lee, are you with us?" Cato laughed. "What's going on in your brainy head? I was just wondering if you wanted some iced tea. No miracles implied."

Both of the guys were staring at her. This was a first for them. The ever-present Lee had zoned out, and they were there to see it firsthand.

"Just kidding, guys. Yes, I'd love some iced tea. I'm just trying to figure out what caused Zin's transformation. Please don't tell me it's the blue algae! But I plan on asking him next time our paths cross—if they cross." Lee opened her laptop on the patio table and slid it around until the shade hit the screen at just the right angle. It was a good way to stall and to deflect from her embarrassing lapse at the same time. "So. The electrical components we found are the same ones you'd use to create a mobile power supply, just as I suspected. Why they would want that is a question I'm still working through. The supply is designed to ramp up the voltage big-time. It's like the one I built with my cohorts at Los Alamos. That one that was intended to power a portable muon tomography device."

"Why portable?" Isaac asked.

"You could take it anywhere, even undetected, if you want. It can work from a battery or regular current. And the mechanism could be broken down or put together in no time. It was easy to transport and made out of simple components. Here's what I'm thinking: they were processing blue algae to combine with the lithium and the GHB. A strong electrical current could facilitate the bond. Cato might be able to address that."

"Yeah, it's just what you said. One example is electroplating—like when they lay a thin gold or copper layer over another metal. For jewelry or something. You think it's a solid precious metal, but it's sometimes just a coating or a bond of two different materials."

"So it could create a bond between the algae and the drugs, maybe at a molecular level. Right? They probably had to experiment with that a long time to get it just right," Lee added. "Now the portable aspect is starting to make sense. They could do this process anywhere. Even in an old shed in the middle of wine country. And . . ." Lee paused to put it all together in her headfirst. "They would have a major power supply—a potent device—that could be broken down into seemingly unrelated pieces that someone else would never be able to identify—like the police."

Isaac put words to the realization that this plan was more evil than they suspected: "If there was an accidental—or purposeful—explosion, or an electrocution, authorities wouldn't see the connection between all of these bits and pieces. Can the power supply be rigged to malfunction?" He was asking but already knew what Lee and Cato would say.

"I guess that was the point. They could kill an intruder or an unfaithful cult member *and* keep processing their blue algae concoction without detection. Kat's friend was supposed to disappear altogether when they realized he was a threat to the operation. They probably got interrupted before they could get rid of the body, so they broke down the power supply and scattered everything around, leaving just enough evidence to convince the cops it was an accidental electrocution. It could just as easily have been an explosion if they had turned on the gas." That last part sent shivers up Lee's spine as she verbalized it, and she glanced at Cato. They had never really explained their whole near-death caper at the BARF/ZUMBA compound to Isaac. *Maybe Isaac will let that part slide*, she thought. *For now, anyway.*

"Okay. And we have to figure out how my sister's friend fits into the whole thing. The guy was young. Kat's age and really smart. I think she said he had been a chemistry grad from UCSB. Now the name makes sense. He was born Alan something. Kat said he called himself Alan Ishara. Go figure. That means he was a faithful supporter to start with."

"Maybe he didn't know the whole picture—what the plan was—until it was too late," Lee said. Isaac was clearly preoccupied at this point.

"So . . ." Isaac said. *Here it is. I know that look*, Lee thought. "What is the story with the gas in the shed? You guys didn't tell me about that part."

Cato took the metaphoric bullet for the both of them, and Lee was glad she didn't have to relate the story to Isaac. He felt bad enough as it was about everything involving his sister. Cato did an admirable job explaining what had happened, and even made Lee feel better about it all. "I guess they always had the option of blowing up the place before the police got there. They were just greedy—or rushed—and wanted to keep the garage in one piece. Maybe so they could keep working as long as possible. They didn't plan on the two of us showing up that day."

"Just your luck, guys," Isaac said. "Sorry."

"Hey, don't worry about it. That was a first for me. Cato's an old hand at climbing fences in a hurry. It was my first time. Now I'm ready for anything." She grinned. "Really!"

"That kind of explosion isn't always as lethal as you'd think. You have to be right on top of it. Sometimes it's a small blast. And there's rarely a fire. But it was good practice to hightail it out of there . . . especially for Lee . . . er . . . Jane Jetson." Lee could see that Cato was trying to lighten the mood. That whole escape from the ZUMBA property was done and over with, as far as she figured.

"Now we need a plan of action. I have to go over to the campus tomorrow to put some things together for the next semester. It shouldn't take long. Can we each come up with a proposal for extracting Kat and meet up tomorrow night?" Lee hoped that would end the session for today, and they could just enjoy the rest of the afternoon on Cato's patio. A slight Santa Ana wind was warming up the air, and she was ready for a few minutes of Zen—not to be confused with ZUMBA . . . or Zin.

CHAPTER SEVENTEEN
THE REVIGATORS IN THE BASEMENT

It's the job of every teacher—no matter what level or grade—to spend the days leading up to a new semester planning lessons and setting up the classroom. Lee was beginning to realize just how much easier it was to be a part-time instructor at a community college than to be a professor at a place like Caltech. Not that she felt she could slack off. She would always deliver 100 percent. It's just that there was a more relaxed atmosphere here. Less competition in the science department, fewer people, fewer egos to contend with—for the most part. With Cato's help she had gotten off to a strong start: two physics classes had the benefit of her expertise and her mentor's hidden chamber of delights. And she still had time to investigate a crime and a cult; the rush of that escapade left an indelible mark, and she was ready for more of the same.

The business at hand today was to decide which of her lessons she would keep and which she would replace. Lee liked her labs but wanted to spice up her repertoire with one or two new experiences. It was hard to pass up all the artifacts in the basement, and a good teacher would take advantage of anything to prove a physics point. While foraging around in the basement two weeks before, she had noticed two "Revigators™" (probably still trademarked) sitting on one of the old Steelcase desks. They had the vintage look that could capture the attention of her students and the promise of radioactivity that would seal the deal. At least, that's what Cato had said about it. She figured it was worth a try.

Lee researched *Revigator* and came up with the scoop: Revigators had been manufactured with the purpose of flimflam and scam. That is, to prove the old adage that there's a sucker born every day. She had never seen one before, and after reading up, she figured the safest place for one is in a museum or in the PCC basement with the other relics, waiting only to be liberated for an hour or two. Ceramic, with a spout and a lid, they looked like something you'd use to serve iced tea or water. Most of these crocks were imprinted with the name Revigator and often the words "Patented in 1912."

The "sucker" part was the interesting thing—maybe even more interesting than the science, but it all presented a simple lesson in measuring radiation and the human capacity for falling victim to quackery. The promise of cures for arthritis, flatulence (yes!), and senility drew the unsuspecting public in. The magic ingredient? The inside lining of the Revigators contained low-grade radiation in the form of radium ore embedded in a ceramic coating. All one had to do was fill the crock with water, let it sit overnight, and drink up the next morning. The actual scientific analysis of the water often showed little to no radon, unless the lining was cracked or chipped: small pieces of the ceramic would have a higher reading on a Geiger counter than the H2O itself. The added bonus was that the drinking water also contained lead and arsenic, which even Lee's students would recognize as toxic.

Lee figured a lab involving measuring the radiation of ordinary tap water, then the inside of the empty Revigators, then water that had been sitting in the Revigators overnight might yield some graphable results. All that was left to do was head down to the basement again to retrieve them. And stash away the Ra-Be at the same time.

"Okay, little guy. Let's see if we can figure out how you ended up in my classroom. I know I left you languishing in the dust." *This is a bad sign. Talking to carpenters' tools.*

She figured she could take the old screwdriver back down to the basement too—just to see what would happen. On the other hand, it could prove to be a handy defensive weapon. "Come on. I'm taking you with me." Armed with cell phone and screwdriver, and a pig, Lee headed for the stairwell. The door that actually led below ground was unmarked; only a few faculty members had keys to the storage areas. Cato was one of them, and he had bequeathed his to Lee. *This is going to be quick. I have things to be and places to do.* She remembered her highbrow professor father used to think that this lowbrow play on words was the funniest ever. *Thank you, Dad.*

Lee had something else in mind at the moment: another meetup with the guys to review any new evidence. That included the DNA. Then hopefully, a "cocktail of the week" somewhere. A little rum or vodka would soften the blow too. Tonight was the night they were also going to come up with an extraction plan for Kat. The Blue Öyster Caper was on.

As she neared the bottom of the stairs, Lee noticed that

another sprinkling of dust had layered itself over her earlier footsteps, and then at some point a larger shoe print had been superimposed over hers. Kind of like the ghost image that one of Cato's holograms would produce if it was out of sync. *Okay, let's not dwell on this. Really.* She pulled out her cell phone and knelt down to take a picture of the prints; the screwdriver popped out of her pocket and bounced down the last two steps. On the steel stairs, even a wooden-handled Phillips screwdriver could sound like a gunshot if it hit the steps just right. The sound reverberated throughout the chamber, bouncing off anything . . . and anyone.

=

The rest of the foray into the basement was uneventful. Lee left the screwdriver where she had first found it, on a shelf near the entrance. The wayward pig went back into its hiding place. There were two Revigators anchoring an old Steelcase desk at the back of the room—just the way she remembered it. The question was whether it was possible to carry two of them upstairs. She cradled them in her arms and realized the peril of trying to make it up the stairs with both. It's not that they were heavy, just awkward to grab hold of, and leaving shattered pieces behind would be irresponsible. Not Lee's style. For a few seconds she stood there trying to make a decision, and then the whole basement went silent. There had been a transformer humming away just like that very first time—and just like that first time, it was background noise that only makes itself known when it stops—or you stop to listen. The dripping water somewhere in the recesses of the basement made her think of her surreal encounter at the beginning of the last semester. But somehow the magic was gone; the familiarity with the place did that—and the traveling screwdriver. Lee felt her favorite admonition coming on: *Get real, Lee. Let's go!* That's all it took: within minutes the Revigators were settling in upstairs, and the evening lay ahead.

=

The plan was to meet up at the Tap Room to advance their rescue blueprint, then transition to The Langham's restaurant. Isaac offered to cover the bill, so Lee figured she'd oblige by dressing the part. She hadn't taken her Ted Baker out on a date for a while. Still fit to a T. *Where did that expression originate?* she wondered. *No matter.* The Louboutins were itching for a night out as well. She rounded out the outfit with a creamy Ferragamo scarf and marveled at how uplifting it was to put on pieces of her mother's treasured wardrobe—things that Lee herself couldn't afford to buy, especially since becoming a bona fide homeowner. There was something about the lines of the pieces and the stitching, more than the labels or the price tags. And the vintage clothing added another dimension: their history, often the history of women and their place in the work world or social world. *Funny how so many of the designers were actually men, though.*

The meeting of the Blue Öyster Crew started the minute they all sat down. It was clear that they had done their homework and were eager to talk. Lee started: "I'd be interested to know about the DNA. The likeliest source would be that post-it note, but maybe some of the items we collected from the garage would have traces too." Drinks came and so did menus.

Cato pulled a paper out of his sports coat pocket. Lee was trying to recall if she had seen him dressed up before. Dark blue suited him. And Isaac. Isaac always dressed well and on the expensive side. Not only had the guys done their cult home-work, but they had received Lee's telepathic memo to dress up.

"It does look like your thinking is correct as far as the amount of DNA evidence goes. Yours was all over the post-it note, Lee; the rest would have to be a second individual. I excluded trace amounts of other people who probably handled the post-it note packaging machines, so it was easy to narrow down Zin as the second individual. But—and this is a big but—his DNA pointed to a different individual, not Gabriel Zinder or Zin Ishara or any combination thereof."

"So he was making that up?" Isaac asked.

"Or maybe he didn't know," Lee said. "Maybe he was never in the system and so there would be no way of comparing him."

"Actually, the report comes up with a different name, so he had to be in the system. And we don't have DNA for Zinder family members as far as we can tell. So there's no tracking him down that way. He could have been adopted, or knowing how some cults work, he could have been fathered by a cult leader who . . ."

Lee chimed in, "Wait. Cults sometimes raise children communally, but he could have been given to an adoptive mother to raise if he was deemed special. He was devoted to her; that doesn't mean he was genetically her child. Again, it's possible he didn't know. Not that it makes him innocent—or a victim in some way."

They could see the server heading their way with a determined look on her face. Either she hadn't read their body language or she was just anxious to get the order in, whether they were ready or not. The special for the evening was a pasta dish with clams, and they figured the quickest way to send her off to the kitchen was to all order the same thing. It's hard to go wrong at The Langham anyway. Isaac picked a bottle of white for the table, as well.

"So, whose name is associated with the DNA, and what do we know about him?"

"Isaac, that's the weirdest part," Cato said. The wine steward had impeccable timing, and Isaac had impeccable taste in wine. A Rombauer. When they were alone again and with glass in hand, Cato continued. "The report lists a Matthew Jacobs, but according to my sources at PPD, there's no rap sheet on him. No way of knowing right now how he got into the system. We would need to do a little more research, and the name's pretty common."

Lee was trying to stay calm. *Lots of Jacobs. It is a pretty common name. Don't muddy the water with speculation. Maybe, like Gabriel, it's just a reference to biblical characters. Lots of people like those names . . . or it could be a cult thing to do that?* Isaac was watching Lee. It was hard not to. She looked classy when she dressed up—even beautiful. Not a new observation on his part, but he couldn't help notice the ever-so-slight change in her demeanor. She was pretty good at the poker face, but not perfect.

"Uh . . . I guess I could spend time online trying to track down the name, but the more pressing issue is what to do about Zin. The Zin at hand. I'm for doing what will get Kat out of there and then trying to bring down the cult people if we can do it safely. My sister is my priority." Isaac was looking at Lee as he spoke. She caught his drift. *He's right. Don't go there, Lee. Forget about my bad boy, John Jacobs. There's no way he is connected.* She put on a reassuring smile, hoping he would accept it. No way of knowing for sure.

Dinner was delicious and offered a respite from the heady

discussion. As if with one mind, the Blue Öyster Crew decided to take a deep breath and enjoy the meal and the wine. The dining room was beginning to fill up, people bringing wine and cocktail glasses with them from the bar as they filed in. Fortunately, the server got busy at other tables, and the three compadres were happy to be left alone. Dessert was a flourless cake, complete with three spoons. Lee was gratified that both guys also liked chocolate as much as she did, and they ate slowly to make the experience last—and also because once they were finished with the meal, they would have to revisit the DNA dilemma.

Cato led the way back to the Tap Room and sank into a settee on the dark patio. With heaters crackling away, the whole place felt like a summer retreat. The expansive lawn was set up for what looked like an impending wedding or corporate event, and the old wing of The Langham was postcard perfect. The best part: they were alone for the time being—the professional sleuth and his investigators-in-training. Lee turned down a cocktail, and so did Cato; Isaac, probably steeling himself for the rest of the DNA report and the plan that would follow, ordered a vodka on the rocks. Lee didn't blame him.

=

As much as they wanted to solve the DNA mystery of Zin, they all agreed that the priority was getting Kat out of the cult. Second would be figuring out what happened to her friend. Isaac was anxious to find out more about this Alan Ishara, whose last name, it would appear, was actually something else. He would take on the job of asking Kat. Lee would follow up on any possible DNA evidence for him on the electrical components from the garage, though the odds of any biological material remaining on the tiny metal pieces were pretty slim. Cato would call in an expert in DNA analysis and ancestry to see if they could get a handle on Zin, and most importantly, he would come up with a plan to extract Kat from the cult compound. The metamorphosis from BARF to ZUMBA, with a side of SOS and HOP, sounded ridiculous—and harmless. But it was a deadly serious matter. Emphasis on *deadly*. They could laugh about it later.

They would all head up to Santa Ynez on the weekend.

CHAPTER EIGHTEEN
SANTA YNEZ REDUX

Lee felt like this would be the last-ditch effort for the group. In any case, she had to get back to the business of teaching in a few days. The Revigators were safely ensconced in her classroom cupboard, and her lesson plans for the next semester were almost done percolating in her head. The guys had a little more flexibility with their time, but there was no way she would let them do this alone. It had to be finished by the end of the weekend. The plan was simple on the surface: get in and grab Kat, get out in one piece, and worry about the rest later. There would always be time to expose the group: social media and the press could handle that part. If the police, ATF, or whomever wanted to raid the place, Kat and the Blue Öyster Crew would be out of harm's way. At least, that was the idea.

Cato had loaded up his car with the usual equipment, plus a few white socks and some clean ziplock baggies sans Fritos. Isaac didn't have a clue what to bring but took Lee's advice about a change of clothes for Kat that included a hoodie and some running shoes. And Lee? She had it just about right the last time, except she made sure she had on a long-sleeve shirt today, given how scraped up she had gotten. All three had charged-up cell phones, set on silent. The most essential new addition was a map prepared by Kat herself. It was on everyone's phone. Isaac had convinced her to provide an address for her new living quarters in the compound. Something about needing to know where she was in the event of a wildfire—a real possibility these days. Google did the rest.

Timing is everything. A year ago it would have been a simple matter. Kat was still living in the forested enclave up off the highway then. Now she was part of the indoctrinated population on the BARF compound. Sort of like a *Children of the Corn* thing, only the "Children" in this case didn't really know what Zin was capable of; if they were feasting on altered blue algae, they wouldn't care. This was the good and the bad of today's caper. Kat would either be unwilling to go with them, or she could be in a submissive stupor. Lee wondered if they could even trust Kat. Would she be capable of setting them up, giving them over to Zin? *Don't go there, Lee.* She had no way of knowing that Cato shared the same concerns. Neither of them wanted to bring it up to Isaac; he was hyped up enough as it was. Even his olive complexion had a decidedly ashen look today.

They had all agreed that Cato's old Land Cruiser would be the best getaway vehicle. The four-wheel drive might come in handy, and anyway, all his equipment—*Star Wars* backpack included—was already loaded up. Han Solo and Chewie had served them well, and so had the meters and measuring rod. Cato decided to leave his big camera at home because of its weight and brought along a small pocket-size Panasonic with a telephoto lens instead. Lee noticed a few green garbage bags up against the rear window. Would they need to dress up like Garbage Men? The group had all agreed that food should be limited to snacks and bottled water—no time for a meal in town. Hopefully, there'd be a celebratory feast in their future.

The trip up the coast was uneventful and very silent. Each of them was introspective, going over the plans in their heads and running a loop of contingencies—Plan Bs, so to speak. As they headed farther north, fog began to set in; Cato took that as a good omen in case they needed to sneak around somewhere. Lee figured her hair would go limp but relished the opportunity to look even tougher than she felt. Isaac was only focused on one thing: get Kat out.

As the Land Cruiser approached the 154 turnoff, Isaac figured he'd better text Kat using the excuse that he was heading up the highway for a conference and wanted to drop something off from home. That sounded plausible to him, and he knew that Kat would likely want to know what the parents were sending her, especially if it included money. Cato and Lee figured that, at the very least, they could determine if Kat was in her apartment on the property.

> Hey, Kat. Hoping you're around today. Passing by. Have something for you from home. Where will you be in an hr?

The few minutes that it took to get a response seemed like an eternity to Isaac, but considering they were climbing into the hills, the signal was pretty good. And Kat didn't seem suspicious.

> Have some errands to do. Hope back here in an hour. You have address–right? Every-thing okay with mom and dad?

So far, so good. Lee glanced back at Isaac. "How does she seem? Do you think she'll do better if Cato and I stay out of sight? Don't say anything about your parents. Keep her guessing." She was trying not to alarm Isaac, not to escalate the sense of danger that was welling up in all of them, though Cato looked pretty calm at the moment.

"Yeah. She seems fine. Do you think I should try to finesse info on getting into the gate or if there's another way in? The map shows her building near a perimeter but not near the entrance."

Cato was way ahead of them. "I have a way to bypass the electrical current on the fencing—if there is one. The last time, the whole system seemed pretty hit or miss. Google shows an access road nearby. I say we pull up there first and take a look. If that's not doable, we may have to go through the main entrance—and possibly Zin or his henchman—which, since we don't have a way to defend ourselves, would be the worst scenario."

I've got my mascara, guys, Lee thought. *Not the time to bring it up. This is serious stuff.* "How do we get past the Garbage Bag Guys? They must have figured out by now that we are still alive. Maybe a diversion of some kind? Can we set off an explosion or a fire somewhere?" She was really relishing this caper, trying to push the grim realities out of her consciousness.

"Cato, you have those green garbage bags in the back. Maybe I can put one on and show up at the gate while you guys set something on fire." Lee was secretly hoping that Cato had a different plan in mind.

Just then Kat texted.

> They won't let you in the gate. Text when you get there.

"Hmm. How do we take that?" Cato said. "She can buzz you in? She can alert the guard or someone to let you in? She can meet you there? All of those options don't seem safe. According to the map, her place is a good walk from the front gate. Plenty of time for someone to intercept her—or us. That has the makings of a trap. No offense, Isaac. I'm not saying *Kat* would trap us; she might be oblivious to the dangers. Tell her you'll be a few minutes late. Stuck in traffic or something. Tell her to just hang around her place. Let's case the perimeter near her apartment first. I think we should get her out as fast as possible before someone gets wise to us. And don't let on that Lee and I are with you. That'll get her suspicions up for sure."

Lee was tracking the car on Google maps when Cato made a sudden turn. They were definitely on an unmarked path, and not near the entrance they had used their first time or the access road on the map. She gave him a "What's up?" look, which she figured he'd sense even if he was looking straight ahead. "Is this the access road? It's not even on the . . ." He nodded before she could get the words out.

The old Cruiser came to a skidding stop, a mix of dried mud and chert flying everywhere. Within seconds Isaac hopped out and yanked aside some errant olive tree branches, which allowed Cato to pull off the road a few feet. The guys looked like they had done this before. It was a smooth move, and the color had come back into Isaac's cheeks. *He's got a bit of Indiana Jones in him too!* This was a side she hadn't seen before. Cato grabbed the backpack and motioned for Lee to get out. Isaac reached in for Kat's running shoes and hoodie. Lee put the hoodie on over her own shirt, figuring it was easier than carrying it. The shoes were another matter. Bigger than her white socks for sure, so they wouldn't fit in her back pocket or Isaac's. The old tie-the-shoe-laces-together-and-toss-them-over-your-shoulder thing she used to do at the beach worked. She strung them around Isaac. "Keep an eye out for security cameras and guys in green trash bags . . . and golf carts," she whispered to Isaac. He was too busy to question the trash bag reference, but the camera warning sank in immediately. With a hand shading his eyes, he looked up into the trees. Nothing, unless some of them were actually those fake cell-phone trees—with surveillance cameras.

Cato cautioned silence and headed through the foliage skirting the road. The rest of the Crew followed, and they threaded their way forward. Every hundred feet or so they stopped to check their cell phone maps from Kat, looking for a sign that they were near her place and hoping there would be a weak spot in the fencing. The GPS was playing games with them, their icons jumping around on the screen. It occurred to Lee that maybe signals were being jammed. *Don't let this caper go to your head, Lee.* Suddenly, Cato looked back. The expression on his face was priceless. The fog had lifted. White whiskers glistening in the sun and a "Eureka" smile.

"We're about as close as we can get to your sister's place,

Isaac. Just a couple hundred feet from here. Are you up for climbing a fence?" Cato whispered. Out came the voltmeter, wire clippers, and some other gadget with black wires and clips attached. Lee guessed it was an improvised hookup that allowed an electrical flow to be bypassed without interrupting it and triggering an alarm.

Lee grabbed Isaac to keep him in the clear while they checked the fence. "Stand back for a minute while we check for voltage." No argument from him on that point. Cato and Lee worked quickly. A beep, a red light blinking at them. The wouldn't-you-know-it moment.

As one six-legged beast, the Crew scrambled along the outside of the fence, keeping a healthy distance from the metal links. "We need to find the most vulnerable spot. Maybe a little lower than the rest and maybe a few gaps," Cato said. And there it was. Probably as good as it was going to get, considering the time pinch. He unraveled his wired-up gadget and gingerly clipped one end of the wire to a link in the fence, jumping back in anticipation of an electrical arc. All good. The other end—six feet away—had an identical clip, which he clamped onto the fence as far away as possible. Lee could see that the idea would be to climb over the fence between the two ends of wire. The good news was that he was using insulated copper wire. The black rubber coating was just enough to contain the charge. Next Cato flipped on a switch and watched as the dial spun. Whatever this MacGyver thingy was, it seemed to be registering a good charge, the same charge as the fence itself. Lee was still not sure how this was going to work. Along with the new wiring, the fence would still be electrified. *Come on, Cato. What are you thinking? We're out of time here.* "Lee, you're fast. Can you run to the car and bring the green garbage bags back? I'll prep Isaac while you're gone. And be careful. We've got to get this show on the road."

In Lee's mind she heard the same urgency from weeks before: *"Don't. Don't turn off the lights!" What's he up to?* She scrambled toward the Land Cruiser, trying to look for perils along the way. Not a good idea. Lee should have been watching her own footwork. She slid around on the rough path, cherts slipping under her footing, then tripped on the tortuous roadway. *Man, good thing I'm wearing an extra hoodie over my clothes. I'd have no skin left.* She fell again, this time rolling to reduce the friction. It had only been a couple of minutes, but Lee could feel the same angst the guys must be experiencing. The garbage bags were lighter than she expected and bounced around silently as she ran back. Skidding to a stop, this time upright, Lee couldn't believe what she saw. Isaac was stripped down to his boxer shorts and listening intently as Cato talked to him. *Oy. I've got nowhere to look. Careful. This is the time to put on your poker face if there ever was one, Lee.*

=

So here's the thing: the fence was still electrified. Cato's gadget allowed for a continued flow of energy even if the fence was sliced top to bottom to allow the Blue Öyster Crew in. Anyone monitoring the fence would not see a disruption; no alarms would sound. The fence could be cut with the rubber-handled wire cutters, but it would take forever to do the whole eight-foot height. Enter the wetsuits. Cato had stashed neoprene wetsuits and rubber gloves in the trash bags. Three of them, if it ever came to it. But the plan was to cut a gash or a square in the fence between the span of wire clips and send Isaac through wearing a Hurley Full-body Warm Weather Special. This is the don't-try-this-at-home part: you need rubber gloves and athletic shoes—no rips allowed. As long as your skin doesn't come in contact with the metal, you should be okay. Kind of like the insulated copper wire encased in rubber—only with a heartbeat. Lee wanted to don another wetsuit and go along, but it was agreed that Kat would be more accepting of Isaac if he was alone, regardless of what he was wearing. That was going to need some explaining, and so far, no one could come up for a reason why he would be wearing the Hurley. Lee agreed to wait on the outside for twenty minutes before heading through the fence herself. And Cato had rubber gloves on and was already busy cutting a slit up from the bottom, careful not to lose contact with the rubber handles of the wire clippers.

Isaac had done this before. He had the perfect technique for putting on a wetsuit. With shoes and gloves, he looked like one of those blow-up balloons that flops its arms and legs around at the used car lots off the freeway. Only handsome. Lee took a big gulp as if going under water and peeled off her jeans and hoodie. She left her long-sleeved T-shirt on to save time, a move she immediately regretted. Her wetsuit was large on her, but getting it over her sleeves was a sweat-inducing exercise. By the time she was cased in neoprene, Isaac was already halfway through the fence with Cato holding up flaps of chain link. He tied them back with extra insulated wire—a time saver if they all ended up on the inside and needed a quick getaway.

Isaac's imagination failed him at the moment. All he could think about were Cato's instructions: (1) keep in touch by text but make sure your phone is on silent, (2) keep low and be aware of your surroundings, (3) be prepared for resistance from Kat but don't give in, (4) surprise is on your side, so if you have to, just grab her and run, (5) as to why you're wearing a wetsuit . . . well, you're on your own with that one. It was that number 5 that bothered him the most.

Isaac found the apartment building with no difficulty. It was the approach that slowed him down. He knew the clock was ticking on the outside—Lee would be waiting for any excuse to dive through the fence and join him—but he couldn't see the front door or windows of Kat's place from his vantage point. It was worth a few seconds, he decided, to case the joint first. He decided correctly: soft voices from behind sounded like alarms in his head, and he dove for cover, ripping his wetsuit along one arm. A silent "Shit!" Then he heard it—Kat's voice. Something about an important meeting for the inner circle tonight. Muted excitement, monotone, really. He would have suspected dulled senses, but she always spoke in a low-key manner, regardless of what was going on. So no way to know if she was under the influence; he'd have to proceed with caution. And if she'd been alone, this caper would be over. He could have grabbed her and headed for the fence.

Isaac sized up the other one: mousy complexion, sixty-ish, dressed like Kat, with eye-catching red hair—not natural red but costume red—like a clown. Just then Kat glanced his way. How would she play this? She had that look. A little startled but in control, the way he remembered her when they had a fight and something crashed to the ground. If it was his fault, she would "own" him with a look—she could rat him out or hold it over his head for later use. Today it could go either way. "I'll be in in a second," he heard her say. Casual and laid-back, a good sign. Maybe. Clown Lady headed up some moss-covered brick steps and, brushing aside hanging vines, disappeared into the building. No wonder he couldn't see the entrance. As kids, he and Kat had created a fort in the bushes that bordered their backyard. They were what? Five and eleven at the time? Fighting off evil trolls entailed a secret doorway and a password, and they fashioned an arsenal of dried-up pepper pods and acorns, ready to fall on any intruders. That was the last time that they had been comrades, playmates. Age and differing interests took their toll.

"What are you doing in there, Isaac? What's with the wetsuit?" She was peering in through the shrubs, and he was peering out at the same time. A cartoon in the making. The looks on both their faces would have been comical, if this wasn't deadly serious stuff. *Okay, Isaac, forget rule number 5, just get her headed in the direction of the perimeter fence.* With any luck Lee would show up in her Hurley and distract Kat even further. He wouldn't mind seeing the look on her face then. The two women hadn't seen each other in years. This could shock Kat into a surrender—or freak her out. He motioned silence and grabbed her hand, heading away from the building and toward escape. It all happened so quickly that Kat went willingly. No resistance. *Don't question it, Isaac, go with it.* But he wrapped his arm around her waist just in case.

Twenty minutes, and no Lee. He checked his cell phone. Nothing. The blood surged to his head as he pictured Cato and Lee at the mercy of Zin. Maybe tied to the fence with Zin getting ready to electrocute them. Or maybe force-feeding them blue algae. Suddenly Kat stopped dead in her tracks. Coming toward them was another wetsuit, with a black hood on top and something resting over one shoulder. Isaac knew who it was, but he had no clue what Kat was thinking. A small man or a large child? With a hump? Isaac continued pulling her toward the all-black figure. The disparity between what Kat knew to be true (or thought was true) and her brother's behavior was raising alarm bells, and, in truth, he could see she was growing increasingly uneasy. "Something's not right, Isaac. Let me go. Stop!" He slapped his hand over her mouth, and she dug her heels into the soft ground—literally; at that moment Isaac realized where the expression *dig your heels in* had come from. As petite as she was, Kat disrupted their momentum, and they both fell backward. If he took his hand off her mouth, no telling what she would do. So he didn't dare put out a hand to soften the blow. It was Isaac's dumb luck to hit his head as he fell. At least, he hoped that's what it was. But for a brief moment before he saw stars and blacked out, he imagined someone had clobbered him with a rock.

Isaac woke to find both Lee and Kat tussling with Ronald McDonald . . . or wait . . . it was that evil clown . . . Pennywise something . . . or both. Nausea and blurred vision set in, and he was struggling to sit up. He had to see who would win this one. Actually, he wasn't sure what the teams were: Kat and Pennywise, Lee and Ronald McDonald . . . you get the idea. He gave in to vertigo and closed his eyes again, grateful that he hadn't added to the chaos and gravity of the situation by throwing up. This was too good to miss. He willed himself to look again. This time it was a three-way fight. He still couldn't make out who was fighting whom. Clearly Lee and Kat were in the pile, but the clowns had morphed into one redheaded figure. The redhead who had been walking with Kat!

Lee seemed to be holding her own for the moment, but Isaac knew he had to get them out of there. From the distance the intermittent low whine of an electric motor and the crunching of foliage floated their way. Lee stopped in her tracks to listen and gave Isaac a look. He was listening too, trying to recall her admonition . . . something about golf carts. That few seconds gave Clown Lady the advantage she needed. She grabbed Lee by the throat and started squeezing with both hands. Kat sat back with a look of horror on her muddied face; she, too, glanced at Isaac, mouthing "Help!" That's all he needed to rouse from his stupor—that and the sound of a sputtering golf cart headed their way. He threw his body full-force into Clown Lady, sending her flying. *That's a lesson in mass times force equals acceleration, if ever I saw one*, Lee thought, still struggling to take in air. It was Kat's turn to pounce: a full-on cat fight—or Kat fight—ensued. She had landed on Clown Lady, who was on her stomach, arms and legs outstretched, face in the mud. The image reminded Lee of one of those fake women's wrestling matches—not that she ever watched them. And she piled on to add her weight to Kat's.

"Grab garbage. . . ! Maybe . . . to tie . . . hands behind her . . . should slow her . . ." Lee struggled to speak, motioning toward the garbage bag she had brought with her.

Isaac pulled the extra wetsuit out of the bag and handed it to Kat. "I'll take over. Put the bottom part on. Just slip into the legs. You may not need to wear the whole thing when we get there." He plopped down on the redhead, causing her to grunt. "Grunt all you want. . . .What's your name?" Kat was struggling into the neoprene, and Lee was helping her as best she could. Isaac tore the garbage bag on its seams and began tying strips around Clown Lady's wrists.

"Ishara. Aphrodite Ishara," Kat said.

"What?" Isaac looked at her, trying not to laugh.

"That figures," Lee croaked.

Kat looked more than annoyed as she stepped within inches of Isaac's face and pointed a finger at him. But all she said was, "Again, Dear Brother, what's with the wetsuit?"

"Can't we leave the clown?" Lee asked, getting antsy to head to the fence and, hopefully, a waiting Cato. It was a risk either way. She could see how conflicted Isaac was, but she said, "Remember our first objective: get Kat to safety." He nodded.

"Yeah. Leave her. The redhead tried to kill you. You don't owe her anything. We can travel faster without her." Isaac was breathing hard, powering both himself and his sister up a muddy path to the perimeter. Blood still dribbled down the back of his head, and his color was not great. Lee grabbed Kat's other arm, hoping to help, but Kat was having none of it. *I knew there was something else I didn't like about you, Kat. You don't realize what we just did for you*, Lee thought.

"Cut it out, Kat. We all put our lives on the line for . . ." The sight ahead was chilling, and Lee felt the air go out of her for the second time today. *Not a way to spend a Saturday, guys.* "Isaac, look up ahead!" They all stopped dead in their tracks. On the other side of the fence, Zin and Cato were struggling. Clearly this was a battle that Zin would win. They watched as Cato sank to his knees, hands tied up with the same kind of wire he had used earlier in the day to bypass the electrical charge on the chain link. Zin was standing over him.

Before Kat could open her mouth, both Lee and Isaac slapped their hands over her face. Isaac whispered, "Kat, I'm begging you. Keep quiet." Surprisingly, she obeyed, but the look in her eyes screamed murder. "How do we play this, Lee? Any ideas? Or do we just barge in?"

Lee's mind was going a mile a minute. And her cynical self had no ideas. "I say we just barge in. Oh, and I'm guessing the fence is still electrified. Kat, pull the arms on and zip up your wetsuit." Lee was getting ready to slap her if she resisted, and she could see that even Isaac was out of patience.

The sight of the three neoprene Musketeers popping out of the woods would have given Cato a laugh, if he hadn't been otherwise occupied. He had a welt on his forehead and looked a little dazed. Lee hoped he was lucid; they would need his wits if they had any chance of escaping. "You all right, Cato?" she heard Isaac say. Cato nodded, but Lee could see that he had something on his mind. Then she saw it: the wires wrapped around his wrists extended toward the fence. Not yet attached, but the intent was clear. She was looking for the wire cutters . . . just in case she needed to jump into the fray. The problem was they were still on the inside, and Cato and Zin were on the outside.

Lee thought chances were that if Cato stayed where he was—a few feet away from the fence—he'd be safe, even if Zin attached the wires to it. She could see that Isaac had realized the same thing. He had a funny smirk on his face; apparently Zin had no clue how insulated wires worked. And Cato was in on the joke too. "Hi, guys, how's the surfing today? Kind of cold out there. Insulation helps, right?"

Yes, Cato, we've got it. Now if we can only get Kat through the fence and out of here. Lee's throat was killing her; she could feel the bruises hardening on her neck, and she was picturing that evening at the Blue Room with its Avatar glow. Not a good color for her. Still rasping, Lee said, "Zin, can we get Kat out of here? Her friend Aphrodite . . . uh . . . Ishara is going to be really upset with her. I trust you want to keep her safe and avoid a scene."

Kat did look pitiful. Caked in mud. Wearing a wetsuit miles too large for her. Wild eyes, possibly indicating she was no longer under the influence of blue algae or something. Somebody's blood was caked onto a few curls. Lee was about to say something more when Zin seemed to give in. He motioned for them to help her through the flaps in the fencing, all the while keeping a threatening eye on Cato. The wetsuit plan worked perfectly: Kat was tiny and slipped right through without a crispy mishap, making sure no actual skin came in contact with the links. Lee was right behind her, and before Zin had a chance to object, Isaac clambered through. He was a little larger in stature, so Lee grabbed his arm and yanked. In the don't-try-this-at-home category: don't grab someone who is about to be shocked. This worked fine, except for the singed arm hairs where Isaac's suit was ripped. With all the peril at hand, he didn't even notice. Still, they all looked pretty ridiculous. Isaac sank to the ground near Cato, a possible concussion mixed in with the scent of burnt skin had done him in. So there they were: two small-ish women and Zin left standing. Cato and Isaac on their knees. *What could go wrong?* Lee thought.

Off to one side, Lee could see the original clothing she and Isaac had come in, snagged on a bush and fluttering in the breeze. In the other direction, she spotted something gleaming in the weeds—the wire cutters. In the unlikely event of an emergency, what would she grab first? Kat was following Lee's line of vision, noting both the clothes—as yet unexplainable—and the cutters. Their eyes met, but Lee had no idea what she was thinking. Zin had been speaking into his cell phone. Something about trespassing and the need for a fatal accident. *That again!* "Ramp up the current as high as it will go. I'll check in with you in a few minutes. As soon as I'm done here."

Cato, Isaac, and Lee knew that insulated wire confines the current, like a garden hose confines water. Only bare wire or metal clamps on the ends could convey a jolt. So unless Zin tried to tie them all directly to the fence, they had a good chance of staying alive. At the moment it was one able-bodied but bruised woman, one woman with questionable allegiance, one older . . . er . . . mature guy with hands tied, and Isaac. *Isaac, get up. Snap out of it!*

If Lee or the others had any doubts about the electric current running through the chain link, they were answered. All five people watched a moth flirt with the fence for a few seconds, and then dive bomb toward incineration. Zin sported a sneer as he turned toward the group. He grabbed Isaac by the collar, lifting him to a standing position. "No moving, or this guy gets it."

"Master Zin, that's my brother. Please . . ."

"Well, I see the resemblance. No matter. You've all got to go sometime." He dropped Isaac, who slowly scrambled back up to his feet. Zin headed toward Kat. "Maybe I should start with you. You've been a big disappointment, Kat Ishara. I had hopes for you, even invited you to the inner circle because I thought it would spark something. And yet, you've remained detached. Even Aphrodite couldn't get through to you, couldn't control you," he snarled.

"You sent her? To keep an eye on me? No wonder she knew so much about me. And why . . . she kept forcing more and more blue algae on me. Was that her job?" Kat was backing up, repulsed by Zin's sneer and trying to stay out of his grip.

"Matthew! Matthew! Kill her. Kill them all!" The red-headed clown lady was bounding through the branches, black plastic strips hanging from her wrists, hair flopping around as she ran. Some wild, tropical bird after its prey. "Matthew!" It was clear to Lee that Kat had no idea who "Matthew" was, but she knew. So did Cato and Isaac. Their conversation about the DNA came back. Matthew was the name associated with Zin's DNA sample. And judging from the look on his face, Matthew was pretty startled to hear his name. He backed away from Kat and turned just in time to see his mother heading for the gap in the fence. Too fast. Her head popped through to the other side before the rest of her struck the chain link. No wetsuit. No protection. The shock caused her to recoil. She went flying backward, landing in mud. Her clothes were in shreds, but the mud had smothered her arms and legs, probably saving her life. Then, without warning—not even a spark—her hair burst into flames. Little tendrils wafted upward like embers, leaving a stench behind. Kat was screaming. Zin was screaming.

Lee dove back through the fence and scrambled to get to her. She scooped up as much loose mud as she could find and dumped it onto Clown Lady—or at this point, apparently, Zin's mother. *Take that, you clown!* The sight was ridiculous, but the question was even more so: Why the delayed burn? "You know why your head burst into flames? Spray-on hair color can be flammable. Just like hair spray. Didn't you read the label?"

=

"Cut the juice to the eastern fence!" Zin was screaming into his cell, his characteristic detachment nowhere to be found. "You two, go in and get her." He was motioning to Cato and Isaac. "Kat stays with me."

"I have to check the voltmeter to make sure there's no residual current. Everyone stay where you are for a minute." Cato was back in his element. The gadget he had put together included its own voltmeter. They all watched as the dial slowly moved to zero. No beep, no light, no current. "There's only one problem. We're not going in there while you still have that phone handy. You could have the current ramped up before we're able to get back out. Hand it to Isaac, and we've got a deal. While you're at it, where are the keys to the golf cart? Give him those too. Just in case." *Way to go, Cato*, Lee thought. The Blue Öyster Crew plus Kat waited to see what Zin would do. He was staring at Cato. Lee imagined that Zin had come to the realization his plans were shot, but he didn't want to look weakened—especially in front of his mother. *This would be a good time for the Jeopardy theme song. Come on, Zin.*

Zin handed the phone to Isaac. "The keys are in the cart." Kat jumped into action and retrieved them. With exaggerated motions, she made a point of handing them to Isaac: a statement that she was done with Zin and his shenanigans.

"Keep your hands off my sister! Kat, you going to be okay here?"

"Go, Isaac, get this over with. You've got Aphrodite as a hostage. He won't hurt me."

Isaac dropped the phone and the keys down the inside of his wetsuit and zipped it up. He went through first. Cato ducked in, and they both grabbed Aphrodite. She cried in pain as they picked her up, shreds of fabric and hair falling to the ground. Lee followed closely behind, thinking this looked like a scene from *The Hunger Games* or something similar. Then she glanced at Kat outside the fence. Something didn't look right.

"Where is he, Kat? Where's Zin?" Kat turned slowly to look at Lee, who could not read the expression on her face. Blank. "Kat, are you in danger?" she yelled. No response.

Isaac chimed in: "I'm coming! Stay there if it's safe." Kat's expression was twisting into a look of despair, and before Isaac could get to her, she burst into tears.

"I didn't understand . . . he is a monster. I'm sorry," she sobbed. "Aphrodite *is* his mother. He said he didn't care what happened to her. That she . . . she had it coming for messing everything up. I'm sorry." Isaac, Cato, and Lee stepped through the now-inert opening in the chain link, carrying Aphrodite with them like a sack of potatoes. They stretched her out on the damp dirt. When Kat saw her lying there, she crumbled to the ground. "Is she alive? Is she breathing?"

"She is, Kat," Cato said. "Luckily, the current wasn't enough to kill her. She has serious burns, though. We've got to get her to the hospital. Where is Zin?"

The sun was starting to go down behind the trees, casting a red-orange pall over the group. In stark contrast the wet-suited trio in black stood out; only Aphrodite seemed to blend in, to melt into the orange haze. What was left of her hair and skirt—and her burnt skin—were all the same orange color. Lee was reminded of that wicked witch scene in the *Wizard of Oz*, the one every child remembers. She could hear the words: "I'm melting . . . melting."

"Where is my son?" They all bent over to hear Aphrodite struggle to speak. As Lee got closer, she thought she spotted a tattoo on the woman's neck. A circle with the letters S and O, but then again, soot and burnt skin mingled to make a hodge-podge of color and pattern that could be anything.

"He's gone, Aphrodite—I don't know where. I didn't want to follow him and leave you guys behind . . . Aphrodite, I'm so sorry," Kat sobbed.

"It's not Aphrodite. My name is Mary Jacobs. Please . . . don't let me die," she whimpered.

Man, just when you think you are all set to hate someone . . . Lee thought. "You're not dying. We'll get you to the hospital in Solvang. It's the closest. But you owe us. We're going to need info on your son and this cult. We're calling the police too. And probably the FBI. Alright?" Lee didn't really care if it was alright with Aphrodite—Mary—or not. She was most annoyed at a world where anyone can take on a fake identity at the drop of a hat. Use it long enough, and you forget who you actually are.

"I think we need the ATF and DEA also. Kat, in what direction did he go? I guess he had to hightail it on foot." Cato motioned to the golf cart still wedged into the bushes. "I don't know if it's worth taking her in the cart; if we have to go out on the open road with it, we could be at a disadvantage. In any case, we've got to get out of here before it gets any darker."

"He shoved me to the ground, pushed me down with his foot, told me not to look. I didn't see where he went, but it had to be straight through the trees. Sorry. Sorry . . ."

The plan was to load Aphrodite/Mary onto the golf cart and take her back to Cato's Land Cruiser. There, they'd all pile in for the trip to the hospital. With luck they could make it in half an hour. Isaac and Kat piled into the cart with a crispy Aphrodite in the back. Cato and Lee walked back to the Cruiser, both of them limping at this point. Lee was gasping for air; the bruising on her neck was solidifying, and the extra exertion was making itself known. Isaac and Kat had beat them to the car and were loading Aphrodite into the back. As it stood, they would both have to take the back seat with her, a distasteful proposition considering how the woman smelled. Lee had grabbed her own clothes on the way and was relishing peeling off the wetsuit. She didn't care who saw her in her underwear. Isaac had left his clothes behind, so he was going to have to explain to the hospital folks and the police why he was dressed in the Hurley. At this point he, too, was past being embarrassed.

=

What ensued was a tiring and repetitive round of questions and examinations. The authorities were alerted and had dispatched a team to the compound. BOLOs were issued to keep a look out for Zin. Mary Jacobs shed her cult name and was admitted to the hospital for evaluation; she would eventually be sent to a burn ward at another location if it was deemed necessary. Lee, Isaac, and Cato—the entire Blue Öyster Crew—were being kept overnight for observation. Only Kat was free to go until further questioning, but she refused to leave her brother's side and was forming a strange, not necessarily welcomed or reciprocated, bond with Lee. That's what happens when you save someone's life.

CHAPTER NINETEEN
BACK ON CAMPUS

When the next class session at PCC rolled around, Lee was still miserable. She had no good way to cover up the bruising on her neck; even a vintage Ralph Lauren cashmere turtleneck wouldn't completely do the trick. Word had gotten around the campus that she and Cato had been involved in some kind of rescue effort at a dangerous cult operating in the Central Coast. Since Cato was sporting a bandage on his forehead— not Snoopy but regular hospital issue—it would be hard to deny the rumor.

Fortunately, today's lab would mostly entail a setup for the following day. All the student groups had to do was (1) measure the radioactivity of plain tap water in glass containers and then (2) measure the dry insides of the Revigators. Extra credit work would entail taking a scraping of the inside lining using a razor blade. The resulting ceramic powder could also be analyzed in a petri dish. Then the *lab-sters* only had to (3) record all the readings in their lab books and (4) measure to the nearest milliliter how much water they were pouring into the Revigator. It would sit until the next class session, when analysis of the water would or would not show radioactivity. Easy. Lee, feeling even more bruised than the day before, was happy to head home early. As she contemplated how fast the academic year was moving and how fast her personal life was changing, Lee was grateful. For a lot of things. Cato was gearing up for retirement, cleaning out his office and organizing any files he would leave behind. He felt good about leaving most of his teaching materials for Lee. While she was happy to inherit Cato's lessons and gadgets—Revigators included—she was also feeling a loss. Kind of like the regrets she felt about her father and his legacy. The good news was that Cato would still be around, comfortably ensconced in his casa on Orange Grove Boulevard and probably looking for things to do. Lee figured that he would always be up for a new caper—should one present itself. He was also a good resource for hard-to-find lab supplies. She was sure he wouldn't be revealing some of his sources, though. Now that Isaac and Cato had risked their lives together, there was that bond. The Blue Öyster Crew was indelible.

For Lee, Isaac was another story. She wondered if Kat would be in the picture. His sister was staying with him for now, but knowing how tidy he was and protective of his space, that wouldn't last long, Lee guessed. His tolerance for anything out of place would be stretched thin, and his small residence was set up to accommodate one man and one cat. Cat with a "C." Lee imagined more meals and happy hours at the Raymond with the Crew, and that did not include Kat with a "K."

Revigator Lab—Part 2

Objectives:

- Students will learn to investigate dubious scientific claims.

- Students will learn to assess the level of radioactivity and other contaminants.

Materials:

- Two Revigators containing the plain tap water added during the previous class

- One or more Geiger counters

- Test strips for contaminants in water (available at Carolina Biological but also Home Depot and Amazon)

- Lab books

Procedures:

1. Same Lab Groups.

2. Measure water for radioactivity and record.

3. Using test strips, measure for any contaminants and record.

Conclusion:

- Discuss with lab group and formulate three (3) conclusions. Write conclusions in lab books.

The Revigator labs on the second day went as expected: no clicks of the Geiger counter for the dry interiors of the containers. Although a more sensitive meter could detect some radiation in plain water—a normal product of atmospheric radiation from the sun—most lab groups had no readings for the H_2O. One lab group chose to pull a little water from the reflecting pool at the front of the campus when no one was looking, and that registered a low "click." The good news was that all the students who chose to scrape the interior ceramic coating of the Revigators were rewarded with a low, single "click" as well.

The lab results were a further testament to the flimflammery of the Revigators' promoters. The water contained no magical radioactivity, no health-inducing substances. The test strips, however, did produce trace amounts of arsenic and lead from the water and ceramic lining—something of an eye-opener for the lab-sters. With all the lab books turned in, Lee started thinking about her basement strategy. She had made two trips to get the Revigators up the stairs in the first place. Tonight, she was tired and sore and in no mood to run up and down from the basement. Time to get home. It was worth taking a chance; carrying both at once was certainly not as perilous as escaping the BARF compound and lugging a burning hunk of woman through an electrified fence. *You've got this, Lee. What could go wrong if you watch your step? You've already had your brush with death—twice over.* Did she say that out loud or just think it? In any case, as she propped the basement door open with a rubber stop, she couldn't help noticing a light bouncing off the walls in a far corner of the storage room. It had the quality of a pendulum, swinging back and forth, and then it went out. A new security light or motion detector, she figured. *About time, people.*

Lee cradled one Revigator in each arm and gingerly felt her way down the steel steps. At one point she decided to lean against the wall, with an elbow steadying her as she moved. That would have worked just fine if something—or someone—hadn't suddenly stopped her in her tracks as she neared the bottom. An arm came out of nowhere and grabbed her. Something out of a bad horror film. A *Chucky* thing. One Revigator went flying. It shattered as it hit the ground, sending pieces of ceramic in all directions. *Shit!* She managed to hold on to the other one, but she started to nosedive toward the concrete landing.

"What the . . ." she mumbled. Lee came face-to-face with her erstwhile nemesis. "What do you think you're doing, Mr. Jacobs . . . uh . . . John? Get your hands off me, or you'll be wearing this other Re . . ." *Damn. Why didn't you take that martial arts class when you had the chance? You're an idiot, Lee. No mascara. Can't even fake it.*

"Chill, Ms. Roberts. Look down. No step. It's like missing. Probably couldn't see it with those things you were carrying." John Jacobs took a step back, both hands up in a defensive pose. The MeToo move. "I'm not here to hurt you. Really. Just heard you coming down. I fell the other day on that last step. Someone took it out."

Lee was not ready to thank him . . . yet. "What are you doing here? How did you get in?" She set the surviving Revigator on the ground, all the while keeping her eyes on the kid. The teacherly, hands on hips, what-were-you-thinking pose made *her* feel better but didn't seem to intimidate Mr. Jacobs.

"Well, like I sometimes sleep down here. Back in that

corner." He shrugged, finally looking embarrassed. "I can't tell you how I got the key. Nothing illegal or anything. Once in a while I can't be at home. Bad situation. Anyway, I kinda like the quiet, and I get off on all of this science stuff." John was watching Lee's face intently at this point, looking for a sign of acceptance. Lee put on her poker face, her old defense.

"I don't get it, John. What do you mean you can't be at home? This place is not meant for habitation . . . except for the . . . uh . . . rats. How long have you been staying down here?" As much as she was disturbed by the whole scenario, she was beginning to feel a little relieved too. This could explain the mysterious traveling screwdriver and the eerie feeling of not being alone on her previous forays.

"Never mind. You don't have to tell me about your personal life . . . unless you want to . . . if I can help . . . well, don't tell me where you got the key. I'd like plausible deniability. Do you know what that is?" John nodded but had the confused look she'd seen before. Lee didn't care if he understood; the fact was she probably took advantage of supplies—Cato's supplies— that weren't supposed to be down here either. That whole issue was a wash as far as she was concerned. This was not the time or place to launch a discussion on John's domestic situation, so she let that go too. "John, thank you . . . really. I appreciate your help. I've got to get this thing back to its spot on the table and clean up the shards of the other Revigator." She handed it to him, sensing that he would know exactly where to put it. He did.

Clean-up was quick. And silent. Lee avoided glancing back to the corner of the basement that served as John's occasional bedroom. And she was beginning to feel sorry for him. *Don't push it, Lee. Unless you are prepared to do something about it.* "Let's head outside for a little daylight. The reflecting pool okay?" She hoped he would go for that idea. She really did want to get away from the tomb-like mustiness. And to be out in public view.

"So, anyway, Ms. Roberts, I was the one down here those other times. I probably like freaked you out. Sorry." He offered up an apologetic shrug. It was at this moment that she realized how dirty they both were. At least there were no crispy critters involved this time. "Yeah, let's go out to the pool," he said.

As they came out through the double doors of "C" Building, the spotty sun hit them—a welcome change from the windowless basement. Lee couldn't help thinking how this radiation, the natural kind, was also welcome. She'd had enough of the Revigators and their dubious scientific value. "Have a seat, Mr. Jacobs." He sat on the rim of the pool. She stood over him—the ploy of a petite female teacher. "So what interests you so much in the basement? What's in there that attracts you?" At this moment, she was sorry she had used that word with a male student: *attracts*. Fortunately, he didn't react.

He was looking up at her, the sun causing him to squint. "I just like the science stuff. Really. Besides when you spend time down there, it's not creepy at all. You know what I mean. Right?" Lee didn't know how to respond. She was still figuring out how she felt about the whole thing. And John.

"But it *is* really filthy down there. It can't be healthy, with the rats and all. Go home tonight if you can. I'll talk to someone about finding you a better place to stay. Okay?" She could see he wasn't convinced. "Look, I have an idea. I know someone who might want some company. I think he's got a little casita out back behind his house. As far as your interest in science goes, maybe we can get you a few hours as a lab tech. I've discovered I might need some help on other projects also. I'll get back to you tomorrow. And seriously, don't spend the night down there again, or I will rat you out . . . pun intended." *He's young. Does he even know what that means? What are you thinking?* Lee didn't even have an answer for herself, something that was becoming more common recently.

=

The text from Cato came in early:

> Thanks for the new roomie. He'll work out fine. He can do work around here to earn his keep.

Lee figured it would work out to everyone's advantage. Plus, they could all keep an eye on John Jacobs. She, for one, still had a nagging suspicion about his name. Any association with ZUMBA, BARF, or otherwise made her arm hairs stand up, and if John was related to Zin, they would eventually find out. For now, he seemed to be a good kid, and Cato would have some company. She might be able to enlist John's help with her final lab: a subatomic cloud chamber. Muons, get ready to make an appearance!

> Glad you don't mind. Yeah, I might put him to work also. Thanks.

> Oh, do you think we can look into the Jacobs link with Zin some time? No rush. Or am I being paranoid?

Cato's response was immediate:

> Ha! I had the same idea. Though I don't think he's gangrenous.

So was Lee's:

> ???

It took a few minutes for Cato to figure out the problem:

> Dangerous. Sorry. Autofill.

Lee hoped Cato was right about that. The dangerous thing, not the gangrenous thing.

=

Isaac, as predicted, was at his wit's end with Kat. Sharing one's place with a down-and-out sister should be a given in a time of need, but he knew that she knew that their parents were minutes away and had ample room for her. She could be just as self-reflective back in her old room, in fact, as in Isaac's living room. The authorities had debriefed her and determined that she didn't need a lot of deprogramming; a few sessions with a therapist specializing in cults would do. She seemed to be taking everything in stride, a sign that maybe she wasn't as committed to the Grand Pooh-bah as she appeared. Isaac had been cautioned to be on the lookout for a delayed reaction on Kat's part and on his own. He felt the need to wrap up loose ends with Cato and Lee but didn't especially want Kat sitting in on any "working" happy hours or dinners. Lee, in particular, was still angry about the danger his sister had put them in—and the whole cult thing in general—and he couldn't really blame her for that. In an abundance of caution, Isaac suggested that Kat spend the night with their parents while he got some work done. She knew that was code for meeting up with Lee and Cato, and she didn't really care.

Isaac texted both members of the Crew at once:

> What say you to a little wrap-up session over drinks and apps? Place of your choice.

> Oh, and Kat won't be joining us.

Lee was tired but figured, since she didn't have any food at her place, she might as well:

> Maybe an early and brief session. 5 pm? Still tired. I don't care where.

That left Cato to make the decision:

> I agree. How about a burger at my place? I'll grill. Bring beer. Ok?

Responses chimed in at the same time:

> Perfect.

> I'm in.

The typical sunny California afternoon had turned cloudy and promised rain, so the meal was moved inside. Cato made it in from his old Weber barbeque, balancing a platter piled high with food, just as big plops of water hit the ground. They sat around the kitchen table eating the quintessential meal: burgers, corn on the cob, and Fritos—Cato's go-to chip. The trio still looked as if they'd been through war, with fading scars and bruises, but the mood at the table was victorious. The Crew had done their job, and they had managed to stick to their planned procedure—a must for scientists. On the win side: Kat was home safe, Aphrodite/Mary would make a slow recovery and had already offered up a flood of incriminating evidence against the cult, and the BARF property had been emptied out. On the loss side: Zin was still on the loose and certain to show up again, blue algae products infused with drugs were likely stockpiled somewhere in the country, and it's anybody's guess if scattered loyalists of ZUMBA, SOS, and BARF were bent on revenge.

Cato and Lee were happy to turn the whole case over to authorities; it could take years to ferret out the impact of this convoluted cult, its history, and its reach into the lives of those seeking something that a normal existence had failed to give them. Then there was the matter of the drugs. While blue algae might have offered promise for who-knows-what, it would be associated with cults, lithium, and GHB in the near term. Lithium, of course, was nothing to be afraid of as a medical treatment; it had been around for decades. GHB was another matter.

Isaac, on the other hand, was still seething with resentment about the peril his sister, Kat, had faced, and maybe a little bit about the peril his friends Lee and Cato had faced on her behalf. He was having a hard time letting go. Kat's extended stay at his condo had worn out its welcome. Even Bernoulli was complaining about this other creature occupying his sofa and possibly vying for the same cricket treats he coveted. He left a dried-up mouse head on the sofa one day. Kat assumed it was a gift; Isaac knew it was more of a warning—*Godfather* style.

CHAPTER TWENTY

CLOUD CHAMBER

Classes and labs came and went as the school year barreled to an end. This final lab was a new one for Lee. Cato had told her about it months before, but she was putting it off until she had a really good handle on how it would work in a classroom. Like the lawyerly adage, "Never ask a witness a question that you don't already know the answer to," teachers follow the same admonishment (if they know what's good for them). She had tried it out, looking for the caveats, the pitfalls. There was nothing dangerous about this one; she just wanted it to go really well. Then she could end the school year on a high note and get on with the business of firming up her forensic investigator "creds."

"Hey, Ms. Roberts, like what else do you need me to do for the lab? I've got the things on your list. It was like pretty easy. There's three setups—all identical." John motioned to the meticulous staging he had arranged around the classroom. Only the dry ice was yet to be positioned. Lee had told him to set that under her demonstration table—no telling where it would end up if left unattended—maybe in the cafeteria in a beverage dispenser or in a faculty toilet. A dramatic presentation in any case. She had to admit that John was neat and efficient, if nothing else. And it was nice to have someone to bounce her thoughts off of when prepping for a lab activity. He had the advantage of being the same age as most of the students and the insight and empathy regarding how to instruct the less-tuned-in ones to keep them on track. "So, maybe if we start with the dark classroom . . . lights out . . . the class will be kinda stoked. Like grab their interest. What do you think, Ms. Roberts?"

"Excellent idea. Let's get the document camera fired up so I can project the procedures and materials on the board. Can you do that for me? Cover it with a piece of cardboard or something until the big reveal." Lee was liking this collaboration. *Good call, Lee. So far.* "I meant to ask. How's it going at Mr. Klein's place?" *What's the adage again? Don't ask unless you know the answer?* She knew. Cato had called, energized by the increased population on his property. He had joined the thousands of Pasadenans who had taken advantage of the new granny flat zoning laws. In fact, the occupant of his casita had already fixed a few things around the place. A win-win so far.

"It's cool. Like he seems happy to have company. Thanks, again, Ms. Roberts." Lee was tempted to tell him to drop the "Ms." thing and just call her Lee, but she wasn't quite ready to give up that barrier to her personal life, artificial as it was. *Soon, maybe.*

"Okay. Glad to hear it. Here's the doc for the projector. We've got five minutes to get this show on the road," a saying whose origin, she was sure, was before his time; *she* wasn't even sure where it came from. The circus?

Cloud Chamber Lab

Objectives:

- Make subatomic particles visible to the human eye

- Postulate how they become visible in this environment

The concept was pretty simple but yielded good results only if done carefully: find a glass tank, like an aquarium, that can be sealed up till it's completely airtight. Soak cotton with lab quality alcohol—not the drugstore variety or the Tap Room variety—and attach the cotton to the underside of the tank lid. Make sure the tank is totally sealed and place a block of dry ice underneath the tank. Using a hairdryer or heat lamp, heat the lid with the alcohol-soaked cotton. With patience, a cloud forms on the bottom. The more fog the better. In a dark room, shining a flashlight into the fog if necessary, bubbles of condensation can be spotted shooting quickly downward from the top of the cloud.

As John predicted, students filed into the classroom looking a little unsettled. Once their eyes acclimated to the dark, their excitement ramped up, and they quickly found their seats. The rest was smooth sailing. Lee put the lights on and projected her instructions on the board. She walked around the room to hand out slabs of dry ice and to observe and answer questions, and John did the same, relishing the chance to prove that her trust in him was not misplaced. With everything set and directions followed, all the lights were turned off. The heating portion of the lab went well, with old heat lamps forcing alcohol vapor from the cotton into the tank. Gasps ensued as students spotted tiny bubbles laden with moisture shoot quickly to the bottom of their tanks. There was nothing magical about it. Thousands of subatomic particles bombard every square meter of the earth every minute. In this lab, the lepton group of muons and electrons, and the heavier hadron particles, were making their presence known as they attracted condensation from the fog. Only the moisture in the form of bubbles were visible, but it was pretty amazing that they could catch a ride on their invisible vehicles—the subatomic particles.

Lee remembered her fascination with the idea that muons traveled through everything, including her own body. It was almost poetic, she thought, that she had come full circle with these clever little bits of matter. She had spent that summer internship at Los Alamos getting acquainted with them, harnessing their power, respecting their ability to pass through lead or concrete, and here she was, casually observing their talent for entertainment as well. She was close to choking up. *Well, Lee, I don't think I'd go that far*, she thought. But she was thinking about how she had made it to the end of her first year at PCC, how far she had come, and it confirmed in her mind that she was on the right track—for now. *Who knew?*

CHAPTER TWENTY-ONE
DEATH BY MASER

J. R. Fillion. She hadn't heard that name in almost a year. It was one that she had tried hard to forget. Forget that he had gotten the job that should have been hers. Forget that he worked down the hall from Isaac. Forget that he was a constant thorn in her side whenever she felt "less than." That feeling had gradually retreated over the past few months: Lee was making her own way at PCC and she was appreciated there, especially since news of the Blue Öyster Caper got around. Students and others on campus thought she was a badass at this point, not really knowing the details of her escape from the madding clown and the rest of the crazies at the Santa Ynez compound. She *was* kind of a badass, and she had the bruises to prove it, but she would have traded that day for one at the Spa—the expensive one in Old Town. Well . . . maybe.

Reinventing herself as professor by day, forensic investigator by night sounded pretty good. Even Alexander would have offered a thumb's up at that, though the gesture itself was something he would have found beneath him. Undignified.

The job had enough potential to almost rank up there with discovering a new subatomic particle. Almost.

This Fillion guy had garnered next to nothing in terms of respect for his work. In fact, very few people even knew what he was working on, and that included the geniuses in Caltech's physics department. The question posed by Isaac when he and Lee had initially bounced it around at the Tap Room remained: How did he get the job?

According to the local paper, an unseemly death would soon be the impetus for a full investigation into J. R. Fillion. The *Pasadena Star-News* promised to reveal all. In the meantime, Lee and Isaac were left to ponder what in the world he was up to. They were right to be suspicious, and Isaac was the most right of all. She remembered that evening.

"I think he's a threat to the Institute . . . a danger . . . an embarrassment," Isaac had offered as the reason Lee should question why he, not she, had gotten the position. She had been in no mood to hear it then. But here it was, staring her in the face. The headline read, **"CALTECH RESEARCHER DIES OF MYSTERI-OUS DISEASE: Physicist's Brain Was Cooked. No Visible Signs of Illness or Foul Play."** Lee knew she would hear from Isaac any second now, but it was Cato who called first.

"Morning. Did you read the local news today? About the guy you and Isaac knew?"

Lee thought she heard a bit of glee in Cato's voice. "Yeah. The paper made it sound kind of sensational. Tabloid-ish. What do you think?"

"I think it depends on his research. What does Isaac say?"

"I haven't heard from him yet. I thought this call was from him, in fact. He was always suspicious of the guy. Thought he was up to no good." Just then Lee's phone beeped. A call waiting from none other than Isaac. "It's him. Let me see if we can conference this. If I disconnect you, stand by. I'll call back." Lee managed it perfectly, and in a matter of seconds all three Crew members were tossing in what they knew.

"I rarely saw the guy at work. Apparently he spent most of his time in the old underground atomic lab near the Rath. The New Rath. Ha! Old lab, New Rath. Anyway, rumor was he was a legacy hire. The family founded the Fillion Think Tank, an organization of deep thinkers, and offered to fund something at the Institute in exchange for the position. Something that the Institute wouldn't go for, I'm sure. So the rest of that story would have to be dug up by the Pasadena PD and the newspaper," Isaac postulated.

"Well, what could he have gotten himself into? Assuming it's not some exotic disease ... or some new cult thing." At this point, Lee had no intention of gloating. She was genuinely approaching this as a problem, not just for Fillion and the Institute, but potentially for everyone in the vicinity. "They need to get the CDC involved, just to rule out disease. And the NSA. There could be some kind of national security risk here," she said.

"Well, who has access to the lab?" Cato asked. "Oh, wait. I do!" *Wise guy*, Lee thought.

"Let me ask around and see what kind of permissions we might get first. They know we were working on the cult case together, and the expertise you both had in portable energy was useful. Maybe they would hire you, Cato, as the forensic investigator. Lee, your background could be useful, whether they originally signed you on or not, and your father's name still has clout here. It's worth a try. What do you guys think?" Isaac seemed really fired up to take this on. She hadn't heard him string this many words together since ... ever.

"I'm in," she said. "Keep me posted."

Cato added his own take on it. "I'm free, as you all know. Give me a call if you get access. If not. . . . Well, let's do this transparently, if we can. The Institute is formidable. Talk to you later." Cato hung up, and it was back to the two-way call.

"What do you really think, Lee?" Isaac asked.

"Well, it's too soon to know, but I really hope we can get in on the investigation. The first thing that came to mind, barring any exotic disease like some kind of encephalitis, is that microwave study or the old maser weaponry thing. The government was involved in both. Actually, I hope it's one of those two things. A new strain of encephalitis could be mosquito-borne. That would mean an epidemic. At least with a microwave or maser attack, it's pinpointed and limited to a particular target. Right?"

"I was thinking the same thing, though I don't have any background in weapons like that, except for the theoretical energy waves." Isaac was still sounding wound up about the whole case. Lee wondered if it was because of some deep harbored resentment toward Fillion or just a desire to get the Crew together one more time.

Lee had to admit it sounded like fun . . . if that was the word. "I know. I did some work on the old-style masers before finishing my internship at Los Alamos. It's like a ray gun. Really old school sci-fi stuff. The so-called 'Death Ray.' You always saw them in the black-and-white movies of the forties and early fifties. We built a rudimentary maser just for kicks. Too weak to do any harm."

"But that's not the same as the microwaves used at the American Embassy in Cuba. Microwaves are . . ."

"Yeah. You're right," she cut in. "The maser was actually

Microwave Amplification by Stimulated Emission of Radiation. It used sort of hyperactive microwaves with infinite range. Regular microwaves are usually more limited. Otherwise we'd all fry every time you heat up a Lean Cuisine. Though microwave ovens *were* originally called radar ranges. Ha! All of this stuff came about because the military was looking for weapons, and they ended up inventing one of the most useful cooking appliances of all time. Especially for someone like me."

=

A three-way text came in the next day. Cato had been on the job:

> Afternoon, guys. How about a meetup at the New Rath? Outside. Got some info for you.

Lee was more than happy to check out the New Rath patio. That's Rath, as in Rathskeller, and New, as in . . . new. The old Rath was the aging student and faculty tavern on campus. The new Rath Patio had no Old World Bavarian charm, but the refashioned outdoor seating offered views of oak trees amid historic academic buildings, so it had a charm of its own.

> Five–ish? Still in my sweats.

> I'm with Lee. Not still in sweats but five is when they open. Sounds good.

She wondered if Cato thought Isaac meant *with* Lee . . . like at her place, as opposed to *in agreement with her.* But she trusted he wasn't thinking that way or even cared. The old Lee would have taken offense at the idea that it was anybody's business anyway. No offense taken here, she decided as she hopped into the shower. The water was cold—characteristically so—the old water heaters in the building were on their last legs, or "last pipes," as one of the neighbors put it. She would have loved the cold water on one of those bruised days—the ones where she crawled into the shower to wash away the dirt and soothe the cuts and scrapes from scrambling over a chain link fence or running from a flaming white sock as it sparked an explosion. Then there was the tackling of a blazing cultist who had started out choking her within a last breath. Even now her neck still bothered her when she thought about it.

=

The Rath was relatively quiet for the early evening hour. Plenty of seating outdoors. The diners gravitated toward the shady spots today. SoCal's "unseasonably" warm weather. The television meteorologists had coined the term, so now it was a real thing and becoming more common than "seasonable." Climate being another topic for another day.

Lee found the *primo* table and set down her tray. Truffle fries and salad sounded like the perfect early dinner, especially when paired with a local craft beer. Crown City Pale. Isaac pulled up a chair and sat facing her.

"We're both early. Must be the promise of food and ale. Not to mention Cato's teaser about info," he said. True to himself, Lee noticed: the kale salad special (Einstein Greens with Quinoa and Corn). *The only thing that would have made it even less desirable is vegan bacon bits and gluten-free croutons*, she thought. *Sometimes you make me feel like a natural glutton, Isaac.*

"Where's the ale, Isaac?"

"It's coming. They're bringing it out. One of my favorites." That sounded more like the old Isaac.

As if on cue, a server—probably a grad student—appeared with Isaac's proprietary ale. They seemed to know each other, which made perfect sense. "One of my Particles students. Good researcher. I wonder if she knew Fillion. I'll have to get back to her about that. There's Cato, looking for us. No tray. We'll have to send him back to the counter to order, I guess."

Isaac guessed wrong. Cato had ordered a gooey grilled cheese sandwich, which would be delivered when it had sopped up enough grease. Lee didn't feel so bad now. He was also waiting for an exclusive ale. Must be a guy thing. They communicate with each other about special secret labels, like insects or dolphins would. No one else can hear them or understand them.

"What's the news?" Isaac asked Cato when he'd devoured the last of his sandwich.

"They still serve a good grilled cheese here," Cato said. "On the other hand, their ales have gotten a little pricey, don't you think? Anyway, talked to the Pasadena PD. Convinced them they'd better be careful with this investigation if it's something other than an exotic illness. They would have to get the CDC involved if it's a disease—infectious or otherwise—but my money's on some radiation device that malfunctioned."

"Or maybe it worked as designed. A weapon. Isaac and I were talking about a maser or an experimental microwave gun. Something like that. I'm glad we're in on the investigation. Do we take orders from the PPD, or can we work on our own? One thing's for sure: we'd have a better chance of identifying what Fillion's got in his lab than the police would. I was telling Isaac that I worked on a basic maser at Los Alamos. Got it running. Fortunately we couldn't do much damage with it. We mostly reenacted Death Ray scenes from old *Star Treks*." Lee looked at Isaac. "What do you think?"

"I'd have to see the lab before I could venture a guess, but the cooked brain thing is sounding like the most solid clue. The police could figure out who Fillion was working with or associating with. They could do the money trail too. And the medical examiner is theirs. Maybe that's the place to start. Cato, if you can get me an intro to the ME, I'll confer with him . . . or her?"

"Her," Cato said, "and I agree that's the best jumping-off point. I did a little brush-up on invisible weapons that could poach your brains. A few could be feasible considering the resources here. But without the military budget and backing, some would be a prohibitive proposition. I'll set up a meeting for you at the PPD."

Lee looked at the two men—the complementary bookends, she once called them. They had downed two beers each and seemed pretty mellow, even as their brains clicked away on the plan. "Uh guys, I'll pull up my old notes on the maser when I get home and send you a copy. What else needs doing for now?"

"Think you can find any test results on death by maser? What happens to human organs when exposed, that kind of thing. Also Google anything on the microwave attacks at the US Embassies. Actually, see what you can find out that's maybe not so public on that. Buried test results. You know." Cato got up to leave. "Talk to you tomorrow, you two. Oh. I might know a guy from way back who did some testing on masers for the military. Maybe Truman or Eisenhower administration. He's about ninety now but still pretty sharp. I'll get back to you on that. Have a good evening, you two."

Lee noticed how striking Cato's shock of white hair was in the filtered sunlight. He was backlit, but it was the shorter cut that made for little tips of silver. Even with that, she thought he looked years younger. Retirement . . . maybe, but she was willing to bet it felt like a new lease on life to dive into murder mysteries and demented cult philosophies. The irony there was how close he—they—had come to death at the hands of some crazies. Hopefully this new case wouldn't be so precarious. Mad Scientists vs. Cultists? Who knew?

=

It had been nagging at her. Lee knew she needed to get back to her classroom to put things away for the summer. She'd been assured that she had the job for the next year, but just erring on the side of caution meant that she needed to organize files and equipment and get any illicit radioactive supplies back in the basement where they belonged. She'd been through a lot of menacing episodes since starting this job and was facing yet another caper with possible gastronomic ramifications: poached, braised, or scrambled brains.

Going down to the basement was nothing to worry about—especially since she had extricated Mr. Jacobs from its bowels. Lee remembered some saying about recognizing your fear and doing whatever-it-was anyway . . . or something like that. *Get over it, Lee. This doesn't even come close to fear, compared to . . . what was the worst? The blazing redhead, the Grand Pooh-bah, the earthquake, or wading through the crowd at Nordstrom's Fall Sale with your bank account and dignity intact?*

Fortunately, the really radioactive materials had already been delivered to Cato's inner sanctum of scientific paraphernalia. There were only some of the bathroom tiles and the Geiger Counter still stashed in the classroom cupboard. Lee made the executive decision to leave them where they were until she needed them again. Not fear—just laziness—she told herself: no one else at PCC uses these things. No particular danger either.

The burning issue now was whether she should boot up her school-issued PC while she was here and see what she could find out about maser deaths and obscure test results on microwave weapons. The school's Wi-Fi network was infinitely faster than her own. Lee was channeling Cato, trying to weigh the pros and cons of using the work server. What would Cato do? *WWCD—a new motto if you go into the investigating biz! After all, he's survived this long. It must mean something.* A sound in the hall could have been anyone but served as a reminder that there wasn't much privacy here. The idea that the server probably records everything in perpetuity and there is no such thing as a complete deletion was one big con. The other was that she really wanted to go home, slip into something comfortable, and have a glass of wine: the best way to face hours of research.

She'd already decided to head home when John Jacobs appeared at the door.

"Uh . . . hi, Ms. Roberts. I thought you were like finished for the semester."

"I am. Just doing some organizing for next year. Straightening things up. You know."

"Well, if you like need some help, let me know. I'm working a few hours at the Casa Viño and doing some odd jobs for Mr. Klein. I might get a part-time at Lucky B's . . . uh Lucky

Baldwin's. Don't know yet, so I have time if you need me to do some work for you too."

"Gee, thanks, John. I'll seriously consider your offer. Right now I don't know what I would have for you." Lee smiled to let him know she appreciated his offer. "Really, thanks. If anything comes up, I'll be in touch. Maybe we can meet in the fall to set up for the new term if you're still available to help." It was tempting to have him do some research for her; she figured he'd probably be pretty good at it. But there was no way she would get him involved at this point. The Crew didn't even know what they were up against, but she was sure the case had to be kept under wraps while they were investigating. And there was no way of knowing the potential danger.

"Okay. Thanks. See you around."

"Bye, John."

Nice kid. Lee was sure she had made the right decision. Besides, she thought, she'd have to explain the whole maser thing to him first. He was no dummy, but the idea of cooking someone's gray matter was pretty fantastical. Even she had a hard time believing that it could happen at the Institute.

=

She was right. Sitting at her kitchen table with a glass of wine was the way to go. No sweats. Lee's vintage air conditioning unit was barely cranking out air—let alone cold air, which didn't bode well for the summer months ahead. The old arched window didn't actually open either, and the others were strangely situated so as to prevent any cross breeze. Her go-to lounging attire in warm weather was boxer shorts and a T-shirt. No haute couture tonight. Maybe tomorrow she could convince the guys to meet up somewhere that required clothing. In the meantime, she could plow through her old notes from Los Alamos and initiate a search on deaths by maser. It was a funny thought. It had to be homicide. How could someone—a physics professor, no less—aim a lethal beam of amplified microwaves at his own head. Unless he accidentally stepped in front of it or the device started spinning around like a pent-up garden hose and he got caught in the crossfire. Assuming it wasn't an accident, who would want Fillion dead? The list was short, but a good distraction from the research task awaiting her attention:

Who Killed J. R. (Fillion, That Is)?
1. Wife (if he has one)
2. Children (ditto)
3. Parents (no way)
4. Coworker(s)
5. Terrorists (domestic or foreign)
6. Girlfriend (see #1)
7. US Government (or foreign)
8. Nancy Grace (so she could do another murder mystery episode on TV)
9. *20/20* (see #8)
10. Google (so they could steal the technology)

Okay, Lee, get to work. Enough stalling. She figured Isaac or Cato would have come up with similar notions, but she saved her list. Just in case. The research into masers was mostly what she already knew. The only recent additions to the Google citations were made in the past couple of years. While the old stuff was exactly what she expected and jibed perfectly with her own Los Alamos notes, a name popped out in some newer references: Jay Fillion. She had paged over to the more obscure titles—ones that were way down on the Google ranking. That indicated to Lee that there was little relevance in the article for the average Googler or that it was too complicated to fit in the Google algorithm. She determined that Jay Fillion and J. R. Fillion were one in the same and set to work wading through the articles.

One was a dud. It was a thesis on the origin of the maser and one of its inventors, Allan Frey. It looked like something Fillion would have written for a grad school assignment. It did have an interesting reference to Pasadena's Jet Propulsion Lab, but nothing secretive. Lee made a note to follow up at JPL anyway. Another article caught her eye: "The Secret Advantage of Death by Maser." It was dated more recently. Most of the verbiage was about secret military weapon research that had been abandoned. Microwaves and amplified microwaves primarily. It seems that he had taken a particular interest in the maser and wrote about its possibilities in modern warfare. He footnoted several other citations. Lee copied the citations into a separate folder, hoping she wouldn't have to actually follow up on all of them. The last article was *about* Fillion, not *by* him. It was written by a colleague of his, apparently, and was none too flattering. It looked like an op-ed in a scholarly periodical. "The Sinister Effects of Maser Technology," by James J. Ray, PhD.

The title spoke for itself. Anytime you see the word "sinister," you know you've got a good plot. The article didn't disappoint. Lee read through it at Mach speed, looking for the evil allusions. It was clear that James J. Ray, PhD, was no fan of Fillion; in fact, much of the piece read like a really bad Yelp review. The part that caused Lee's arm hairs to bristle was a subsection on deadly effects. It pointed out that maser weaponry was discreet if nothing else. One could use it without detection: no sound and no visible marks or burns left behind. Just cooked guts. There were additional references to the human brain as a target, but nothing very specific. It looked to Lee like she would have to do her own research on that. It was the last paragraph in the op-ed that was most enlightening:

> In any event, those who carry out these kinds of experiments in the name of humanity are doomed to end up the victims. It is karma rather than science that prevails, and J. R. Fillion—a charlatan, a Dr. Frankenstein, if you will—is sealing his own fate as much as that of mankind.

Whoa, Lee. Keep calm. If this isn't a threat, I don't know what is. The first thing to do is to check out James J. Ray. If he's still living, the Crew would have to pay him a visit. If he's dead, then he either has a demented follower doing his bidding, or he's a fortune teller. She copied the article into a folder and then also printed it out. This was too good for a text message; she had to call the guys. An expert at conference calls now, she could manage that in a minute. The hard part was containing herself until everyone was connected.

"Listen to this, guys—an op-ed from two years ago about Fillion from a Dr. James Ray. Quote: 'In any event, those who carry out these kinds of experiments in the name of humanity are doomed to end up the victims. It is karma rather than science that prevails, and J. R. Fillion—a charlatan, a Dr. Frankenstein, if you will—is sealing his own fate as much as that of mankind.' End quote. What do you think? Of course, I'm going to look up the author and see if he's still alive, but this looks like a lead."

"Man, that's a pretty harsh assessment. Definitely worth a look. If he's still around, I say we all go to talk to him; nobody go alone. Good work. Anything else?" Cato asked.

"Well, there might be a JPL connection from way back. I'm just getting started on the digging. What about you guys?" Lee said.

Isaac was next to chime in: "I checked around at the Institute. Just as we thought, everyone was suspicious of Fillion. He was a loner—more so than your typical eccentric professor. He did have some visitors who looked a little suspect. Security is looking for sign-in logs and video for me. Hopefully, they'll come up with something too. Whatever he was up to, it didn't sit well with the rank and file or the admin people. So Cato, do we have an appointment with the ME yet? We have to check out the brain and get a closer look to see if there are any marks on his face or skull. That could tell us a lot."

"My preliminary research suggests that masers were considered a valuable weapon for the military because they *don't* leave a mark and they are silent. But you're right," Lee added. "It would be something to look for, Isaac." Lee made a mental note to add to her list of possible perps: (11) Mad scientist (who gives bad Yelp reviews).

"So guys, I'm thinking I might want to be in on the medical examiner thing. Let me know what's going on with that." Lee regretted the request the minute she said it. Crispy critters were one thing, but fresh brain was another. "Well, I'm headed to JPL tomorrow morning to run down the research and see who's still around that can talk about it. I know someone who can get me in there. If that doesn't pan out, Isaac, I might need a reference from you. Oh . . . and I'll look into whether this Dr. Ray is still alive. And what about breakfast Saturday? I need a break from the Happy Hour thing—at least for a few days. Have you guys been to Mary's Market up in the Canyon? Food's decent, and it's like being on a mini-vacation for an hour or two. Worth the drive over there. I grew up a couple of streets over. House is gone, but I still like the vibe in my old neighborhood."

"I think I was there pre-earthquake, Lee. Sounds like a plan," Isaac said. "If I remember correctly, there's not much parking. I'll pick you guys up. Nine a.m.? See you then. That is, unless we end up at the coroner's office that day, poking at some boiled gray matter instead. Hmm. I'd rather be looking at a plate of scrambled eggs and bacon."

Cato was laughing. "Better to eat *afterward*. Don't you think? That image—not to mention the odor—will stay with you for a while. See you." Cato was off the conference call.

"Seriously, Lee, are you up for an autopsy? I'm not sure I am. The only thing I ever did that was remotely similar was a few frog dissections. You could barely find the brains in the little guys."

Lee thought back to her own high school labs. She'd handled those okay. And Cato's crispy critter photo albums too. Besides, they'd just be looking at the brain, and she'd seen pictures of a brain before. *Piece of cake, right?* "Yeah, I'm in. You can do it too. Just Google 'brains' and take a look at the photos before you go. It should help . . . I think." When she hung up, she wished she'd sounded a little more confident.

With an appointment at JPL all set, Lee went about reading up on that part of the maser story. Nothing suspicious: just articles about Deep Space Navigation and Communication. No weapons mentioned.

Before she knew it, the sun was starting to sink behind the

building next door, and the air in her condo seemed cooler. She noticed how much darker her kitchen had grown. *Don't be a sloth. Go for a run . . . if you still remember how*, she thought, elated that her snark was still intact.

=

The usual route east on Del Mar seemed longer than she remembered. Probably because she was out of condition. The sun was behind her, and she watched her shadow—strangely misshapen—undulate over the cracks and bumps in the sidewalk. Rush-hour traffic was anything but rushing, the sad joke in Southern California. And the hour wasn't an hour at all, but three or four, depending on the day of the week. When you're running on the sidewalk, it's an annoying fact that you will be moving faster than the cars. Today was the perfect day for a run, Lee thought: a balmy temperature and enough daylight to still get somewhere and back before dark.

Don't waste the time, she told herself. *While you're running, sort through this cooked brain mess and see if there's any other angle.* Lee's mind went back to the Perp List. It all sounded silly, but . . . really . . . what else could it be? Someone offed Fillion, she was sure. The key might be in security tapes and visitor logs at the Institute. She made a mental note to remind Isaac about it when she got back. If the guy was knowingly working on a weapon, the idea of terrorists was not far-fetched. Or even if he was unaware of the ultimate purpose of the maser, it could still be terrorism. Intellectual jealousy seemed off the mark: the device itself was nothing new. Another mental note. Get a good look at the maser in Fillion's lab. Even though it had been a few years since she had worked on one, a rudimentary one at that, the components would have to be the same.

Instead of a lens, masers amplified their beams through ruby crystals and the like. Even sapphires were used. Maybe there's some new kind of beam. Final note: Who's this guy James Ray, and is he still alive?

By the time Lee reached her usual turn-back point, she was feeling better about life. She had done the distance and waded through her list of research tasks simultaneously. Looking into the sun could be unbearable at this time of day, but the trees and buildings created a heat shield as she headed west. More Maser Tales awaited, and the thought of microwave beams made her hungry. Surely there was a Lean Cuisine in her freezer.

=

With no news on the medical examiner thing, she was on her own. The visit to JPL was just as she expected. Lee sat in one of the public areas where special VIP tours traipsed by at regular intervals on their way to the famed "Control Room." A couple of old-timers had agreed to meet with her. They seemed eager to talk about their early research into masers for deep space use. Both admitted that talk of maser weapons had come up, but nobody was openly interested—or authorized—to pursue it. In the aftermath of WWII and the detonation of two atomic bombs, the lab sent out a directive that the emphasis on maser technology was for peaceful purposes. Navigation and communication, just as the articles suggested. The two men seemed to Lee to be skirting around the fact that deep space was probably the battleground of the future, but they were pretty clear that they had not done research in that direction themselves. At this point, nearing full retirement, they clearly were not going to discuss it. They both had the nerdy, gentle demeanors that suggested they were being honest with her. One of the men offered up the contact information of a former colleague who had supervised the work on masers but cautioned that advanced age and progressing dementia made his expertise less than reliable. Lee appreciated the inference as she thought about her own father's battle with dementia. The whole JPL angle moved to the bottom of her list for now.

Next up was taking a look at James J. Ray, PhD. With the cult thing in mind, Lee had learned to be suspicious of initials—letters that might be hiding a true identity . . . or a false one. A Google query turned up only a few references, one of which was the article she had already read. A bit of digging revealed the "J": Janusz. A little more research showed that it was a popular Polish name and often anglicized to John. Not much to look at there.

The most recent articles on Ray indicated that he was still alive. A BluePages.com search showed him living nearby. Lee followed up on Google Maps and figured it was an hour or so by freeway to get to his Orange County home. Distance in miles, much less kilometers—was something that no native Californian could relate to—kind of like the metric system. Necessity dictated that drivers speak in terms of time: an hour midday but an hour and a half during early rush hour. Holiday weekends? Fuhgeddaboudit. That kind of thing. Scientists were exempt from the rule, however. Lee would be true to Cato's admonition that the Crew all go together. No telling what would set this guy off. Especially if he was the perpetrator of the cooked-up crime.

Lee sent the driving directions and address for Ray to her cell phone and got back to reading up on him. He had the normal resumé for a physicist and seemed pretty even-tempered, except for his rant on Fillion. She wondered if it was personal. Only one way to tell. A three-way text was called for:

> Hey guys, Dr. James Ray is alive & well & only an hr. from here. I have the address. Want to pay a visit after breakfast tomor-row—unless we end up meeting with the ME?

Isaac got back to her first:

> Still no word on the ME. I say we do it. Do we call first? I'll defer to Cato on that. See you at 9.

It was a couple of hours before Cato texted back. He always subscribed to the element of surprise, but the long drive could be a waste if Ray wasn't there. His plan was to do a little sur-veillance first using an old cop buddy of his. He would have an answer at breakfast. Lee forwarded Ray's contact info to both guys. She was beginning to feel like they were finally getting things moving.

CHAPTER TWENTY-TWO
VACAY IN THE CANYON

Mary's Market was not a market, and local legend Mary was long gone. A succession of owners since then had paid careful attention to the culture of the Canyon, but it was a tenuous deal to take on running a café with a small kitchen and only ten tables total, inside and out. Food was simple but skillfully prepared; it was the décor that made Mary's Mary's. No two chairs alike, vintage household items lining the shelves, the old upright piano. Lee always liked the grainy photos on the walls too, but it was the box of old Fisher-Price toys that best embodied her childhood. Saturday was the day when everyone brought a dog or a rabbit on a leash. She remembered bringing Chloe once; the two had feasted on crispy bacon—the little dog's favorite.

Today was all about fortifying themselves for the drive to Orange County and firming up their approach. Cato's buddy had come through. Ray was at home today and not likely to take off; he was sporting crutches—supposedly the result of a mishap on a ladder. And he was alone, though he apparently had a wife somewhere. Isaac and Lee let their imaginations go wild: What if he had actually injured himself in a maser mishap?

"Yeah, pretty funny, you two. My experience tells me that the most obvious explanation is the truth . . . unless it's a lie." Cato laughed but decided he would try to take a close look at Ray's injuries, just in case. "So what's good here?"

After breakfast the Crew headed out over the footbridge to walk off the meal. A real stream rippled by underneath, a rarity in SoCal. And a rag-tag bunch of cottages lined the narrow roadway, interrupted every once in a while by a large home sporting expensive renovations. It was pure nostalgia for Lee and something totally new for Cato. Isaac was somewhere in the middle, trying to look relaxed but visibly itching to head down the freeway for a visit with Dr. James Janusz Ray and his dubious injuries.

The conversation on the way down to the OC, as Orange County is known, centered around whether the microwave attacks at the US Embassies were the same as a possible maser attack. The consensus of the Blue Öysters was that regular microwaves were much lower in intensity and involved "sonic" beams. They were first detected in the fifties and sixties and nothing new. While recent news was about attacks on the embassies in Russia, China, Canada, and Cuba, it's not known if they represented "spy craft" gone wrong or were deliberately designed to cause permanent harm. Both Isaac and Cato had looked into the official and unofficial reports of ill health in embassy employees and their families.

"Some analysis indicates that bad actors were trying to listen in to classified conversations and their equipment ended up blowing out the auditory nerves of their victims," Isaac said.

"Something must have gone very wrong, because a lot of those people have a whole host of ailments, and nobody knows if they'll ever get better," added Isaac. "I'm betting that China and Russia didn't care about possible damage."

"Maybe they were experimenting on unsuspecting Americans just to see how it would work, guys. Is that possible, or were they really developing a new weapon?" Lee was still on the weapon track rather than the spy track.

Isaac shrugged. "It doesn't matter that much in terms of Fillion's death since masers are a different kind of microwave. The embassy workers reported hearing deafening sounds, and their brain scans, for the most part, show alterations, but nobody has cooked brain matter."

"Well, the fact that they're alive means that researchers can keep looking into the cause. The story will come out sooner or later—unless there's a cover-up of some sort." Cato was not laughing this time; he was dead serious.

Lee offered a different take, she hoped: "It's hard to keep anything secret these days. My money's on one of the news outlets getting the scoop, or maybe a late-night comedian will hit on the truth."

The traffic slowed as Isaac hit the transition corridor from LA County to OC—sometimes referred to as the Orange Crush or "going behind the Orange Curtain." Lee appreciated the comfort of his luxury car, as small as it was. The black BMW was an older model, but the leather seats were carefully maintained, and the air conditioning was working really well, even in the back—something she had learned to go without in her own car.

A buzzing phone interrupted the stop-and-go motion, and all three reached for their pockets. Cato was the winner. "A text from my stake-out guy. Says he has to leave in a few minutes, but Ray is still home."

"We'll be there soon anyway." Isaac had plugged the address into his nav, and it looked like he could get off the freeway and still make the estimated time of arrival. "Half an hour maybe, or twenty minutes if we get a break."

"Good. So we need to figure out what we're going to say, how we're going to approach this. I have my investigator's license, so I'll start. That should get me in the door at least."

Lee flashed on that image of Zin tossing Cato's ID in the bushes. The funny thing was it was really his PCC faculty card, something Cato didn't need anyway. Hopefully, this would go smoother. No methane gas, no explosions. "Are we honest about the purpose of the visit? There was no love lost between Fillion and Ray, so unless he's actually the murderer, Ray might be fine with the discussion. He might not even know Fillion is dead," Lee said.

"Yeah, I vote for honesty," Cato responded and looked at Isaac. "You okay with that?"

"Sure."

The rest of the drive was quiet. They pulled into Ray's neighborhood, a complex of '70s-era modest homes and mostly manicured lawns and did a drive-by first before parking down the street. A temporary wood ramp had been installed over Ray's front steps, but everything else indicated business as usual. Lee felt a rush of nerves as they started up the walkway; she thought Isaac looked a little nervous too. Cato motioned for the two to stay back on the lawn while he headed up the ramp. "Don't want to overwhelm the guy," he whispered.

The first knock got no response, but Lee thought she saw the front window curtains move—or maybe she imagined that. *Get a grip, Lee.* The second knock got a voice: "No sales-men—or religious zealots."

"Doctor Ray? My name's Cato Klein. I'm from Pasadena. An investigator looking into J. R. Fillion's death. I wond . . ." The door swung open to reveal a diminutive man, age-wise somewhere in between Cato and Isaac, it appeared. The crutches were no joke, and Cato stepped back in case Ray decided to weaponize them. "Uh . . . these are my colleagues, Lee Roberts and Isaac . . ."

"I know about Isaac. Saw him speak. Read a paper by him. Caltech's Particle Physics Department, right?"

Isaac stepped forward. "Yes, sir. Can we come in and talk?"

"What's the girl here for?"

It took all her restraint to avoid a snarky answer. This was the time for finesse, since they weren't even in the front door yet. "Physics prof at PCC—Pasadena City College—uh . . . we all work together."

Ray stepped back to allow the threesome to enter and hob-bled to a nearby dining chair. "Not very good on these yet. Still hurts a lot too." Lee noticed the guy wince as he sat and wondered if the injury was worse than reported—like way worse. She could tell that Cato had seen it too.

"Could we sit, Dr. Ray? We have a couple of questions that you might be able to help us with." Cato didn't even wait for a response; he forced the issue by plopping down on another chair and taking out a small notepad. Lee followed suit—no notebook—but she was thinking that sitting would dispel some nervous energy. *Her* nervous energy.

Cato started the conversation; he was uncharacteristically polite, careful in his wording. "Dr. Ray, we appreciate the opportunity to talk to you under these circumstances." He pointed to the crutches, but Lee figured he was also thinking about the probable murder of Fillion, a man who qualifies more as a nemesis than a colleague. "I assume you knew that he was found dead in his lab a few days ago. Authorities are looking into the possibility of an accident, but they've agreed to let us also look at another angle . . ." Cato waited to see if Ray had a reaction or a response. The guy remained passive. Cato continued, "We all have expertise in the field of physics, and I'm a licensed forensic investigator. We're . . . uh . . . delving into the theory that Fillion might have been murdered because of what he was working on—or why."

Ray's good leg began to bounce in that quick nervous move that teen boys have when they're sitting down. Finally, he coughed, and the angry words came spilling out: "I couldn't tell you a thing about that, but I'm glad he's out of commission. He was a menace. We used to be friends, or at least friendly colleagues, but I could see him getting deeper and deeper into some kind of downward spiral. He became obsessed with finding a modernized maser. I think he had some backers, some dangerous characters, egging him on. I tried to warn him, but he became threatening. I'd say he was bordering on mental illness. How he ever . . ."

This was where Lee thought Ray was going to say something like, "How he ever got that job at Caltech is a mystery." That's pretty close to what actually came out of his mouth: "He didn't deserve that position at Caltech. I think his parents had some influence, but the Institute is too ethical to knowingly allow something like that."

It was electric music to her ears, and Isaac's look confirmed that he understood too. Isaac asked, "How *do* you think that happened? Rumors abound about the way that kind of hiring occurs. He wasn't a legacy in terms of family who attended or taught or researched there. Unless someone falsified records." Ray's face lit up.

"That's what I think, but it wasn't up to me to figure that out. No access to the data frame, no 'in' with faculty or administration. It is hard to imagine that the Institute knew what was happening. I bet they're pretty annoyed now."

"There are a lot of smart people over there. They'll get to the bottom of it, but in the meantime, we need as much information on this new maser as possible and who Fillion might have collaborated with. It would save us a lot of time," Lee said. "I did work on rudimentary masers at Los Alamos, but they were too weak to do any harm. I checked with JPL, and they haven't worked with them in years. On the way down here, we discussed the acoustic microwave at the US Embassies. I'm wondering if you think there's a connection."

Ray was looking pale, but the Crew hoped they could get a little more out of him before they left. "Sorry, I'm not much help there. I don't see a connection, except that both devices would be used without the intended victims knowing. I'll do some thinking on it and let you know if anything occurs to me. Now, what else do you want before you go?"

Ray's coke bottle lenses weighed down the wire frames that held them, and Lee could see how the pull of gravity would eventually get the better of him. Within seconds he had to grab them before they slipped off his nose. She figured he was beginning to get uncomfortable at the thought of a long, drawn-out Q and A session, and she felt kind of sorry for the guy: a three-to-one ratio was probably overwhelming. "Can I fix you some coffee or tea, Mr. Ray? I think I can find my way around your kitchen."

"Oh, yes. Thank you. It's kind of hard maneuvering in there with the crutches." He lifted one crutch in the air, and the Crew, as with one mind, must have wondered again about the nature of his injury. "Tea would be nice."

"Anyone else?" she asked. No takers, which was fine. Lee did manage to locate tea bags and cups, and she hoped that the microwave would be acceptable for warming the water. *Can't escape those waves*, she thought. *They're everywhere.* She hadn't realized how prevalent, omnipresent, the radar range was. And how easy it would be to disguise a weapon as a household appliance. Within minutes she appeared with a tray of Oreo cookies and microwaved tea for the beleaguered Dr. Ray. "I hope you don't mind. I found some cookies in the cupboard." *That'll soften him up*, she hoped. "So, Dr. Ray, exactly how did you injure yourself? It seems like it's pretty painful."

She could see Cato and Isaac look at each other for just that nanosecond but remain expressionless. *Well, guys, someone has to ask. It might as well be "the girl."*

There it was: beads of sweat. Two possibilities: the tea was too hot, or Ray was hiding something. Isaac's turn. "Janusz is Polish, right? Is that a family name? We have a couple of profs at Caltech with the same name." Small talk was never a skill he managed to hone, but even Isaac could see that line of questioning was making things worse. "So how long will you need to be on crutches? Is it a clean break?" The comfort gauge was heading back up, and Ray's color had returned.

"They say I'll probably need surgery. I'll know soon."

Cato figured he'd give it one last try before they had to leave: "I had the same kind of injury. Fell off a roof investigating a case. Had to wear a splint till they could put my leg back together with pins. Are you splinted or . . ." Success—sort of.

Ray lifted one pant leg to reveal a splint and a lot of bruising, but it looked legit. Nothing resembling crispy skin or overcooked meat.

Lee had one last question: "Uh, Dr. Ray, I noticed some beautiful English china in your cupboard. Is that your wife's? I hope she's here to help you get around."

"Yes, that's her china. She's uh . . . out of the country, visiting family outside of London. Couldn't be helped. Uh . . . death in the family."

There's the "tell," Lee thought. Ray's neck and face were beet red. Not a good liar.

"Dr. Ray, thank you for your time. I think we have enough for now. Please call me if you think of anything else." (The classic police line, but you never know.) Cato handed him a card with the PCC address crossed out and his personal number scribbled in Sharpie. Lee realized she was going to have to get some cards made up too. Lee Roberts, Girl Physicist. Something like that.

They headed down the makeshift ramp, leaving behind a very drained James Janusz Ray, PhD. All three had the same thought: he seemed innocent enough—not the maniacal murdering scientist type, but he was clearly hiding something.

The trip back up to Pasadena was grueling. Slow and go was the term for it. Talking business filled the first half hour. The conversation included (1) What was Ray hiding? (2) Who's going to work on that? (3) Who's going to pester the ME's office for a look at Fillion's brain? (4) When/how does the Crew get access to Fillion's lab? and (5) Finally, what's the time frame for a happy hour meetup to go over findings for above numbers 1–4?

The answers came in reverse order: (5) The Crew would reconvene at Edwin Mills in Old Town for happy hour after the medical examiner visit and the lab look-see. This was an easy one since, as Cato put it, it's better not to eat first where dead things, dissections, and crispy critters are involved. (4) Cato would take the lead on the medical examiner. Everyone knew how backed up they were, but someone in the department owed him a favor, and he would cash it in. Tomorrow. (3) The whole Öyster Crew would meet with the PPD next to get the go-ahead on entering the lab, and then with the Institute's admin and security as a courtesy to get the keys—even though Cato found his old key in the bottom of a sock drawer. (2) Isaac and Lee would be back in touch with Ray in a day or two to see how he was doing. Gaining his trust would take some time, so they were going to have to cultivate a rapport with him. (1) Be prepared to fail on getting any more out of Ray.

With that settled, Isaac put on some music—country western, a decidedly uncharacteristic choice, Lee thought. She liked that she was getting to know more about him, even under these grim circumstances. Sitting in the back again, a concession to Cato's aging knees, she could get a good view of the traffic slogging by and of the mountains to the north. There were still small pockets of snow at the higher elevations—surprise gifts left by a late spring storm—and most of the upslopes were still green. The sky was clear, the kind of clear that Angelenos were lulled into thinking would last, always to be disappointed. Like Lucy and Charlie Brown and the football. Lee knew what would happen in a month: dry brush and the return of smog. She remembered her father complaining about the inversion layer, the heat that pushed air impurities down toward the valleys and against the mountains. He would launch into a description of the days that were so bad children had to stay inside.

"Taking a deep breath felt like inhaling pool chlorine," he told her, "but stricter air quality regulations were largely successful here—until recently." He was right. There was a slight worsening of smog now, and people were in denial, calling it "haze."

Isaac was the right person to be driving today. He was more patient than Lee would have been. Cato was nodding off, so not a good option for driving on the freeways. She wondered if this caper was taking Isaac away from something else. He was close to his family, even his sister, but Lee had never heard him talk about other friends. He was likeable, good-looking, so he would have a lot to add to the landscape. It was tempting: she could do some snooping now that she was an investigator-in-training, but she respected Isaac too much to invade his privacy. No LinkedIn or Facebook searches, much less the Instagram route. She hoped he felt the same way.

Isaac looked at his nav. "Okay, guys. About fifteen minutes if the 210 cooperates."

"On the Road Again" came on the radio. A song written for places like Texas but appropriated by Californians, probably because they spend so much time on the road; whether they are actually getting anywhere is another issue. Cato woke and began to sing. Before long the geeky trio was harmonizing with their fake twangs. *If only Dad could see me now*, Lee thought.

It was a toss-up whose house Isaac would get to first. He decided to drop Cato and then swing down to Lee's place. There was a tangle of legs and seat belts as Cato got out and

Lee moved to the front, but it was worth it as far as she was concerned.

"Thanks for driving. We'll have to come up with a plan to get into Ray's good graces," Lee said.

"I think he likes you, so no problem, I bet. It was the kindness you showed him. People forget about that. It goes a long way, and he impresses me as a lonely guy. You can take the lead when we get back in touch with him."

Lee hadn't thought about it that way; she really was being sincere—mostly. She knew something was brewing inside Ray. "I kind of felt bad for the guy. He could be hiding something sinister or something mundane."

"Define 'mundane.' "

"You know—he cheated on his wife, she cheated on him, he's behind on his Netflix bill. Anything. We all have something to feel guilty about. Well . . . maybe not you." Lee smiled. *So sappy. Cut it out, Lee.*

Isaac didn't respond. They pulled up in front of the Mountainview Gardens, and Lee knew she had been saved from the abyss of words she would have regretted later.

=

The call came the next morning, and it was electric. The Crew was on its way to the medical examiner's office. Each drove separately, figuring it was quicker. The parking around the PPD was another matter. Lee fed a meter on the street and headed toward the old Italianate building at almost a run. She'd dressed down for this appointment, not knowing what to expect with bodily fluids and all. She figured old tennis shoes were in order, and she thought for a moment that she had worn this same pair while scaling that fence at the cult compound. *Maybe you shabby things'll bring us luck today.* Lee caught a glimpse of Isaac coming out of the parking structure behind the building and Cato cutting through the park at City Hall. They both had the eager look that she understood so well today and were walking at a decidedly brisk clip to meet up with her. Cato always dressed down these days, but Isaac looked more prepared for a lunch meeting than a coroner's meeting. Lee hoped his shoes would survive.

It was silly, she realized once she got into the examining room. No pools of blood, no slimy stuff, no guts. The attendants in the room all wore sparkling white aprons—clean aprons. The female ME, Dr. Dee Jones, was shapely, muscular, with long dark hair tucked into her cap. Green eyes peering through protective safety glasses. Beautiful, really. Lee figured her to be in her fifties.

It was the odor that stopped Lee cold. It was something she expected but still found hard to handle. She'd read that chewing peppermint gum might help or sniffing Vicks VapoRub. She had both with her. And it wasn't enough. Cato was used to it; Isaac, another story. Lee handed him the Vicks and the gum, hoping they would help. The adrenaline of the moment actually seemed to work the best, especially when Fillion's body was rolled out.

The whole experience seemed surreal to Lee. Naturally, the surroundings were sterile. The cold blue of the LED lighting, punctuated by little blinking red lights in various parts of the room—sensors of some sort—gave the place an otherworldly aura. The beams of color bounced off the steel tables. The three donned masks, caps, gloves, and aprons—and booties. *Isaac's shoes are saved!* It could have been an alien abduction scene or something befitting the maser death of J. R. Fillion. Lee, like the rest of the Blue Öyster Crew, was determined to make the most of this opportunity. It had been made clear to them that this was the one and only time they would get a look. And they were not disappointed.

The ME pulled back the sheet unceremoniously to reveal a brain sitting on a steel tray next to the skull, which was attached to a stitched-up body, Frankenstein style. *Just like TV*, Lee thought. *Nothing to it.* It was exhilarating and disgusting all at the same time. Not at all like a gutted frog. She glanced at Isaac to see how he was doing. Even Isaac looked spellbound, though a little green around the edges.

Cato leaned in to get a closer look. "How would you describe the consistency of the brain, Doc?" The Doc nudged it with a probe.

"Want to give it a try?" She handed Cato the probe, thinking it would be declined. Lee knew better: Cato grabbed it and started poking.

"I didn't expect it to hold its shape so well. Must be because it's so firm," Cato said. I'd say it feels like a hard-boiled egg— or poached tofu."

"I wouldn't know about the tofu part." Jones laughed. Lee thought she seemed happy to have an audience. The doc probably saw Cato as someone with the same sense of macabre humor—soul mates in all things gruesome. She continued, "But it's definitely been cooked. It would take a temperature of one hundred seven degrees to start the process, and I'd say this one was a little overcooked."

Isaac was looking a little better—color-wise—and decided to outdo them all. "Uh . . . can I touch it? I need a better idea of what cooked . . . uh . . . overcooked brain feels like." Lee was getting prepared to spot him in case he keeled over, but he did just fine. "More like pot roast, I think."

Lee had had enough of the culinary analysis. "Okay, guys. I know that raw brain is soft and squishy. Like Jell-O. Right? So let's all agree this one is definitely cooked. Can you tell us any more, uh, Doc?"

"Well, it weighed two point six pounds or about one point eight kilograms at some point. Well within normal range. We have to assume it lost some volume when the moisture was boiled out. The brain has more water than gray matter in it actually. No other visible signs . . . not even on the skull or skin. That's some weapon."

Cato said, "Yeah. It's designed to kill at the speed of light without sound and without a trace. Any other abnormalities?"

Lee was trying really hard at this point *not* to laugh. She remembered the scene in *Young Frankenstein* where the mad scientist sends his trusty but dimwitted sidekick Igor to procure a normal brain. Igor is so proud of himself, returning with what he thinks is the brain of one "Abby Normal"—translate that *abnormal*. She figured she must be giddy from the formaldehyde or some other preservative. *Get a grip, Lee.* But then she noticed that Isaac had a strange smirk on his face too. *Don't look at him, or it's all over.* "Uh . . . did you notice if the eyeballs were affected? That might tell us which direction the beam came from." Both Isaac and Cato gave Lee a "good job" nod. Then she hoped the ME wasn't actually going to pluck them out for show and tell.

The ME said, "Yes. I thought about that too. It's standard to look closely at the eyes. Windows to the soul and all that. They appear cooked to a much less degree—basically only a little firmer than normal. With the expected amount of cloudiness, considering the number of days post-mortem. So if your theory is correct, the beam would have come from behind. I don't pretend to understand this device. Is it a laser, a microwave like the embassy attacks?"

"Actually, we suspect a maser. Similar to a laser or microwave but much more intense and capable of pinpoint precision. Think Death Ray," Isaac explained. He was in his element now and with a rosy bloom on his cheeks, Lee thought. Smart boy makes good in the investigative biz. He went on, "We'll be examining Fillion's lab equipment next. Anyway, could he have done this to himself . . . accidentally . . . or otherwise? Did you get fingerprints from him?"

"Hopefully, the PD checked for prints on the maser and in the lab," Cato chimed in. "That would be standard protocol. Right, Doc? Though nothing is standard about Fillion's death."

"We did chemical testing on the deceased's hands. Not all the results are in, but it looks pretty normal so far. He hit the ground when he went down, so we have dirt and dust on his palms and fingers. I'll check on that right now for you. Give me a sec."

When the ME left the room, all three of them were bursting to speak. "Dirt and dust? How is that possible?" Lee asked.

Isaac had the same thought. "It should have been a 'Clean Room.' Who would do an experiment like that with contaminants on the floor . . . or in the air? That old lab is like the others: it has a filtration system. Even if it was broken, you'd still have a near-perfect clean environment. There are mats that clean the shoes, and most people would put on booties anyway."

"Uh . . . maybe someone tracked in dirt later. Or during his experimentation—or murder," Lee said. "If not, we need to find out where the dirt came from."

As soon as the examiner walked back in, all three started peppering her with questions about the residue on Fillion's hands.

"Whoa. One at a time, people. What are you asking?"

Lee piped up, "The dirt shouldn't have been there unless someone tracked it in later. The lab was a 'Clean Room.' Would the PD have tracked dirt in? Or could there have been something about the process of getting Fillion's body here that would . . ."

"Uh . . . no. No way. The procedures assure that no contamination of the body takes place during transport or handling. And the PD would have been careful to wear booties. They should have samples of anything that was on the floor. Check with them. Our lab doesn't have a complete analysis of the dirt on his hands yet. I'll tell them your concerns, and we'll add some more sensitive tests. We can sometimes pinpoint *exactly* where the dirt originated. That's what you want. Right? As for whether this could be an accident, you physicists will have to figure that one out." Lee noticed that the ME looked a little offended at her questions. *Better make this right, Lee, if you hope to work with this woman again.*

"Uh . . . I was pretty sure that you'd take every precaution, Doc. I know we didn't even have to ask. We're in good hands. Or rather, Fillion is in good hands. We just feel like this might be an important development. Thanks for your time. Please let us know when you get the analysis finished."

The police department was in the same building, so in a matter of minutes they had tracked down the detectives responsible for the Fillion case. They were set up in a small squad room with inexpensive modern furniture that contrasted with the classic 1930s architecture. The aesthetic was typical for most big city police stations but still kind of a disappointment in a building this beautiful, Lee thought. Cato knew most of the guys, and it was like an old homecoming. After introductions were made, he got down to the dirt business: how to explain where it came from and how it ended up on Fillion's hands. The files, complete with photos and graphs, were displayed on a large flat screen monitor, but there were also old-school baggies of dirt and other artifacts spread out on a large table, waiting to be catalogued.

"Looks like our timing is perfect," Cato said. "We need some info on this dirt. It doesn't add up that Fillion would have dirt on his hands. If he fell as he was dying, he would be landing on a clean floor. The whole lab was a Clean Room. He would have washed his hands and cleaned the soles of his shoes before entering. Do you have notes on exactly where the dirt was?"

"Yeah, we had two sets of fresh footprints in the dirt on the floor under the body and behind the device. No dirt anywhere else. We dusted for prints, of course, and found multiple sets. No telling how old some of them are. We matched one set to Fillion, and it was corroborated by preliminary testing of DNA taken from his body. One other set and some DNA samples seem to be contemporary, so we ran them through the system. No hits yet. Waiting for the FBI to get back to us. This device— what we all assume is the weapon—had only two sets of prints on it, and they were Fillion's and the one I just told you about. No other prints on it. So is it like a laser or something? I've never seen anything like it. I hope this is the only one out there."

Detective Tom Washington was a veteran officer, with two decades of experience, and a decade of military before that. He still sported the shaved Marine-style haircut. A tattoo on his dark forearm looked like a woman's smiling face and a name. Lee couldn't make out the letters but assumed it was a wife or girlfriend. "Let me show you guys another thing we found. We're not sure what it is. It's here somewhere."

While Washington was sifting through piles of baggies, something on the monitor caught Lee's attention. She motioned to Isaac and Cato, and all three headed over to the screen to take a look. "Detective Washington, can you zoom in on that object in the lower right corner?" Lee pointed to what looked like a screenshot from a laptop. There was no mistaking that it was a site on the dark web; the address on the URL bar made that clear, but the angle and height of the monitor made it hard to read the text that followed. The image that *was* clear looked like a logo. A black, white, and lime-green orb, with the stereotypical extraterrestrial head in the center. Blasting the big-eyed cranium were two weapons, guns that looked strangely familiar. Under the orb, in bold letters, were the words Masters of Alien Defense. *Sheesh*, Lee thought, *here we go again. Kill me now!*

Washington zoomed in, but the pixelated images were even less useful. He said, "That's what I was going to show you. We have a whole file on the dark web sites that were on Fillion's laptop. Our cyber guy is going through them. There's the encryption software that we have to use, and it takes time. Funny thing is the victim only accessed them the day before his death but not before, as far as we can tell. The very last thing he saw before his death—or during—was this site you're pointing to."

"Have you heard of this group or seen this logo before?" Cato asked.

"No, this is a new one on us. Usually these groups are just nut cases who meet at Denny's Coffee Shop or someplace similar to compare notes on their 'abductions.'" Washington highlighted the word *abductions* with air quotes, clearly communicating his thoughts on the idea. "I've never heard of a group that has turned to weapons like this . . . or murder. Is that some sort of Ray Gun or something?" he asked. *That's it! Ray Guns. How did you miss that, Lee?*

Isaac started to laugh. "This *is* nuts! It has to be more than a wacky alienophobia organization. There *has* to be a deeper purpose for the maser."

"Well, the question is, where do they get their financing? It takes big money to build or buy a mase . . . unless they tricked Fillion into building this and planned all along to take it from him," Cato said. "That's the most likely scenario right now, I think."

"How in the world would he have come in contact with these people? It's not logical to be a physicist and to fall in with a bunch of . . . what did you call them, Isaac? Alienophobics? Is that even a real thing?" Lee asked. "They must have had something on him to get him to agree. And furthermore, how was he able to work on his maser without someone at the Institute finding out what he was up to?"

"Nobody there would have been complicit in something like this," Isaac pronounced. "I'd like to know more about this web site. I don't deal in the dark web. What was this site that Fillion supposedly looked at?"

"Maybe the murderer or murderers knew Fillion accessed it on the day before he died. They felt they had to get rid of him before Fillion went to the authorities or the Institute. Their timing was just right. They had a working weapon," Lee said. "They must have been keeping really close tabs on him."

"My money's on *that* theory. It makes sense that they duped him into this whole project. He got suspicious and started nosing around. Or maybe someone tipped him off first. I see James Ray doing something like that. We know he's not the murderer. But maybe he heard something about the group and got nervous. As much as he hated Fillion, he probably foresaw the ramifications of a weapon like the maser. He said he tried to warn Fillion. Tom, can we get some printouts on the dark web sites? I don't want to put my laptop at risk. Those encrypted sites can destroy your files—your whole hard drive—if you're not careful," Cato said.

"Sure. We'll keep looking at the alien group. You can do that too. The more the merrier on that one. If you see a blinding light or hear something landing on your roof in the middle of the night, call me. Better yet, take a picture for me." Washington laughed.

"Uh . . . before we leave, we still have one thing to clear up. The dirt. The lab was a Clean Room, so how did the dirt get in?" Isaac asked.

"And do we need special permission from you guys to get into the lab? We have yet to see this new maser up close and personal," Lee added. "And we need to determine if this death could have been accidental, though odds are it was on purpose. The fact that another person—or multiple people—could be involved leads to deliberate murder, especially if this dirt comes from somewhere else. Uh, though hopefully not from Area 51. A joke. Just a joke. Really."

CHAPTER TWENTY-THREE
UNDERGROUND AGAIN

I can't believe this. Underground again. Her descent into the old lab was not unlike the visits she'd paid to PCC's basement. The big difference was how clean the room was. *That's why they call it a "Clean Room," Lee.* Only a small amount of dirt near the worktable belied the name. She could hear the guys chattering behind her. The flickering of the lights—old-school fluorescent tubes that obviously hadn't been included in the energy updates at the Institute—added to the atmosphere. A perfect place for secret experimentation, illicit experimentation.

The whole point of an underground lab was protection. Not for the scientists inside but for the civilians outside. The windowless concrete walls, likely encasing a layer of lead, must be several feet thick, Lee figured. This would have been the place where researchers of the thirties, forties, and later came to work on all things nuclear. She smiled broadly—almost laughed—at the thought that her father would likely have ventured into this room during his tenure here.

"What?" Isaac was looking at her, smiling back. He had

learned not to ask what was going on in her brain, but this was too good to miss. "My father. Picturing him here. Even though he was a theoretical particles man, he would have come down here with his colleagues or his students, I'm sure. He loved this stuff too much."

"Yeah. I get it." Isaac shrugged. "I've never been down here before. Good place to hide something—or someone."

Cato was already examining the maser, snapping pictures, taking his own measurements. "Not that I don't trust the PD. I just think we might be looking for a different set of facts. See the markings on the floor. The cops left those. I'm looking at the angle of the device. It's portable but not easy to swivel. You almost have to pick it up to change the trajectory. It looks like it was aimed at the bottom of the steps. The size of this thing is amazing. So much smaller than the originals."

"The one we worked on at Los Alamos was almost ten times the size. I guess it's like everything else. Miniaturized with small components like today's laptops or cell phones. And this one travels with its own power source. What do you know?"

"That's what makes this one so much more dangerous. It can go anywhere," Cato said. "No wonder Dr. Ray was so worked up about the possibilities."

Fillion's maser was about the size of a blender, excluding the power source—again the portable power unit that ramps up the voltage—and an awkward tripod base designed to steady the whole thing. The components were encased in thick cylindrical glass. Lee carefully detached the power source, which was so similar to the one she had built only a few years ago. Then Isaac flipped the "blender" upright to get a look at the inside. "I guess it's okay to take this thing apart now. The cops don't want it. We could always reassemble it if anyone cares,"

Isaac said. "It's crazy to think that naturally occurring masers in space can be the size of a small galaxy. Even the early prototypes built in labs were exactly what Lee was saying: ten times this size. With lots of individual parts wired together. This one's compact, everything in a neat container. Wait a minute. . . . Do you see any tools around? Pliers maybe? Swiss Army Knife?"

"Ha! You're in luck." Cato pulled a vintage Victorinox Swiss Army Knife out of his back pocket. "Never leave home without it." He was grinning ear to ear as he handed it over. "Have at it, Isaac. Uh . . . careful, don't break it. The knife, I mean."

Isaac gingerly pulled out a large crystal—the heart of the maser, in a sense. "Uh . . . this is probably a diamond. I know that most common crystals, rubies, or sapphires . . . even ammonia . . . are used to focus the beam into a pinpoint. I've never heard of diamond for this purpose. This must be what makes this maser so powerful. I'm not saying it's the Hope Diamond or anything . . . it's certainly industrial grade . . ."

"Isaac! This is your Indiana Jones moment," Cato said. "Hold it up to the light. See if it glows or something. Just kidding." Lee was thinking how alike these two guys were sometimes. And she was thinking Isaac would have to go to that shop in Old Town for his own Indiana Jones hat. Or maybe her Christmas gift list for the guys was all set. "We need to get a gemologist in on this."

"Maybe he could determine the source of the diamond. Uh . . . Isaac, don't hog it. Pass it around," Lee said. She had to admit it was a first for her. Jewelry to go with one of her black Valentinos. She handed it to Cato, who was already snapping more photos. "I think you should hold on to this," she told him.

"Yeah. No problem. Fillion must have been researching

diamonds. We're going to have to check with the PD about his laptop and any other computers he owned. I'm sure the PD confiscated those, though Tom didn't mention it."

"Isaac and I were talking about getting back to Dr. Ray after he recuperates from our visit. He might know something about the diamond. Where one would get this size. What's its advantage in focusing the beam? Or he might crack if he realizes we know about it too," Lee said.

The Crew started a cursory look around. There wasn't much else in the lab other than the maser, some spare parts, and the dirt on the floor. No personal items as far as they could tell. The cops had already removed anything they deemed relevant also. Lee went about taking her own cell phone snapshots—practice, she told herself. She'd learned that looking at the photos on a computer screen has advantages. Not just that the pictures could be enlarged, but the mind's eye sometimes sees things in a new perspective after a few hours or days have passed. Details can take on new importance.

Cato said, "Good job, everyone. I say we meet up tonight at Edwin Mills for a recap and a night cap. Jazz night and the food's pretty good. Six o'clock?"

They had reached the parking lot on California Boulevard, a good ten-minute trek, when Lee realized she had no phone with her. "Uh, guys. I think I left my phone in the lab. I really need to go back for it."

Cato pulled out a key and handed it to her. Same pocket that held the Swiss Army Knife. *What else have you got in there, Cato?* "Here. My spare. I'm heading out."

"Do you want company?" Isaac asked.

"I'm fine. See you in a couple of hours," Lee said. And she *was* fine.

=

Heading back to the old underground lab, Lee couldn't help reflecting on Fillion's death and the creation of the weapon that preceded his untimely demise. The use of the maser could be considered an act of terrorism. What was so compelling that he would have risked everything? What did his parents think when they heard the news? *That's it, Lee. Who talked to the parents?* She wondered, could they be complicit? They ran a worldwide think tank, a well-regarded brain trust. What connection could there be with a group like Masters of Alien Defense? She made a mental note to bring that up with the guys tonight.

It was still daylight out, and yet, when the door slammed behind her, it could have been midnight in the lab. No windows, no other light source. Pitch black. She thought she had noticed blinking smoke detectors during their earlier visit—or maybe not. And the motion-sensing lights above the stairs had not gone on this time. They could be overridden and turned off if experimentation required a really dark room, but she was pretty sure no one had touched them. She reached for her back pocket—that reflex thing people do to pull out a phone—no phone, no flashlight. *Idiot! Finding the light switch, Lee? No problem.* But there was a problem: she felt along the wall, both walls surrounding the stairwell and found two sets of switches. Neither worked. That prickly thing was happening again. The hair on her arms was at attention, and her heart was pounding. She should be used to this fight-or-flight reaction by now. "Get a grip," she said out loud.

A familiar vibrating noise from below made her feel foolish. The phone was there. All she had to do was follow the sound.

The buzzing was louder than usual, amplified because it was sitting on a metal table. Lee was working her way down the stairs, consciously on guard for any loose steps; she could hear the crunchy sound of dirt under her shoes as she approached the bottom. The pulsing glow of her phone each time it buzzed should have given her comfort, but it illuminated enough of the room for her to realize that things had been moved. The maser and the components were scattered around. There wasn't much else in the lab that could be disturbed; it had been sparsely furnished to begin with, and she remembered that there had been no other equipment. The buzzing stopped and so did the glow, but the phone was within reach.

The flashlight app has to be the most valuable—even life-saving—application ever invented. She checked. Plenty of battery life left. Lee was telling herself just to leave. She'd gotten what she came for. But curiosity was winning: as long as she had her flashlight on, she thought she'd take a quick look around. Aside from the traveling maser, which *was* a big deal actually, nothing seemed to be missing. There has to be a logical explanation—other than alien terrorists or anti-alien terrorists. The logical possibilities were that the cops came in right after the Crew left and took a second look or someone from the Institute was looking into getting the maser back up-stairs. *This is ridiculous. The sixties called, and they want their Death Ray back?* Cato had the diamond and plenty of pictures; the cops had fingerprints and DNA, so Lee decided they could all hash it out over drinks tonight. She was feeling better about the lights, or lack of lights too. There could be a mandated nighttime "power down" for some parts of the campus or a genuine power outage.

Armed with her phone, she started back toward the stairs,

images of appetizers and cocktail umbrellas dancing in her head, not unlike the pigs. But friendlier. A noise came from the storeroom at the side of the lab. They had checked earlier and there was nothing in it. It wasn't even locked at that point. "Damn! Wouldn't you know it. I was almost outta here," she heard herself say. Lee set her key down on the table along with her phone, screen facing up and flashlight still on. Out of harm's way, just in case. And just in case, she hit Record.

Investigators, Lee had learned, open suspicious-looking doors a certain way, though anyone who watched *CSI* knows it too: you slam the door open all the way against the wall as hard as you can in case a perp is hiding behind it. All bets are off where aliens are concerned, but she figured she'd give it a try. No one ever mentions, though, that the door could bounce back, hitting you in the face with equal force. But Lee knew. A simple Newton's law of action-reaction. She was prepared to jump back if needed. What she wasn't prepared for was being grabbed by her shirt and yanked into the storeroom. She went flying against shelving that gave way with the impact. The flashlight in the other room offered little illumination at this angle, but it was clear no alien was involved. This was a hulking human. A man, or a really strong woman, had yet to be ascertained, but Lee figured she would find out soon. Whoever or whatever, two hands lifted her up by her waistband and tossed her into another row of shelving. Lee's arms went up to protect her face. She had no intention of coming out of this battle with a broken nose. She also was *not* in the mood for another choking, for that matter. *Time to put your wits to work, Galilea.*

If she couldn't see well, then this perp couldn't either. That was a "pro." This hulking thing was bigger and stronger than she was. That was a "con." She had the power of physics on her side. That was a "pro." Unless the guy or gal was also a physicist. Then all bets were off. This game of logic was going to take too long; Lee had to act. *WWCD? What Would Cato Do? Or Isaac for that matter?* The husky figure wasn't moving. He/she was looking around the small storeroom. Lee was doing the same. No windows or vents. A light switch that probably didn't work. Wooden shelving. Steel shelving. That was about it. *Forget about Cato and Isaac. WWGD. What Would Galilea Do? Right Now?*

Lee backed up until she felt the dislodged wooden shelf behind her. If she could get momentum going, she could wield enough force to knock her assailant off guard with the plank. One of the slatted steel shelves might have been better—lighter to swing—but she had to work with what she had, and besides, the solid mass of the wood might be more effective. She grabbed the shelf and swung full circle with as much force as she could muster. "Keep your eye on the ball," she remembered from PE teachers past. Her father had probably told her something similar when it came to riding a bike, she thought. So she did.

It was a solid hit, though Lee couldn't tell if she had slammed the front or the back of the murky figure. A steadying hand went up against the wall, and Lee thought it looked more female than male and gloveless. She felt empowered by that knowledge—for a minute, until she realized that, in this narrow room, she had to slip past her assailant to get to the exit. The other problem was a steady trickle of blood running down her forehead.

"Two can play at that game," Lee heard from behind as she grabbed the door frame to balance herself. Well, definitely a woman—with a wooden shelf in her hand. Lee ducked, expecting the swing to come high. It hit her squarely in the back, knocking the air out of her. *And probably breaking a rib to boot,* she thought. *Still, it's better than a whack to the head.* As she lay on the ground, reminding herself to take breaths, she could hear her phone vibrating again. Then it stopped. *Damn!* There was no way she could make it to the table. Suddenly, she was alone. She'd fallen in the storeroom doorway, half in and half out. The female goon had taken her phone and headed outside, slamming the lab door behind her.

"Don't let the door hit you on the way out," Lee gasped. Then she heard the sliding of a deadbolt from the outside. *I'm thinking I'm delirious right now. And phoneless. And locked in. Stay awake, Lee. Talk to yourself. Out loud. Okay. Large woman with gloveless hands. That would mean fingerprints. Got her pretty good with the board. Possible injuries. No broken nose for me. My vanity will be intact. If I ever get out of here, I'm going to start working out, though. Then there's that martial arts class I never took.* Lee listened for sounds, any sign, from the outside that there were people around. Nothing. She was in an underground bunker. What would she hear? *Okay, it's crunch time. What else do I know? My phone was on. Someone was trying to get a hold of me. If anyone is looking for me, they might track the phone. That's only a good bet if they're worried. How long have I been here?* Lee made a conscious effort to assign times to every event: *Two minutes to get down the stairs, including searching for light switches. Three minutes looking around with the flashlight. One minute letting her curiosity get the better of her and planning her approach to opening the storeroom door. Seven minutes whacking and getting whacked with lumber. Lying here thinking? No idea how long I've been on the floor. Grand total? Too woozy to add it all up. Oh, the hulking woman had an accent like Julia Child. No, that's nuts. More like . . .*

=

Lee figured she must have been out for a few minutes. The blood on her forehead was still wet. *Where was I? Oh yes. Five minutes, maybe, lying on the floor?* Then she heard it: a sound, coming from far away, as if through a vent. It would be a good thing that the power was out. A fan could obscure any noise coming from outside. She tied her shirt into a knot at the front, trying to create a tight brace around her waist. Her pain was telling her she had been right about the broken rib. The table was only a couple of feet away, and she was able to slither toward it. Getting up was easier than she thought. It was the breathing part that was difficult. Walking along the edge of the metal table, Lee stopped to feel for her key. Not there, of course. A couple of feet and she stopped again to see if she was heading in the direction of the sound. Closer? Definitely closer, but she had run out of table. *Take a short breath, stagger a few feet, wait a few seconds, and start all over again. Another couple of minutes to add to the blasted time frame.*

A few inches above the floor, on the north wall, was a small vent. There was just enough light coming through it for Lee to recognize that it had a filter mechanism in it. *Think, Lee. This would be one of those MacGyver moments.* The whole opening was about the size of a manila envelope. No way to crawl through it, especially with the grate and the purifier in it. And it seemed to be attached to a narrow air duct. No screwdriver, not even a handy Causemetics Mascara wand. If she could dislodge the pump inside, she might be able to get more light and catch someone's attention above ground at the same time. It looked like wire would work. *Don't turn out the lights, remember?* Electrical wire is pliable and strong. This is the don't-try-this-at-home part: Lee was thinking about the nearest light switch. No power. It could be safe to pull the wire out of the receptacle, cut it (still working on that one), and then make a loop to lasso the pump and dislodge it.

Without a screwdriver there was no way to remove the screws holding the vent covering or the switch box on the wall. It would take something heavy to knock it free. Or maybe Lee could make a screwdriver out of something. Considering how much pain she was in, she opted for the second idea. She could tell that the grate over the vent was held with four slotted screws. There were lots of goodies scattered around on the table, but getting there was a struggle. Lee worked her way back to the edge and pulled herself up. With almost no light, she had to rely on her sight memory. She did have a good eye for details: what to grab first? The transformer that powered the maser had plugs sticking out, a larger flat one, a smaller flat one, and a round one, just like on most power cords. If only there had been a cord, that would have saved her a lot of time looking for wire. *First things first, Lee.* She yanked the transformer loose and headed back to the vent. The going was easier and faster now. Lying on the floor, Lee used one of the flat plugs to loosen the screws. As usual, it's always the last one that won't turn, but at this point, all Lee had to do was jiggle the vent cover loose.

Lee could tell that there was enough space to fit a wire noose around the fan. Now the other part of the plan—the one *not* to try at home. She made her way back to the storeroom with her makeshift screwdriver in hand and, feeling along the wall, quickly removed the two screws holding the light switch in place. Just to be sure, she flipped the switch about a dozen times. No power. Then she yanked on the wires attached to the switch until she had pulled out about two feet. The old copper wiring, much like that in her condo, was thick and stiff: two useful attributes for her plan. Lee bent the wires back and forth repeatedly until they snapped. No cutting needed. Considering how painful it was to travel the distance to the storeroom, she stopped to take stock of what else she would need for her trip back to the air vent. Much to her relief and her annoyance, she was beginning to get acclimated to the dark; while removing the vent cover helped provide some light, she thought she must be morphing into a rat or a bat. And being familiar with the feel of the electrical components didn't hurt either.

She grabbed the wood plank that had caused her so much grief and dragged it back to the vent opening. Plan B—just in case. As she suspected, the wire loop went in and curled around the fan like clockwork. What she soon found out was how hard it is to budge something like that when one has a broken rib. No amount of yanking worked. Plan B to the rescue: Lee wedged one end of the plank into the bottom of the vent opening. Then she tied the loose ends of the copper loop around the upper end of the wood. Picture a crowbar (sort of). *A Class II lever. This'll make a good lesson for Basic Physics—if I ever get out of here.* Just to prove her point, she gingerly sat on the upper end of the board. The extra weight meant she didn't have to struggle to pry the fan loose. Her body did the work nicely, and the fan plopped out onto the floor. *Let there be light!*

It was definitely easier to see with the addition of a little light, but the gloom of her situation almost brought Lee to tears. That and the searing pain. At the moment she couldn't even muster the strength to yell into the air duct. She slid down along the wall into a sitting position and then decided she needed to just close her eyes. *What's a few more minutes in the time frame?*

=

What a waste, she thought. "What the . . ." she mumbled, water dribbling down her chin and soaking into her shirt. "Where's my watch?"

"Hey, take it easy. Stay still, we've got EMTs coming for you."

"Am I dead? I liked that ME from Pasadena—the woman."

"No. Not ME. I said EMT, Lee." She recognized that voice.

"Is that you, Isaac?" With the fluorescent lighting now working, he looked like he was wearing a halo.

"Yes. Cato's here too. He's upstairs waiting for them." He placed his hand on her forehead. "Lie still. You're a mess. Geez, you scared us. We thought you were . . . well . . . we'll talk about it later."

"I don't think I've ever heard you say 'geez.'" She tried to laugh, but a groan came out. "Ribs. Head."

"I can see." Just then a commotion outside the door and then a clatter down the stairs interrupted their conversation.

"She's semi-alert, Cato," Isaac whispered.

"Hey, I'm right here and pretty alert, if you ask me," Lee whispered back.

Cato whispered, "Why are we whispering?"

Just then there were hands all over her, checking vitals, wrapping a very unstylish collar around her neck, poking until they got to the broken rib. And a very painful lift onto a stretcher.

"I wish I were unconscious for this part. How are you going to get me upstairs, guys?"

"That's our job, ma'am," one of them said.

Watch who you're calling ma'am. Did I just say that out loud?

There was discussion about how to maneuver the steep stairs, and Cato had to get in the middle of it with his physics calculations, but it all went off without a hitch. The fresh air felt cold on Lee's skin, but she relished feeling anything at all. The trip to Huntington Hospital was quiet. No siren. No one spoke. And Isaac sat beside her all the way.

CHAPTER TWENTY-FOUR
SO, WHO *DID* KILL J. R.?

Dr. Mary Ray, PhD, was arrested by Detective Tom Washington that same night. Using Lee's cell phone signals, he had tracked her to the meeting place of Masters of Alien Defense, in a church basement on Hollister Avenue. She gave up peacefully, and the cops were glad it went that way; she was a "bruiser" of a woman. When they booked her, she still had Cato's key to the old laboratory; they took it with no promise that Cato would ever get it back. He was fine with giving it up, considering what had happened in the underground storeroom.

Lee did have a concussion and a broken rib, and a new collection of bruises.

"You've got to stop making a habit of this," Cato told her when he got to the hospital. Isaac said nothing.

"No promises, Cato, as long as there are wacky cults out there," she replied, offering a slightly sedated smile.

"Actually, that's the thing. In this case the alien defense thing was just a cover-up. The group pretended to form for the purpose of defending the world against nefarious extra-terrestrials, but they were actually part of a cabal that was planning domination of the Arctic Territories. They wanted the maser prototype to sell to a mercenary group of domestic terrorists who would supposedly safeguard America's rights to every natural resource, along with the strategic right to build military bases there. But they were looking to benefit from the riches and dominate militarily—to threaten other countries, not safeguard."

"That's not so farfetched, actually; it's becoming a sought-after frontier already, though I don't agree with their tactics if they're going to kill and maim people," Lee said. She was trying unsuccessfully to sit up, deeming lying in a hospital bed a sign of weakness. Especially since she had come out on the losing side of the battle tonight.

Isaac said, "What are you doing? You have a concussion. If you don't lie still, you'll get nauseous—or worse."

Lee thought the indignity of vomiting *would* be worse than the pain she now felt. "I know. I know. I'm wondering what anybody found out about the hulking woman who got the better of me. Please tell me she had superhuman powers."

Cato was paraphrasing a text he'd just gotten from Washington: "Tom says the woman weighs two-hundred pounds, so no surprise she beat the crap out of you. Get this—she's James Ray's wife! She's part of this cabal. James Ray was leery of the whole idea and pulled out of the group. They both had been part of the Fillion Think Tank and apparently got swayed by a few fanatic geniuses. The brain trust started spiraling down-ward, and the Fillions kicked them all out. Says he doesn't know yet how Jay Fillion got involved or recruited—or mur-dered. More on that tomorrow."

"Huh. What do you know? What is it about geniuses that makes them so vulnerable to real-world conspirators?" Isaac asked.

"You talkin' at me?" Cato said with a really bad Brooklyn accent. Just then his phone vibrated. "Another text from Tom. He'd like to come see you tomorrow morning, Lee. Get your statement. He'll probably give you your phone back. There's no evidence other than Mary Ray's fingerprints on it, so he'll give the go-ahead to release it."

"Hmm. By the way, her whole palm print is on the side wall of the storeroom if they want it. That's where I whacked her." Lee smiled at the thought. "Closing my eyes now," she whispered.

=

The next day is always the worst. Lee could barely sit up, but she wanted to get back home, to her own migrating bed. Hopefully, it hadn't moved too far westward while she was gone. Tom Washington got to the hospital early. He handed her the cell phone with an evidence tag taped on the back and fingerprint powder still stuck in the grooves, and he proceeded to update her on the case. It was pretty much what Cato had already said, with the additional news that Mary Ray had confessed to killing J. R. Fillion accidentally. She'd also caused James Ray's broken leg when the two were fighting passionately about the whole cabal thing. She had pushed him down the front steps of their home, and, not knowing her own strength . . . the rest is history. Tom called her a one-woman wrecking crew.

"I don't feel so bad about getting beaten up now. She had a lot of practice as a bully," Lee said. "So how did she actually kill Fillion? And why was she hiding at the crime scene?"

"She didn't actually know much about how the maser worked. She followed Fillion into the lab and confronted him with a do-it-or-else proposition: give her the maser, or she'd see to it that he would probably end up dead. The 'probably' part was because members of her cabal were falling by the wayside and she didn't know who was left who'd be capable of murder. Turns out, she was."

"How *does* an accident like that happen?"

Just then Cato and Isaac filed into the room. They had bagels and coffee. Isaac handed Lee her favorite: Caramel Macchiato, light on the caramel dribble, heavy on the foam. "The foam dissolved on the way over, and this is a single espresso. You probably don't want a double today if you're on painkillers, I imagine," he said.

He was right. She planned to do a lot of sleeping if she ever got home. "This is perfect. So Tom is filling me in. Looks like Mary Ray is the murderer, and she gave her husband the broken leg. I guess I'm lucky."

Cato asked, "What happens with the whole group, the Masters of Alien Defense? Ha! Just got it! MAD!"

Washington filled in the rest of the gaps. "They've all been rounded up. They had amassed a fortune from poor unsuspecting dupes. They were going to fund more masers. The bulk of the money would go toward procuring those industrial diamond crystals. Speaking of which, Cato, where's the prototype diamond?"

Cato feigned innocence with a shrug. "Gee, Tom, I had it here somewhere. Oh yeah. It's at home in my safe. Can I drop it by the department tomorrow? Not to change the subject or anything, but do we know anything about the dirt that showed up on Fillion's hands? That's still out of place in a lab setting."

"And I'm still curious how this whole thing happened at the Institute without their knowing," Isaac said.

"And I'm curious when I can get out of here. I'm planning on that happy hour at Edwin Mills—or anywhere for that matter. And soon. I think I've earned it," Lee added.

Breakfast came for Lee. She was glad that she'd already eaten two bagels; the cuisine at the Huntington is decent for hospital food, but it didn't compare to Starbuck's fare delivered by her two favorite people. Tom continued with his wrap-up, reading from his phone as he went: "Just got more forensics. Traces of carbon, among other things, were mixed in with the dirt. The lab can't pinpoint why. It's not the naturally occurring kind, they say. The dirt itself was likely tracked in by Mary Fillion. They'll keep working on that. Could be something as simple as dirt from her backyard, or maybe she was hiding in the bushes at Caltech. Oh . . . more here. . . . Let's see. The Institute states categorically that they knew nothing of Fillion's plans and is taking immediate steps to recoup their expenses. The old lab is closed for good. The Prosecutor's Office is supporting the In-stitute; Fillion's records and resumé were masterfully falsified. They suspect someone in this group did it."

"What happens to the Fillion Think Tank?" Isaac asked.

"Don't know, but they're probably pretty embarrassed," Cato said.

"I don't have an answer for you, Miss Roberts. I don't know when you're getting sprung from this place, but no happy hours while you're on those painkillers. Okay? And be sure to let me know when you head over to Edwin Mills. I could go for some good jazz."

"Absolutely, Tom." Lee smiled at the idea that their Crew might have a new sometimes-partner.

"Well, I need to ask you a few questions—officially—so the guys have gotta go for now."

"Let me know if you need a ride home," Isaac said on his way out. "Really."

Tom set his phone down, ready to record, but he also pulled out an old-school notepad and pencil. "So, off the record, you are in an unusual situation. You were an unofficial investigator on the case, but you will also be considered a percipient witness, should we go to court. If we *do* go to court, that could be some time next year. Just letting you know. Now, please state your full name, age, and occupation for the record."

"Galilea Roberts. Thirty-two. Physics professor at Pasadena City College."

"Uh . . . beautiful name. Off the record, why don't you use it more often?"

"Hmm. I think Lee sounds more powerful, professional. Maybe also, I have always tried to shed the trappings of childhood. I don't know."

"Okay. Back on the record: What involvement did you have in this case prior to the assault last night?"

"I was consulting with Cato Klein and Isaac Sades on the physics aspects of the case. The maser and its components."

"Okay," Washington said. "Now can you tell me from the beginning what happened in the laboratory last night? Be as specific as you can."

"The specific part's no problem. I always make a point of noticing details—unless I'm unconscious." Lee recounted the whole assault, including Newton's law of action-reaction and the Class II lever. That was probably more information than Tom Washington was looking for, but he took it all in stride.

"Thank you, Miss Roberts. We'll need to follow up with

you again in a couple of days. Will you be able to make it to the PD? And off the record again, you're pretty gutsy. I know you're curious about how Fillion actually got cooked, so we should be able to share that with you. You've earned that. See you midweek, Galilea." Tom was a big guy. Reassuring. Really likeable, so she didn't mind the reference—this time.

Lee wondered how he managed to get her thinking about her childhood, off or on the record. It's possible that she had misunderstood her father. While her mother was an open book, Alexander had probably been trying to prepare her in his own way, not necessarily to follow in *his* footsteps, but to make something of her steely self. His genius, and later his dementia, may have contributed in some way to forming a bond that was indelible but hard to fathom all at the same time. In any case, she could see a nurse heading her way with a file folder. *Please be my walking papers!*

=

Edwin Mills had that Old Pasadena vibe, and it came by it naturally. It was in a historic part of town and in a historic brick block of buildings that harkened back to the 1850s. The bar/restaurant had once been horse stables, and later an assembly point for Model T Fords. In the twenties it had the honor of serving as an after-hours joint for a Hollywood crowd that came in looking for the opium den that was accessed by tunnels under the building. Tonight, the Crew was celebrating a successful end to the maser caper. It seemed fitting that the mysterious nature of the now-bustling place was their spot for the night.

"Let's all agree that Lee earns the gold star on this one, though I think we should always work in pairs from this point on. No offense, Lee," Cato said, hoisting a craft beer in the air. She was happy to be off pain meds so she could imbibe, but she was also conscious of how sore she still was. Lifting her own lager into the air was a case in point.

"No offense taken. I did get some new info from Tom today. Apparently, Mary Ray was fighting with Fillion when the death occurred. He wasn't prepared for how strong she was when he tried to wrestle the maser out of her grip. She wanted to take it with her, and he wanted to know why. He had accessed some papers on her so-called alien group and gotten suspicious. He thought he had been doing real research based on the number of Fillion Think Tank members who had signed on to support her. After James Ray warned him, he started looking into the whole thing. So anyway, a struggle ensued, and she whipped the maser around and fired at Fillion. The weight of the thing would preclude most people from being able to do that, but . . . well . . . you've seen her. And by the way, Tom said we owe him a visit to this place when they're playing jazz. He's a jazz fan, remember?"

"So the only loose end is where the carbon came from that was mixed in with the dirt. I guess we'll never know since the rest of the case is now settled. Do you have to appear in court as a witness?" Isaac asked.

"Don't know yet. It'll be months, maybe a year, if it happens. Yeah, the carbon thing . . . Tom said there are always a few loose ends in every case and not to worry." Food came and more beer. Then Lee said, "And, guys, thank you for rescuing me—though I'll have to kill you if you repeat that."

CHAPTER TWENTY-FIVE
RIDER'S RETREAT

The expansive oak trees were the first thing Lee noticed as she turned in to the narrow driveway off Edison. They obscured the cottage and much of the nearby stable. When the light trickled through the leaves, it was as if they were on fire—not Aphrodite/Mary red hair fire—more of a reassuring golden glow. Luminosity. That was the word. The driveway took her into an even narrower car port, where she could barely open the driver's side door, and she knew there was no chance of getting her overnight tote out of the back seat. Pulling forward a little brought her into the sunlight again and face-to-face with the presumed owner of the property.

"Weather's good. No need to park under the shed. Leave it there. Want help with your bags?" *Pecos Bill himself. Or better yet, a grizzled Robert Redford.*

"Thanks. I'm good. Just a small bag—two night's worth. Uh . . . are you *WebRenter* number 131515? I'm Lee. Love the place already. Nice to meet you." She extended a hand through the window but was really thinking she just wanted to get out of the car and head inside—no fanfare.

"Okay, Lee. The key's right inside the door on the hook. Let me know if you need anything else. Oh . . . and firewood's out back. Enjoy your stay. Uh . . . you expecting any company?"

That's not a good sign, dude. How do I play this? "Not sure yet. I didn't catch your name. Or do I call you Number 131515?" No smile. He didn't get it, apparently.

"Call me Ezekiel." *Oy, another biblical name. Can't be! Chill, Lee. Get over it!*

She had picked this place because it promised sol-i-tude, not nose-y dude. In fact, counter to her once life-long philosophy of no mulling—better yet, no mindfulness—Lee had been planning a weekend of mental regrouping, an opportunity to clarify where she was going from this point. She didn't need company. She just wanted to give Santa Ynez another chance to charm her. Her past experiences here were anything but charming, and she still had the emotional bruises to prove it. But she was not one to let things lie. She always figured she should have the last word—even if that meant a two-and-a-half-hour drive to do it.

The cottage was nice enough. In fact, it looked roomier than the Instagram photos. Probably a good place to commune with nature and plot a course for the near future. Lee hoped to see both Santa Ynez and herself in a new light. The drive up the coast had been an opportunity to set out some mental bullet points: What about her job at PCC and the forensic investigator thing? What about that slot at Caltech now that Fillion was gone? What about Cato and Isaac? All good questions; she should be able to resolve them in the next couple of days. For now, a walk around the ranch would be in order.

Lee pulled some suede cowboy boots out of her tote bag. She had only worn them a few times, so they still looked like new. The "curated collection" from Zappos. When she stepped outside, she knew immediately why she had brought them. The sound of horses—and the accompanying odor—served to remind her that she was nothing if not a city girl at heart. But that's what Santa Ynez had to offer: a chance to be someone else for a weekend.

The boots served her well, but they would never be the same again. The five-acre property surrounding the cottage sheltered rescues of all colors and sizes, along with privately owned horses, all waiting to be fed or trained or cured of something. The city girl grabbed some hay from the barn and made the rounds, gingerly holding the fodder in an open palm. It was a tentative offering at first, but before long Lee was feeling pretty good about not losing any fingers. A power walk around the property would set her up for an afternoon glass of local wine and a nap. The trick was to avoid stepping in piles of manure, which were, she told herself, nothing more than hay in the end. Literally, in the end.

Lee liked the fact that most of her neighbors were horses, with a couple of dogs thrown in. They had nothing intelligible to say and didn't care what she was thinking at the moment. No judgment on anybody's part. Maybe when they got to know her better . . .

Lee's first move when she got back to the cottage was to pour a glass of chardonnay, courtesy of the winery that sat just across the highway. The simple kitchen was stocked with an assortment of complimentary wines of every color and variety; some appeared to be pretty decent vintages. Brochures advertising tours and tastings were fanned out across the dining table, along with coasters and napkins adorned with grape leaves: a sure sign that someone other than Pecos Bill had staged the place. She didn't mind. Outside on the patio were more coasters and napkins on a redwood table and something that made the whole trip worthwhile: Samba, as advertised. At least she looked like the horse from the website, offering up her own equine testimonial. This was an up-close-and-personal encounter.

"Well, Samba, maybe I can run all my thoughts by you, just to see what you think. Nod if you agree—or do that hoof-on-the-ground thing you always see in the movies. One if you agree, two if you don't." *Can't believe you're talking to a horse, Lee. Get real.* In a moment of uncharacteristic embarrassment, she looked around. No one listening in, as far as she knew, but then again, she imagined everyone talked to their horses up here. "What do you and Pecos Bill talk about, my friend?" No answer from her brown-and-white neighbor.

=

It could have been the glass of wine or the sounds of nature—and no traffic anywhere nearby—but Lee's nap was deep and long. It was dreamless, almost comatose: just what she needed. The sky was darkening, and the radiant oak trees were becoming black silhouettes. She poured another glass of wine and set up her laptop at the kitchen table. Time to create some sort of brainstorming pros and cons list:

Unresolved Issues—and I've Got Plenty

1. Stay at PCC

Pros	Cons
Okay money and some benefits	Could I make more just doing forensics? *
Almost no academic pressure	Could I make more at Caltech? **
I have Cato's plans & equipment even if there's no way of knowing how legal they are	Cato's not on campus
Students (even Mr. Jacobs)	Students
The basement	The basement
No atomic weapons	No atomic research
?	?

* I'd have to get my you-know-what in gear to get the training I need.

** Maybe now they'd actually hire me—or not. Who says they'd actually want me there after the maser thing?

This is looking like a wash. Move on, Lee.

2. Just pursue forensics

Pros	Cons
The Neoprene bodysuits are flattering	Your hair could catch on fire
Isaac seems like a different guy when on a case	Isaac's sister Kat
Cato seems like a different guy when on a case	You could get your brains poached
It's nice to belong to a club—even if it's just the Blue Öyster Crew	I'll need more white socks, and my hair could catch on fire, and my brains could get poached
More chance to catch up to the Grand Pooh–bah, aka Zin	All of the above plus getting blown up
Dinners with Cato and Isaac	No downside here

Well, maybe I'll run this next one by Samba in the morning.

3. Isaac–CONFIDENTIAL.

Pros	Cons
Too nice	Too nice
Not bad looking, especially in Neoprene	Even better in his boxer shorts (Figure out why this is a Con)
A connec	

A horse whinnied somewhere nearby, and Lee's wine glass went flying off the table. A kind of elbow-jerk reflex action. The glass was intact, but the wine splattered, along with the peaceful aura. *Time to get some food, Lee. You're definitely not thinking clearly.* She dug through a stack of order-out menus and found one that promised quick delivery. Pronto Brothers' Barn. The emphasis seemed to be on slabs of beef and pork smothered in secret "atomic" barbeque sauce—an omen maybe, and she was in the mood for something self-indulgent. A long walk tomorrow through the wineries lined up across the highway should burn off a few calories.

While she waited for the delivery, Lee wiped up the mess, mourned the wasted wine, and stepped out back to check on Samba. She seemed distant in the dark of night and asleep as well.

"How you guys sleep standing up is beyond me. See you tomorrow, Samba," she whispered. *Talking to a horse? This is downright creepy, Lee. Snap out of it!*

"And they sleep with their eyes open too." A voice in the darkness: familiar and a little foreboding. *Please be my imagination.* She turned to see Pecos Bill peering over the fence. The name Ezekiel was still a little discomforting to her, having run the gamut of biblical names when wrapping up the BARF/ZUMBA cult case. Zin's family tree did read like a bible—despite the family business. Even in the dark, Lee noticed that Ezekiel had an unsettling way of looking at her. Maybe it was the slightly torqued smile, as if he were missing teeth or had had a stroke. The interplay between his pale leather skin and graying blond mop of hair was shocking when seen up close—a ghostly image. So he was definitely more Pecos Bill than Robert Redford.

"Uh, hi. Didn't see you there." *Stay cool, Lee. Time for your dispassionate vibe.* "Just waiting for a delivery. Dinner. Have a good night, Pe . . . uh . . . Ezekiel."

"Have a good night, Lee . . ."

But she had already slammed the screen door shut—and the solid wood door behind that and the deadbolt. Lee busied herself setting a table for one. Still no food. A sense of calm was slowly returning, but she decided that letting someone know where she was would be a good idea.

> Hey Isaac. Just letting you know I'm out of town for a couple of days. Santa Ynez. Yes. Crazy I know. Doing nothing—lazing around at Rider's Retreat. Sooo not me! But lots of wine here.

The "send" chime on her phone and the front door chime were almost simultaneous, and so was the flinch. *Sheesh. Get a grip, Lee.* On tiptoe she could see through the small curtained window. The moon had risen. The metal rooftop of the barn was shining silver, like the moon had melted onto it, and a skinny kid with "PB Barn—Home of the Atomic Sauce" emblazoned on his T-shirt was standing a few feet from the door but looking off in that direction.

"Miss Roberts? I have your order. Thought I heard someone in that barn. Probably a horse or something. Sounds travel at night here. It's all paid for by credit card, so enjoy." It's clear he was looking for a tip, and Lee didn't disappoint. As she closed the door, her phone buzzed. *Good timing, Isaac.* Just then the image of him diving through the electrified fence in his black wetsuit flashed through her head, and for a moment she felt foolish—but just for a moment.

> Glad to see you are relaxing. Don't fall off a horse or something. And watch out for cult followers. I hear they are everywhere. Ha Ha.

If you only knew, Isaac.

> Gee, thanks. Be back in a few days. Any wines you like?

> Nothing special. Be careful. Let me know if you need anything. You know the pass‑word. Ha!

> Gonna eat now.

She *did* know the password. What had started out as a joke at the Raymond dinner table became an indelible bond.

A red wine—a new California Malbec—worked well with the half slab of ribs. The corn on the cob was charred beyond recognition, but that's what made it so good, and the barbeque sauce lived up to its reputation. Spicy and out of this world, as far as Lee was concerned. The plan was to put leftovers in the fridge for the next night; the monkey wrench was that she devoured the whole meal at one sitting. More than just a fresh air thing, she thought. Maybe a little release of demons too. She was regretting not ordering dessert from this place.

Tomorrow's another eating day, right? And the pros and cons thing can wait too.

At another time and place, she would have grabbed a jacket and set out through the dark for a head-clearing walk. Something told her this was not the night for that. Besides, she had always wanted to try her hand at starting a fire in a real wood-burning fireplace. This *was* the time and place for that, she decided. Someone had left a couple of logs on the hearth, which meant she didn't even have to search for the wood pile "out back." And there was a starter too—one of those Bic things. Was that cheating? *Dummy! You're in luck!*

It was a battle royale—another one of those expressions whose origin escaped her—but Lee prevailed, and wads of lit paper brochures and napkins didn't hurt either. Paltry, but it was a legit fire. The air inside soon grew smoky, even with the flue open, so she set to work raising windows where she could, which defeated the purpose of the warming fire.

How's this supposed to work, Lee? She didn't even have a good answer for her own snark. A knock on the door. Clearly not Samba, and the kid from the restaurant was probably already spending his tip somewhere. That left Pecos. She grabbed the fireplace poker—such a cliché—and set it by the door.

It was the old guy himself. "Ma'am, need help? I noticed there's a lot of smoke. Not normal." *It's his place*, she realized. *He has a right to see that it doesn't burn down.* Reluctantly, she opened the door. Now he was standing between her and the fire poker. She was glad she had already unlocked the back door for fresh air and contemplated how long it would take her to get to it. The old cheerleader calculation popped into her mind. Whose head would land first? she wondered. As he entered the place, mucky boots and all—*a cowboy's work is never done*, she thought—Lee noticed how much taller and bulkier he really was, especially with the cowboy hat on. "It might be something's caught in the flue. Or maybe the wood's damp." Notions that made sense but wouldn't have occurred to her.

"Uh, sorry. Really sorry. I guess I didn't check." Lee could see the security deposit evaporating before her eyes. Eyes that were still focused on the poker at the front door. And she spotted a piece of wood that had yet to be put in the fireplace. Maybe good for whacking a hulking assailant if needed.

"Happens to everyone. It'll air out pretty quickly." He knelt over the ashen mess, nearly tipping his hat into the faltering embers. "Yeah. It looks like the wood was damp. I'll have to talk to my ranch hand. He should've known better."

It was then that Lee's blood went cold—icy cold. On the back of the guy's neck was a quarter-sized tattoo. Round, with letters rotating along the circumference. Even through the adrenaline rush and the smoke she could recognize them: SO-SOSO.

Shit, Lee. What have you gotten yourself into? What were you thinking coming up here? She felt for her phone. It was in her back pocket but probably useless, even if she could pause this moment to type in "Blue Öyster. Now!" Instead she edged toward the front door and the oh-so-cliché poker.

"You alright, Lee? You look a little peaked." She turned to face him, aware that she must have looked like she was going to pass out—that's how she felt anyway, sweat dripping down the inside of her shirt. Visions of her recent underground battle flashed in her head and spasmed in her ribcage. He was inching toward her as if to catch her should she faint. Or maybe to get a better look at her. Or who knows. "Really. It's okay. No harm done." Both palms open in a "no worries" gesture. She was within grabbing distance of the poker, striking distance of Pecos, and was fairly confident of her reflexes even as she felt perspiration prickle on her scalp. Could she afford to trust him?

"Um. I'm . . ." Just then her pocket began to vibrate. Saved by the cell. Or only a momentary reprieve from something perverse? She motioned with her pointer finger—that *just a moment* sign every mother and teacher knows. Fortunately, the ghostly cowboy was still a little unsure about whether Lee was going to take a header right then and there. He stopped in his tracks while she extricated her phone from her back pocket. It was Isaac. He had texted again, but she felt like she could get away with calling his number and Pecos would be none the wiser. She clicked on the call icon. It was only a second before he answered. Lee was making a concerted effort to steady her voice, but the inflection gave it away. She had overcompensated, sounding like the teens do when they upspeak—that annoying upswing at the end of every sentence.

"So . . . um . . . hi. You know that phrase we like to use? The Öyster one? Uh . . . yeah. I was just thinking of texting you." She wasn't sure if Isaac was understanding. Frankly, she wasn't sure what he was saying to her either, but she needed to keep going. "I'm here in my guest house . . . with the owner of the property. Ezekiel. Yes. It is late. He came to help with a fire. No. A fire *in* the fireplace. But he . . . I'll ask." Lee was pretty sure she was no good at this code talk and also pretty sure that Isaac was getting the message anyway, so she forged ahead. "Ah, Ezekiel, what's your last name if you don't mind? My friend is a little protective." She held the phone out and he obliged. *Okay, everyone, keep your cool!*

Pecos offered up, "Ezekiel Shara. Your lady's okay. Just a little smoky." He laughed as if there was a joke hiding somewhere in there. "I'm leaving now. Night, all." Lee had gone deaf after "Shara." Actually, her ears were ringing at this point, but Pecos had already hightailed it out the door with a tip of his hat. *Now there's a cliché if ever there was one*, she would have told herself if she could.

"Don't hang up!" she yelled into the phone and dropped it on the kitchen table. In a matter of seconds—not minutes—Lee had locked and bolted everything and returned to Isaac's call, fireplace poker in hand. "Shit! I don't believe it! Shara! Did you hear that? Like Ishara." She was hoping he felt the same urgency.

He did. "Want me to come up and get you? Can you just pack up and leave? Do you have something to protect yourself?" she heard him say.

"No, no, and a fireplace poker. Yes. Just like in the movies. Believe me, I was prepared to use it, but I don't think he knows who I am, or our relationship with Zin and his crazies. And yes, he's definitely one of them. He had a tattoo. The mandala with the SOS. The Shara thing is too much of a coincidence too. Agreed?" She was sounding crazed herself, but her heart rate was slowing and the ringing in her ears had stopped. As for the sweat, she would live with it. No showers tonight. The *Psycho* shower scene lives in every woman.

=

It was agreed, before she hung up the phone, that Isaac would come up early the next morning. Lee had to admit she wanted that. If only she could sleep tonight. She packed up and set her tote by the door in case she had to *vamoose*. The cowboy lingo was growing on her. After checking every door and window twice—and choosing not to think about the fact that Pecos had keys to the place—Lee plugged in the phone charger by her bed and crawled under the covers with her clothes on. A hall light was just annoying enough to keep her from falling asleep but a necessity tonight. Her sweaty clothes—duds—gave her chills until the layer of quilts warmed her up. And the smoky smell in her nostrils conspired to further agitate her. It was a certainty that this would be a bad night. For hours, every sound caused her arm hairs to stand on end, and every time she turned over, her heart rushed. Maybe this was better than dreaming, especially the recurring pig dreams—or tonight, cowboy hat dreams.

At some point in the early morning she must have fallen asleep; the last thing Lee remembered was a little light peeking through the gauzy filter of the fog, and later, the knocking on the door. Isaac's voice. And there he was, coffee and bagels in hand. A vision to be sure.

They sat in the kitchen, at first silent. Then the words tumbled out. Lee was recounting everything she could think of, and Isaac was listening patiently. The smell of ash hung in the air, and Lee was sure her own sweat was mingling with it. Isaac picked up his phone to look up the name "Ezekiel Shara" and finally called Cato to see what he could find out. The appeal of a hot shower was too much, and Lee begged off a second bagel in order to wash the acrid smell out of her hair and change her clothes.

=

Lee had to admit it was kind of nice sitting across from Isaac. They talked over the possibilities for future employment at the

Institute and whether it was even a good move, in light of her newfound interest in forensics. He didn't seem to mind her straggly wet hair and wrinkled T-shirt, even as he was dressed like someone out of a Ralph Lauren ad—Country Style 2020. He needed one of those hats too. Which reminded her of that wretched tattoo on Ezekiel's neck. Which reminded her of the nightmarish encounter. Which reminded her of the mare—the one out back. And so on . . .

"Isaac, are you waiting to hear from Cato? In the meantime, step outside with me. There's someone I want you to meet." She pulled on her boots, noting that Isaac had on an old pair of loafers. Perfect. "Meet Samba. She's good to talk to. She hasn't answered back yet, but I can only take so much magic anyway." As she was speaking, she was also glancing around, on the lookout for Pecos Bill or a legion of tattooed minions who might file out of the barns and outbuildings. All quiet on the front. So far. Samba was there in a flash, looking for a hay-ish treat. "What do you think, Isaac? Pretty girl. Right?"

Isaac seemed stumped. How to answer that. Both girls were pretty. "Uh . . . yes. Definitely. What do you say we pack up and head to some tastings? It's wine time somewhere in the world. We could grab an early lunch after. I'll phone Cato from the road. We'll have to caravan since we've got two cars." Lee could see he was on the lookout too. He'd only heard about Ezekiel but didn't have a clue what he looked like. And if past is prologue, Ezekiel would be nearby.

"Sure. I'll leave the key to this place on the table and a note explaining . . . uh . . . something about why I'm checking out early. I've already paid, though I think the security deposit is a goner if he needs to get the smoke out of the curtains. I'm packed. Let me grab a couple of things and I'll be right out."

Isaac was already out front—with Ezekiel—when Lee closed the front door behind her. It looked like a friendly conversation. At least that's what she hoped. She just wanted to get out without broaching the subject of cults in general or one in particular. She was resigned to the fact that this was once BARF/ZUMBA territory and there was nothing she could do about it. As she tossed her bag into the car, she caught the drift of the conversation and chose to keep her distance from the two men as they talked.

Isaac: "About the incident at that compound?"

Ezekiel: "Yeah. The leader was an okay guy. Never bothered no one. You know . . . (something, something) . . . knew his family . . . (something, something) . . . did you know about it?"

Isaac: ". . . (something, something) . . . read about it too . . . (something, something) . . . to take her away so abruptly. A thing at work . . . (something, something)."

Ezekiel: "You two . . . (something, something) . . ."

Isaac: "Maybe . . . (something, something) . . ."

Damn! This is where I could have used lip-reading skills—if I had them. Make a note to learn lip reading, Lee said to herself.

Isaac hopped in his car, and the old grizz-ler stepped aside as he started it up. Lee revved her engine and rolled down her window. "Key's on the table. Thanks."

"Thanks for comin'. Come back sometime and bring your friend. We could talk more. Tell him the leader's still around, by the way." *I did not just hear that.* Lee nearly rear-ended Isaac as they approached the exit gate for Rider's Retreat. She could see him look into his rearview mirror. Her expression spoke volumes, she was sure. It was that wide-eyed thing she always tried to avoid—so cloying.

The car phone rang. "You okay?"

"Yeah. Fine. How about lunch at *Sides?* Plug it in your Nav. See you there."

GLOSSARY OF
SCIENTIFIC TERMS

(IN ORDER OF APPEARANCE)

Richard Feynman—An American physicist who worked at Caltech from the fifties to the eighties. He lived near the campus and was known for livening up any party. After seeing it firsthand, he made a famous speech warning his fellow Americans about the destructive properties of The Bomb.

Matter—Stuff. The material that makes up something. Mass, by the way, is the amount of matter in something. Like the mass of a pig is the amount of pig in the pig.

Radioactivity—Refers to radiation that is being active, as in certain kinds of matter actively emitting rays. This runs the gamut from X-rays at the dentist's office to the atomic bomb, only with The Bomb you don't get a lollipop.

Half-life—The amount of time it takes for radioactive atoms to decrease to half (obviously) of their original mass as they disintegrate. Why do we care? It represents the rate of decay and can therefore be used to identify a particular substance or to date ancient organic things like teeth or bones, but not an ax blade. Do you know why?

Uranium—Probably the most famous—or infamous—radioactive substance. It can be found in nature in relatively large quantities. Its half-life is 703,800,000 years (no kidding), so it obviously has been around awhile.

Geiger counter—It's named after a guy named Geiger and measures how radioactive a substance is. You can actually buy one on Amazon! I wouldn't pull it out of your purse in a nice restaurant though.

Radium chloride—A combination of, you guessed it, radium and chlorine. It was what Marie Curie used in her radiation experiments. It ultimately killed her, since the radium part was lethal and could cause cancer. Strangely enough, even though it caused cancer, it was once used to treat cancer. Go figure! The American Chemistry Council even named it "Chlorine Compound of the Month."

Particle physicist—Physics people who study particles and subatomic particles in theory, like Leonard Hofstadter, who didn't really work at Caltech. I'm sure you knew that.

Energy—It's the ability to do work, whether you can see it moving or not. It takes energy to swim and energy to produce light or sound. The "Law" is that energy can neither be created nor destroyed by ordinary means. As you know, Lee was skeptical, but then she's that way. The "ordinary means" is the loophole that explains the power of the atom bomb.

Big Bang Theory—It's the TV show, of course, but also the widely accepted assumption that the universe started with a big explosion that disseminated the building blocks of life and the planets some 13.7 billion years ago.

Electromagnetism—This is a physical interaction that occurs between electrically charged particles when they are magnetically attracted and repelled. It's the stuff of electricity, sound, and light.

Dark matter and Antimatter—Don't ask. Actually, it makes up about 90 percent of the universe but is so dark and dense (concentrated, not stupid), it's not visible. If you can't see it, how do you know it's there? Again, don't ask.

Subatomic particles—The parts of an atom, such as neutrons, protons, electrons, leptons, muons, etc. Picture something you built out of Legos when you were a child, or maybe an adult. The smaller pieces that make up your object are like the subatomic particles, and the object itself is the atom—if that helps.

Hadron particles—Made of quarks. They are notable for being forced to smash into other subatomic particles; they have very short lives. *See the music video: https://www.youtube.com/watch?v=j50ZssEojtM

Bernoulli's Principle—It explains how objects move through fluids such as air and water and how speed is related to pressure. Think about it the next time you fly in an airplane. It's what keeps the wings up.

Apex—When tossed in the air, the highest point before falling back down (due to the pull of gravity) is the apex.

Galileo—The famous scientist of the 1500s who figured out that all objects fall (accelerate) toward Earth at the same rate, regardless of how much mass they have, due to the pull of gravity. Yes, *Queen* did sing about Galileo. That's because lyricist Brian May is no slouch when it comes to astrophysics.

Accelerated—Most people think this refers to going faster, but in physics it also refers to going slower or changing direction. In other words, it's any change in velocity. A good trivia question.

Newton's Third—Sir Isaac Newton thought this one up. It has nothing to do with a fig cookie, as you know by now. The third law of motion states that for every action, there is an equal and opposite reaction. Lots of people can quote this one but then not actually know what it means. In short, think of a rocket. As it expels fuel in the form of gas and fire downward (the action), it moves upward (the equal and opposite reaction).

The Bomb—Not an expression referring to how excellent something is, as in *da bomb*. It refers to a nuclear-powered explosive device that derives its energy from smashing nuclei together (fusion) or slicing nuclei into fragments (fission), thereby releasing unfathomable amounts of energy. Enough said.

J. Robert Oppenheimer—A theoretical physicist who was credited with being one of the creators of The Bomb. He later said, "I am become death," a Hindu expression referring to massive destruction. He was often called Oppie—not to be confused with Opie who lived in Mayberry.

Einstein—He was mostly right about everything he said.

Force, mass, and acceleration—Newton's second law is all about the relationship between force, mass, and acceleration. The formula is force equals mass times acceleration. There won't be a test on this, but think about what's involved in launching Cato's flaming sock missile.

Inertia and momentum—When something gets going, it's hard to stop it. The opposite is true too: if something doesn't want to budge, it takes extra force to get it going—like a boulder rolling down a hill or your brother who won't get off the couch and get a job.

Periodic Table of Elements—That chart that always hung in the back of your high school science classroom. If you create your own element, you might be added to the chart. The most recent additions are usually named after people or places. Take a look. And krypton, by the way, is not the same as kryptonite, which doesn't really exist. Sorry.

Paleontology—The study of really old stuff, namely fossil remains of ancient life.

Carbon-based—Carbon is one of the first elements listed on the Periodic Table. It is a key component of *all* life on Earth. It's also coal and diamonds. You might be related to a piece of coal or a diamond—your pick.

Muon tomography—A big favorite of Lee's, it's also a real thing. It uses muons to create 3D images, sort of like X-rays do. Another kind of tomography is the one that looks through you to find all sorts of things: a CT scan.

Muon—By now, you know. It is an atomic particle that has more mass than an electron. Muons are extremely penetrating and can travel thousands of meters below the surface of the Earth. As you sit here reading, they are going right through you at the rate of ten thousand per square meter every minute. They are Da Bomb!

Theoretical physics—See Particle physicist.

Circuit—Like it sounds, it's a circular pattern that directs electricity from one point to another.

Hologram—A three-dimensional image produced by light that can be seen by the naked eye. Picture Princess Leia's image popping out of R2D2's head. A fake one was used in *Star Trek* to simulate being beamed up, although the famous phrase "Beam me up, Scotty" was never actually spoken on the show.

Superconductor—A substance that conducts (transports) electricity without any resistance or friction, thus being a super way to save energy.

Liquid Nitrogen—It's the liquid form of nitrogen that is so cold it could freeze your . . . well, it could cause frostbite if any part of your body is exposed to it. In fact, it's good for freezing your entire body if you want to come back a hundred years from now. You'd have to be properly thawed, though. It is handy for removing warts and for science projects.

Magnet(ic)—A body, such as a piece of iron or steel (and now rarer earth materials such as neodymium), that has the ability to attract or repel certain other substances by way of positive and negative poles, sometimes introduced by moving electric charges. Not to be confused with a magnetic personality, which Cato certainly had.

Mascara—You never know!

Pig—Not yet.

Trinitite—Very unspectacular-looking rocks that were found at the Trinity test site after The Bomb was detonated. It has a slightly green-ish hue and was the result of The Bomb's ability to lift the sand off the desert floor as it detonated, raining down melted sand and whatever else was in the atmosphere.

Radium Beryllium—Ra-Be, for short. It's a combination of radium plus beryllium. It emits neutrons and is radioactive. (See Radon and Radium Chloride.)

James Chadwick—A British physicist who moved to Los Alamos to work on The Bomb. He won the Nobel prize for discovering the neutron and was instrumental in theorizing how nuclear energy works.

Pig—Actually a container made of solid lead that is used to store radioactive materials because the lead keeps the radioactivity in. Not sure where the term pig came from, but some say it is related to an old-fashioned term used when smelting iron. Where "smelting" came from, I couldn't say.

Ollie Smoot—A real person, whose real name is Oliver. His particular area of expertise is measurement, so naturally . . . the Smoot, which is also a real thing.

Etymology—The origin of words or names, not to be confused with entomology. You know, the study of bugs.

Methane—It's the most potent of greenhouse gases; cows are notorious for emitting it after they eat, if you know what I mean. It's also the main component of natural gas that is considered safer for the environment than coal after it is burned. The gas company adds a scent to natural gas so you can detect it. It's also explosive, so don't smoke near the posterior end of a cow.

Nitrates—Along with nitrites, they are cancer-causing preservatives that are added to processed foods to keep them from spoiling. Most notably, they are in bacon and hot dogs, though now those foods are readily available in any market without the two bad-boy ingredients, so you have to wonder what took them so long.

Voltmeter—Kind of what it sounds like. It measures if and how much electricity is flowing through a wire. Your electrician has one and should be using it for his own safety.

White sock—You never know!

H_2O—Plain old water. It's made up of two hydrogen atoms attached to one larger oxygen atom in the shape of a Mickey Mouse hat.

Crystal diode and transformer—Components that are found in different types of circuit boards to control the flow and voltage of electrons.

Constants and variables—Remember your grade school and middle school science labs? Constants are the things that never change, like the same kind and size of light bulb. Variables are the things that are different, like different size batteries used to light the same bulb.

Richter Scale—Named for Charles Richter, who devised a scale for measuring earthquakes. Actually, it used to be the standard for talking about magnitude and intensity of an earthquake, but the folks at Caltech often use the Moment Magnitude Scale now.

Lithium—On the Periodic Table of Elements, it's used in batteries and in treatments for mental health problems.

Gamma-Hydroxybutyrate (GHB)—It's commonly called the "date rape drug." Stay away from it.

Revigator®—A crazy jug that looks like one of those five-gallon water bottles you see at the office, commonly called the "water cooler." Only it's ceramic and promises to cure you of what ails you using radioactivity. There's a sucker born every day.

Maser, or MASER—Stands for Microwave Amplification by Stimulated Emission of Radiation. Sort of like *laser*: Light Amplification by Stimulated Emission of Radiation, but not. The military tried creating "Death Rays" with masers. Obviously, it didn't work, or we would have wiped out every alien who ever stepped foot on Earth. The Russians actually figured out how to use regular microwaves more effectively on US Embassy staff in Cuba recently. And every kid who ever cooked marshmallow cream in Mom's microwave learned a lesson firsthand. Not to be confused with *mazer*, which is a large wooden Germanic drinking vessel, possibly used for drinking beer. What else?

Class II Lever—A simple machine such as a lever contains a rigid bar or plank that pivots over a fixed point such as a fulcrum. Class I is a seesaw, Class II is a crowbar, and Class III is a wheelbarrow.

Vamoose—Okay. Not a scientific term, but fun to use anyway. It means get going, skedaddle (another fun word), make a break for it. The origin goes back to the Wild West when cowboys mispronounced and misspelled *vamos*, a Spanish word.

ACKNOWLEDGMENTS

I would first and foremost like to thank Keith, who was my mentor, muse, and technical consultant throughout the process of writing my first novel. His accounts of forensic investigations and classic physics gave birth to two main characters and gave wheels to the story. The company id365 provided invaluable marketing expertise and support. It *does* take a village.

I would also like to thank Marla Daniels of NY Editors who, even from three-thousand miles away, had an amazing grasp of the story and the character in a SoCal milieu. Claudine of Claudine Mansour Design created a fabulous book design with a sensibility for what I was thinking. She nailed both the smart vibe of my main character and the allure of science in her graphic designs.

Samantha of Sam Hardy Photography—an up-and-coming photographer and a native of SoCal, is a former student of mine who has the most amazing talent and gift for making anyone look good.

Nicky Loomis—another native of SoCal, a writer and

teacher now, was also a student in my sixth-grade classroom when we first met. Her early support and encouragement launched *Galilea*. Student becomes the mentor.

I would like to thank Laura Raulinaitis, an avid reader and long-time friend, who printed out and bound the very first version of my manuscript. Even after a year of revisions, it remains a cherished memento of her support and enthusiasm. She once described the story as a cross between Nancy Drew and Scooby-Doo, and that stuck with me as a vision for the character Galilea.

Devon Crowe, a native of SoCal, provided copyediting and proofing. She's the comma detective extraordinaire.

Next is the man whose name I don't know. You know who you are if you attended Sam Eisenstein's writing workshop at the Pasadena Senior Center and handed me an article about Ollie Smoot, a great geeky story.

Last, but not least, I would like to thank my children Deborah, René, and Jason, who took time from their busy lives to offer invaluable encouragement and advice in all things big and small. A quirky sense of humor does run in the family, and I hope they laugh as they read this book.

ABOUT THE AUTHOR

Norma Richman has lived her entire life in the Pasadena area, working as a teacher and blogger. She has spent the bulk of her teaching experience with sixth graders, where she learned to love their snark. Over the course of twenty years, she has taught every subject, including physics. When she transitioned into a new position at her school, she discovered the joy of using a different "voice." This little bit of "voice freedom" unleashed the beast, as they say, and she fell in love with creative writing. In any case, when she discovered the character Lee roaming around in her head, she put her to work in her first novel, *Galilea, Galilea*. Richman enjoys travel, photography, printmaking, and her family and friends—including her wheaten terrier Sadie (not in any particular order). She continues to live in Pasadena and is already planning more capers for her physicist characters.

Made in the USA
Middletown, DE
29 August 2020